A Table for Two

A Table for Two

SHERYL LISTER

FOREVER
New York   Boston

Copyright © 2022 by Grand Central Publishing

Cover design by Susan Zucker Design. Cover images by Shutterstock. Cover copyright © 2022 by Hachette Book Group, Inc.

Hachette Book Group supports the right to free expression and the value of copyright. The purpose of copyright is to encourage writers and artists to produce the creative works that enrich our culture.

The scanning, uploading, and distribution of this book without permission is a theft of the author's intellectual property. If you would like permission to use material from the book (other than for review purposes), please contact permissions@hbgusa.com. Thank you for your support of the author's rights.

Forever
Hachette Book Group
1290 Avenue of the Americas, New York, NY 10104
read-forever.com
twitter.com/readforeverpub

Originally published as paperback and ebook in August 2022.
First mass market edition: March 2023

Forever is an imprint of Grand Central Publishing. The Forever name and logo are trademarks of Hachette Book Group, Inc.

The publisher is not responsible for websites (or their content) that are not owned by the publisher.

The Hachette Speakers Bureau provides a wide range of authors for speaking events. To find out more, go to www.hachettespeakersbureau.com or call (866) 376-6591.

Grand Central Publishing books may be purchased in bulk for business, educational, or promotional use. For information, please contact your local bookseller or the Hachette Book Group Special Markets Department at special.markets@hbgusa.com.

Library of Congress Cataloging-in-Publication Data
Names: Lister, Sheryl, author.
Title: A table for two / Sheryl Lister.
Description: First edition. | New York : Forever, 2022. | Series: Firefly lake; 1
Identifiers: LCCN 2022004308 | ISBN 9781538755273 (trade paperback) | ISBN 9781538755266 (ebook)
Subjects: LCGFT: Romance fiction. | Novels.
Classification: LCC PS3612.I863 T33 2022 | DDC 813/.6--dc23/eng/20220225
LC record available at https://lccn.loc.gov/2022004308

ISBNs: 9781538755273 (paperback), 9781538755266 (ebook), 9781538724187 (mass market)

Printed in the United States of America

OPM

10 9 8 7 6 5 4 3 2 1

For Shellie and Michelle,
my sisters of the heart.

A Table for Two

PROLOGUE

Mmm. The taste, the texture. It's rich, decadent, satisfying…almost orgasmic."

Serenity Wheeler chuckled at her neighbor and friend, Andrea Cunningham. "That good, huh? Never heard my truffles compared to an orgasm, but I'll take it." She bit into her own, thinking it would be the only way she'd experience one these days.

Andrea stuffed the remainder of the truffle into her mouth. "Please. This is just like every other thing you make. I'm so going to miss these dinners and desserts."

She frowned. "What are you talking about?"

"I got the promotion!" Andrea said with a huge grin.

Serenity returned her smile. "Oh my goodness, Andrea, I'm so happy for you." She leaned over and hugged her. The two other women seated around the table, Natasha Baldwin and Dana Stephens, expressed excited congratulations as well.

"We need to toast your good news." Natasha lifted her wineglass. "Wishing you the best of everything in your new position as Vineyard Foods' latest regional manager." The four women touched glasses.

Andrea took a sip of her wine. "Thanks. I'm really excited, but there's something else. The promotion means I'll be moving to the Seattle office."

They all froze. Dana slowly lowered her glass. "Moving? You can't leave."

"My sentiments exactly," Serenity said. When Serenity had moved from San Diego to the small town of Firefly Lake, California, six years ago, Andrea had been a godsend. She would be sad to see her go.

"Believe me, I'd rather stay here. I don't know what I'm going to do without our semimonthly supper club nights. Serenity, you know I live for these fabulous meals you always serve."

Serenity chuckled. What had started out as a way for her to share her love of cooking with friends had morphed into so much more over the past few years. Andrea had even nicknamed their get-togethers Serenity's Supper Club because she said they reminded her of the old underground places where people spent hours eating, drinking, listening to music, and generally having a good time.

"I just wish Terri could've been here tonight for the announcement." Terri Rhodes was the fifth member of their group. She worked as an ER nurse at the local hospital and was missing the dinner because she had to sub for another nurse who'd called in sick.

"I'll make sure she's off for your going-away dinner," Serenity assured her. "So does this mean you're going to put the house up for sale?"

"No. I talked my brother into moving here because I don't want to leave Nana alone." Andrea shifted in her seat to face Serenity. "I hope this isn't an imposition, but, Serenity, could you do me a favor and help him get settled in? He's a city boy through and through, and making this transition is going to be a big shock for him," she added with a laugh.

Serenity met Natasha's smiling face and knew exactly what her best friend was thinking. From the moment she'd come to town, Natasha had tried—and failed—to get Serenity to date again. Jumping back on the horse was how she'd phrased it, but Serenity wasn't interested. Andrea had mentioned her brother a time or two, and Serenity seemed to recall her saying something about him not wanting to be in a committed relationship. In Serenity's mind, that spelled trouble. She'd finally found a Zen-like balance in her life and had no intention of letting anyone upset that equilibrium. However, Andrea had been a wonderful friend, so she couldn't deny the request. "Sure. I'll be happy to help out if he needs something. I'll even invite him to a supper club dinner."

"Oh, that would be great." Andrea hugged Serenity. "I know he'll enjoy it."

She smiled. "I hope so." She also hoped he understood the only thing she planned to offer was a neighborly acquaintance.

CHAPTER 1

Pay up."

Gabriel Cunningham glanced briefly at the door where his three best friends stood, then went back to connecting the ports on his computer. "What?"

Brent Ward sauntered over to the desk. "I bet Darius and Glenn that you'd be in here working."

"I'm not working. I was just setting everything up."

Both Darius Houston and Glenn Turner shook their heads. "Mm-hmm. Five more minutes and you would've been knee-deep in coding. You could've at least waited until we were gone," Darius said. They always gave Gabriel grief for working long hours.

"Sorry. You're right." His three friends had been nice enough to help him move from Atlanta to Firefly Lake. The least he could do in return was see them off before he jumped into things.

Glenn propped a hip on the desk and folded his arms. "It's Saturday, Gabe. Being here is supposed to give you a chance to learn balance and relax more, not continue on the same path to burnout you were on at home. And you agreed to take off two or three weeks. You haven't taken a vacation in years."

"No, I moved here because my sister got a promotion, and I agreed to look out for Nana. And I consented to cut my work hours down for a few weeks, not cut them completely." He hadn't really wanted to leave Atlanta, but he agreed that someone needed to keep an eye on their seventy-eight-year-old grandmother. Andrea had uprooted her life several years ago and stepped in to care for Nana after a stroke had left her with weakness on one side. Although she'd made a complete recovery, neither had wanted her to be alone. His sister had put her dreams on hold, and now, at thirty-two and four years his junior, it was time for her to live them. And as she'd pointed out during their phone conversation two weeks ago, Gabriel could do his software engineering job anywhere, particularly since he owned the company with Brent and Darius. And, yes, he'd been working…*a lot*…okay, nonstop for the past couple of years, but work helped him forget about things he'd rather not remember.

Brent waved a dismissive hand. "Semantics. The goal is the same. I agree with Glenn, and since he's the doctor here, he knows what he's talking about." Glenn worked as a physician in his father's family practice.

"Thank you," Glenn said. "I didn't go to school all those years for nothing. The slower pace of a small town will do you some good."

"Whatever." Gabriel stood. "I don't know why I keep y'all around," he said, trying to hide his smile. They'd all met at Morehouse, pledged the same fraternity, and were as close as brothers. No matter how much they got on each other's nerves at times, he knew there was nothing they wouldn't do for each other.

Darius shrugged. "Somebody's got to keep you in line." They all laughed. "Speaking of small towns, are there any women here under the age of fifty? We've been here for twenty-four hours, and I don't think I've seen one. The two women I saw down the block were definitely over forty."

Chuckling, Gabriel said, "I have no idea. Why is that always your first question every time we go somewhere?"

"Because I like women. And you never know when I might luck up on my Mrs. Right. I can't leave Glenn in marriage-land all alone."

Glenn grinned. "Don't hate. But he does have a point. At least Darius and Brent make time to play, but you work all the time. When was the last time *you* had a date?"

"None of your business," Gabriel grumbled. His love life—or lack of one—had been an ongoing conversation since he'd broken up with his ex a couple of years ago. Sure, he'd been brokenhearted and had buried himself in his job to cover the hurt. Though he wasn't consumed by the pain anymore, he hadn't changed his work habits. He found the long hours kept his mind off his nearly nonexistent social life.

He dated sporadically and rarely asked a woman out more than once.

"Now that we agree Gabriel doesn't have a love life," Brent said, "do you know anything about the neighbor Drea mentioned?"

"Nothing other than she's supposed to be a nice lady who does this dinner thing a couple of times a month with a small group of friends. Drea said she can throw down in the kitchen. This morning when I went out to the car, I found a note from her inviting me to a welcome dinner tonight. Nana's invited, too." Gabriel considered himself a foodie of sorts and enjoyed great food. He'd go once to check it out and hoped his sister was right.

Darius made a face. "Nana's going, too? So, basically, that means she's probably old enough to be your mother or grandmother. I don't know any women our age who'd be cooking like that for people on a regular basis."

"I guess I'll find out tonight and let you know."

Glenn glanced at his watch. "We'd better get on the road. I checked the traffic and it's a little slow, and I want to get to the airport in plenty of time. I'm eager to get back home to my beautiful wife." He and his wife had been married for only two years and were still in the honeymoon phase.

"What time does the flight leave?"

"Five. It's going to be a long night because we don't get in until early tomorrow morning."

"I hear you." Firefly Lake was about half an hour

from Napa Valley, and the closest major airport was in Oakland. The flight wouldn't leave for another four hours, but depending on the traffic, it could take two or three hours to get there. "I appreciate you guys making the trip to help me out." He'd hired a moving company to transport a few larger items like his bed, his favorite recliner, large flat-screen TV, and his gym equipment. The guys had helped him out by renting an SUV, and between that and his Acura SUV, they'd managed to transport the rest of the things he would need for the duration of his stay. He followed his friends to the living room where they'd left their bags, then out to the car.

Brent clapped Gabriel on the shoulder. "That's what friends do. I hope you enjoy small-town living."

Gabriel scanned the neighborhood. The house was located in one of the newer subdivisions and had a more modern feel, but it still screamed *small town*. "Yeah." Temporarily. He hadn't told his sister, but he couldn't see himself relegated to this place forever. Gabriel had paid the mortgage on his condo for the next four months, and the guys would keep an eye on his place until Gabriel returned to Atlanta. He planned to return by fall and figured he'd use these three summer months to convince his grandmother to move back with him. He didn't think it would be too hard.

"We'll talk on Monday about the new account," Darius said. "I'm thinking around noon or one since you'll be behind three hours."

He'd forgotten about the time difference. "Sounds

good. I can send the video conference link tomorrow evening."

Brent and Darius nodded. The three men loaded the bags into the trunk, then after a round of handshakes and one-arm hugs, climbed in and drove off.

After taking another look around the area that would be his short-term home, Gabriel went back into the house. As soon as he closed the door, his cell rang. He dug it out of his pocket and sighed.

"Yes, Drea."

Andrea's laughter came through the earpiece. "Hey, big brother. Just checking to see if you've gotten settled in."

"I've talked to you three times in less than twenty-four hours, and the answer is still the same."

"Okay, okay. Have you met Serenity yet?"

"No, but she invited me and Nana to dinner tonight."

"Oh, good. Nana came with me a few times, so she'll be able to introduce you to everyone. You're in for a treat. The woman can cook her butt off, and I know how much you like to eat."

He had to smile at that. "Hmm. Is she a chef?" Gabriel stretched out on the sofa in the living room.

"No. She's a nurse. When she first came to town, she worked in the hospital's ER department. Now she works in Dr. Jacobs's office. Serenity said she was getting too old for those erratic hours."

"Isn't that Nana's doctor?"

"Yep."

Great. Darius was right. The woman is probably pushing fifty. He'd be polite, but he didn't plan to spend hours with a bunch of old ladies. Changing the subject, he asked, "How are you liking the new job?"

"So far, so good. A lot of training for now, though. I just hate that I didn't get a chance to see you and show you around. Things are a lot more updated since the last time you spent more than a day or so there."

"Same here." The siblings had planned to spend a week together before Andrea began her new position, but the company moved up her start date. "And what are you talking about? I was here for Thanksgiving."

"Ha! Is that what you called it? You were here about as long as a flight layover. You got in on Wednesday evening and were gone Friday morning. And please don't try to tell me you had to work because nobody works the day after Thanksgiving unless you're in retail with all the Black Friday sales."

Okay, he'd concede to her that point. Growing up, Gabriel had never taken to the town and whenever his family visited, he'd been ready to leave almost immediately. For a city boy, those week-long visits to a place where everything shut down when the streetlights came on had lasted a week too long in his estimation.

"By the way, Serenity said she'd be available if you needed help with anything."

"That's nice of her, but I should be able to manage. I would like to take a bottle of wine for dinner. Do you know what she likes?"

"That's a great idea. I'll text you the names of a few."

"Thanks, Sis. I need to get going. I want to do some grocery shopping before picking up Nana." Last night he'd stopped at a store in Oakland and bought only enough to get him through the night.

"All right. Let me know how it goes. I promise I won't call you for at least a week," she added with a giggle.

Gabriel smiled. "Liar. You won't be able to hold out until Monday." With their parents gone, he'd become even more protective of her, and they rarely went a week without talking, either by text, phone, or FaceTime.

"Oh, hush. You wouldn't know what to do if you didn't hear my lovely voice on the regular."

He laughed. "Yeah, whatever. You're a pain in the butt sometimes, but I love you anyway."

"You'd better. Love you, big brother. Later."

Gabriel disconnected and thought about how proud he was of his sister. When their parents had died in a car accident eight years ago, Andrea hadn't hesitated in packing up and moving to Firefly Lake. Their parents had purchased this house so their family would have somewhere to stay during their semiannual visits when Nana and Grandpa's small two-bedroom home had become too cramped as he and Andrea had gotten older. His parents had eventually relocated to the town a few years before their deaths, shortly after Grandpa passed away. He took another glance around. Although he had always been in a rush to get back to Atlanta then, he had to admit there had been a lot of laughter between these walls.

His phone chimed, and he read the text from his sister listing the wine choices. Pushing away his memories, he went to grab the grocery list and his keys, then drove the three miles to the town's lone grocery store.

Once there, he was pleasantly surprised by the size of the store and the variety of foods available. He'd been worried he wouldn't be able to find everything he needed but was happy to be proven wrong. Several people called out "hello" as he passed, and he responded in kind. *Gotta love small towns*. He glanced around, and Darius's comment about there not being any women his age here flashed in his mind. So far his friend had been right. Gabriel added steaks and chicken to his basket and headed for the produce section.

As he rounded the corner, his steps slowed. A smile curved his mouth. *Looks like Darius was wrong.* Just ahead of him, a petite woman with skin the color of rich cocoa stood picking out corn. His gaze roamed down her curvy body in the short-sleeved dress she wore, which stopped just above her knees and gave way to slim, toned legs. She definitely wasn't pushing fifty. She tossed her long braids over one shoulder, and he got a glimpse of her face. Gorgeous. Intrigued, Gabriel started in that direction. The moment he was next to her, the sweet scent of her perfume floated to his nostrils. "Looks like a good crop of corn," he said, picking up one and testing its weight.

She smiled up at him. "It is, and this is the best time of year to buy it. Sweet, juicy…yummy."

Her smile and sultry voice intrigued him. "Is that right? Any cooking suggestions?"

"Depends on how you want to prepare it—boiled, grilled, sautéed." She added the ear of corn in her hand to a plastic bag holding three others.

"All of the above," Gabriel said with a chuckle. "Does this mean you're offering cooking lessons?"

She gave him a sassy smile. "You never know."

Gabriel lifted a brow. *Well, now.* She peeled back the husk a little and pierced a kernel. The juice squirted out and hit him directly in his eye, startling him.

"Oh, I'm sorry," she said.

He swiped at the liquid. "No problem. I just hope there will still be a little juice left once you get done." A grin kicked up in the corner of his mouth. "And um…on second thought, maybe I should hold off on those lessons until I can be sure of your cooking skills," he added teasingly. Her slight smile faded as a glare took its place.

"I'm sure *one* little burst kernel won't ruin the entire ear, and you don't know anything about my cooking skills." She shoved the corn into the bag, dropped it in her basket, and stormed off.

"Wait. I'm—" She didn't turn around or break stride. Gabriel stared after her, stunned. He'd been enjoying their banter, but obviously that was the wrong thing to say. He guessed he had a lot to learn about women living in small towns. He shook his head and finished shopping.

Two hours later, he drove over to pick up his grandmother. She was out the door before he got out of the car.

"Gabriel! Oh, I'm so glad to see you." She grabbed him in a crushing hug.

"Hey, Nana." He kissed her smooth brown cheek. Her familiar floral scent surrounded him. Even in her late seventies, Della Williams was still a striking woman and wore her age well. Had his mother lived, he knew exactly what she would've looked like at that age.

She reached up, palmed his face, and studied him through eyes that mirrored his. "How are you, baby?"

"I'm okay. Still a little tired from the drive, but I got everything put away."

"Good. Come on in. I need to get my handbag, and then we can go."

He followed her inside and watched her walk down the short hallway to her bedroom and smiled, grateful that she had no lingering effects from the stroke she'd had a year after his parents' deaths. He wandered over to the photos hanging on one wall of the living room. His heart clenched, seeing a picture of his parents that was taken at one of the lakes in town. Losing them had devastated him, but he'd kept his grief hidden in an effort to be strong for Andrea.

"I'm ready. I can't wait to see what Serenity has on the menu tonight. Ooh, she can cook!"

"So I heard." He could do this. It was just one dinner.

CHAPTER 2

Serenity muttered under her breath about rude people as she cut the corn off the cob.

"Girl, you've been fussing since I got here," Natasha said, taking plates from the cabinet. "What are you so upset about?"

She blew out a long breath. "While I was picking out corn at the grocery store, some guy came up to me and made a snippy comment about the corn being dried out because I pricked a kernel. I had accidentally squirted him in the eye and apologized, but after that remark, I wanted to squirt the entire ear in his face. Then he had the nerve to diss my cooking skills."

"Whoa. Who was it?"

"I have no idea. I've never seen him before." Living in a town with a population of just under two thousand, she knew pretty much everyone here. "Probably one of the employees from that new manufacturing company that recently opened right outside town."

Natasha leaned against the counter next to Serenity. "A few of them came into the office looking for houses to rent or buy, and they were rude, acting like because we live in a small town, I wouldn't know how to sell a house." She rolled her eyes.

"I don't know what's wrong with people." She picked up the next ear of corn.

"What did he look like?"

"Who?"

"The guy in the store."

Serenity shrugged. "He was all right. I didn't pay that much attention." Okay, that wasn't *exactly* the truth. The man's hazel eyes framed by those long eyelashes had grabbed her attention the moment their gazes locked. That had also been part of her irritation. She was far past the age of being worked up over a man. Any man.

Natasha chuckled. "In other words, he looked good."

Serenity threw away the cobs and wiped the counter where some of the liquid had splattered. *Dried out, indeed.* Ignoring her friend's comment, she said, "I think we'll eat outside, since the weather is nice." The early-June temperatures had climbed into the low eighties, making it perfect for outdoor dining.

"Okay. I'll set the table, and you can let me know which candles you want to use."

"Great. Thanks."

Natasha started toward the sliding glass door, then stopped. "Serenity, don't let him get under your skin.

You're a great cook, and it doesn't matter what he thinks."

Serenity nodded. "You're right." She found the candles she wanted and took them outside, where Natasha was setting the table. Serenity had several different sets of china, ranging from casual to elegant, as well as a variety of patterned cloth napkins. Her friend seemed to always know the best combinations. "I think you need to forget real estate and take up table decorating. You always make everything look so beautiful."

"Thanks, but I'll stick with what I know best," Natasha said with a smile. "Then again, maybe I can use this as a step toward finally using my interior design degree."

Laughing, Serenity went back inside to roll out the dough for the French bread. Soft jazz played in the background, and soon she was lost in the one place that soothed her. She'd gotten her love of cooking from both her grandmothers and, as a child, while her sister and cousins were outside playing, preferred spending her time in the kitchen beside them, learning and listening. They'd shared not just recipes but also their hearts. Every ingredient was filled with love and the taste, divine. Serenity applied that same love when she cooked. By the time she finished the sweet, sticky teriyaki glaze that would accompany the grilled salmon, she had forgotten all about her earlier encounter.

The doorbell rang, and Natasha, who was just

finishing tossing the ingredients for the kale salad, said, "I'll get it. It's probably Dana or Terri." She placed the bowl in the refrigerator and headed toward the front. She came back with both women.

"Hey, y'all," Serenity called out.

"Hey," the women chorused.

"Oh my goodness. It smells so good in here." Dana hugged Serenity, then claimed a stool at the kitchen bar. "I really hope you made an extra loaf of that bread because I'm starving. Everybody and their mamas brought their car to the garage today, and I haven't eaten since breakfast." She worked as an auto mechanic at her father's garage.

"I always make extra when you come, Miss Bread Queen." Dana had been known to devour an entire loaf of French bread, but she never gained an ounce.

"I was just telling Dana the same thing," Terri said, laughing. "The ER was busy all day. I had time for half a granola bar and a bottle of water, and then it was off to the races again."

Serenity gave Terri a quick hug. "I'm just glad you could make it. You've been working a lot of extra hours lately." She retrieved a small charcuterie board filled with assorted cheeses, crackers, spinach dip, and chunks of sourdough.

"Me too, and I know. I've been taking a few extra shifts." Leaning against the counter, she scooped some dip onto a piece of bread and asked, "Have you met Andrea's brother yet?"

"No, but I invited him to join us for dinner

tonight—sort of a welcome-to-town thing. Ms. Della's coming, too." She checked the two loaves of bread in the oven.

Natasha laughed. "That means we're in for a *good* ole time. I hope you've got the old-school R & B playlist ready. You know Ms. Della's going to have us all up dancing."

Serenity smiled. "You know I do." She glanced over at the microwave clock. "They should be here in a few minutes. I told them to come around six."

Dana, munching on cheese and crackers, reached for one of the wine bottles chilling in an ice bucket. "In the meantime, I'm going to start with a glass of this delicious chardonnay."

"Pour me one, too," Terri said, holding out a wineglass. "Matter of fact, just pour four, and we can toast to this fabulous food."

Once everyone had a glass, Natasha held up hers. "To friendship, sisterhood, and Serenity's Supper Club."

"Amen!" Serenity said. The four women touched glasses, and she thought about how blessed she was to have these beautiful women in her life. She and Natasha had been college roommates, and Serenity had visited the small town a couple of times during their summer breaks and been introduced to Natasha's childhood friend, Dana. The two women had been the ones to encourage Serenity to relocate after a bad breakup, and it had been the best decision she'd ever made. Adding Terri and Andrea to the mix had been icing on an already decadent cake. The doorbell rang again. "That's probably our guests." Her heart started pounding, and she didn't know why she felt so nervous about meeting a man. She placed her glass on the bar and headed to the front. Taking a deep breath, she smiled and opened the door. Her smile faded. "I don't believe it."

He had the nerve to smile. "We meet again. I'm Gabriel, and you must be Serenity." He stuck out his hand.

Serenity glared at him until she remembered that Ms. Della was standing there and pasted her smile back on. "Yes, I'm Serenity Wheeler. It's nice to meet you, Gabriel." His large hand engulfed hers and held on slightly longer than politeness dictated. She gently but firmly pulled away. "Hi, Ms. Della." She engulfed the older woman in a brief hug. "Please, come in." She stepped back so they could enter.

"Hey, baby," Ms. Della said. "It sure smells good in here. Gabriel, I told you."

Gabriel stared intently at Serenity. "Whatever you're cooking does smell good."

She shook herself and tore her gaze away, irritated that he could affect her this way. "Thank you. We're eating on the deck tonight, so come on back." In the kitchen, everyone greeted Ms. Della and Serenity introduced Gabriel.

He nodded toward each woman. "Nice to meet you, ladies. Andrea spoke highly of you all."

"We miss our girl, but we're happy for her," Natasha said. "Can I get you two a glass of wine?"

"Please," Ms. Della said.

"Sure." He handed Serenity a gift bag. "Here's a little something to add to your ice bucket. I asked, and Andrea told me these were your favorites."

Serenity peeked inside and found a bottle of her favorite chardonnay and a Moscato. *Okay, he gets a point for this one, but it still doesn't make up for that smart-aleck comment.* "She was right. Thank you." She placed them in the ice bucket and ignored the knowing smile on Natasha's face. She pointed to the snack tray. "Dinner will be ready in a few minutes. In the meantime, help yourselves."

Dana picked up the tray and her glass. "We can take this outside and get out of Serenity's way."

As they exited through the sliding glass door, Gabriel turned back. Once again, his eyes held hers for a lengthy moment. A slow smile spread across his lips, and he saluted her with his glass. "Thanks for the invite. I'm looking forward to the meal."

"You're welcome." She spun around and marched over to the stove, then slid the salmon under the broiler, took the bread out and placed it on a rack to cool. The double oven was one of the things she loved most about her spacious kitchen.

"Girl, that man is *fine*! Andrea didn't mention that part, and I saw how he was looking at you."

Serenity startled. She glared at Natasha. "He wasn't looking at me any kind of way."

Grabbing the bowl of salad and bottle of dressing out of the refrigerator, she chuckled. "Mm-hmm.

Whatever you say. But I saw him." Natasha waggled a finger Serenity's way. "Who knows, he might be the one to get you back out there again."

"*Lalala*, I can't hear you." She reached into the still open refrigerator to remove the container holding the corn and some butter. She melted it in a skillet, then added the corn and a dash of salt.

"I so love that fried corn, especially in the summer."

"So do I. Having all these fresh vegetables and fruits makes living here worth it for me."

Natasha shook her head. "Spoken like a true cook. Most people think of the small-town ambience or our beautiful lakes and mountains as a selling point, but not you." She mixed the dressing in the salad.

Serenity shrugged and stirred the corn. "Hey, what can I say?"

"I'll take this out and be back to slice the bread."

She finished cooking, then placed everything on serving dishes and carried them outside. After going back to bring out the wine, she cued up her playlist and took her seat. Everyone filled their plates and, for the first few minutes, only the sounds of forks scraping against plates competed with the music playing through her outdoor speakers.

"Serenity, you've outdone yourself again," Ms. Della said. "I haven't had fried corn in so long."

Smiling, she said, "I'm glad you like it. It's not too dry, is it, Gabriel?" She probably should have taken the high road, but him smiling and acting like he hadn't been rude to her earlier had started grating on her nerves. Yes, he brought wine, but he'd forgotten the apology.

Gabriel held up a forkful of corn. "Not at all. It's really good. Everything's great." He chewed and angled his head thoughtfully. "Have you ever thought about adding bacon to the corn? They say bacon makes everything better."

Everyone around the table laughed. Except for Serenity, who kept her gaze on her plate. When she finally looked up, he was studying her with a puzzled expression. Maybe he'd meant it as a joke, but the backhanded comment stirred up painful memories she thought she had lain to rest. She couldn't wait for dinner to end.

CHAPTER 3

Monday morning, Gabriel had three hours to kill before his noon meeting with Darius and Brent, so he decided to tour the town to see what had changed over the years. His body hadn't yet adjusted to the time, and he'd been up since six. Backing out of the drive way, he saw Serenity and waved. She hesitated briefly, then threw up a quick hand in reply before getting into her own car. He shook his head and sighed. *So much for trying to be friendly.*

He drove to Main Street—it seemed that every small town had one—parked his car, and started up the block. As he walked and took in his new environment, his thoughts went back to Serenity. To say he'd been surprised that the woman from the grocery store was his new neighbor would be an understatement. He was still confused by her attitude after he complimented her cooking and even more now with her reluctance to merely wave back. His sister and grandmother had raved about her being sweet and kind, but so far he hadn't seen much of that. Was she still upset by his teasing comment about the corn and her cooking? Maybe he should apologize.

Putting her out of his mind, Gabriel checked out the stores lining the surrounding streets. An hour later, he had gone several blocks and was pleasantly surprised to see an auto shop, two clothing boutiques, a pharmacy, the doctor's office—where he assumed Serenity worked—and an ice cream parlor. But what caught his attention was the bakery and family-style restaurant.

At the corner, he crossed the street and entered Ms. Ida's Home Cooking. Gabriel had eaten breakfast earlier, but the amazing smells that engulfed him made his stomach sit up and take notice. Sort of like it had on Saturday with Serenity's food. It had taken great effort not to moan out loud as he ate the flaky salmon covered in that sweet glaze. He had never been a fan of kale, but the addition of the dried cranberries and whatever dressing she'd used had him rethinking his position.

"Good morning. You want a table or booth, honey?" a cheerful older woman called out as she approached the hostess stand.

"Would it be possible to do takeout?"

"Of course. I'll get you a menu." She took the three short steps necessary to retrieve one and handed it to him. "You're new around here."

Gabriel raised a brow. With everyone that came

and went, how could she possibly know how long he'd lived there? "Um...yes."

She laughed knowingly. "It's a small town. We pretty much know everyone who lives here. Take your time and let me know if you have any questions."

"Thanks." He guessed if he lived in a town with fewer than two thousand residents, he might get to know everyone after a few years, too. Taking a seat on a bench near the front door, he scanned the menu and found everything from French toast and waffles to sandwiches and comfort foods like pot roast and chicken and dumplings. The foodie in him wanted to sample just about every item, but his saner mind reminded him that at thirty six he was closer to forty than not and his metabolism didn't work quite as fast anymore. After serious debate, he settled on fried pork chops, candied yams, macaroni and cheese, and collard greens. He'd save the meal for dinner and wouldn't have to worry about cooking.

"Would you like cornbread or a biscuit?" the woman asked as she input the order.

"Cornbread, please."

"Okay. It should be up shortly."

While waiting, Gabriel went back across the street to the bakery and purchased blueberry and apple-cinnamon muffins. Due to his impromptu food purchase, he elected to head back home instead of carrying the bags through town. He didn't remember his family ever eating at the restaurant, probably because his grandmother and mother had prepared all the meals during their visits. This time he planned to sample all the food joints to his heart's content, though Nana had already extended an invitation to dinner for later in the week. He looked forward to doing both.

When Gabriel returned home, he couldn't resist one taste. He bit into the still warm pork chop and groaned. Samples of the other foods elicited the same reaction. Macaroni and cheese and candied yams were among his most favorite foods, and he'd thought no one could come close to preparing them as well as his mom and grandmother, but Ms. Ida's wasn't far off. He had to make a concerted effort to close the container and not devour the entire meal right then.

He grabbed a bottle of water from the refrigerator, then went to power up his computer for the meeting.

Darius logged on first. "What's up, D? Did you manage to survive not being able to go anywhere after seven?"

"I see you're starting already. It hasn't been that bad."

"What hasn't been that bad?" Brent asked, coming online.

"Firefly Lake."

"Ah. Oh, yeah, you were supposed to have dinner at the neighbor's house. How did that go?"

"Food was off the chain. The woman can cook, and, Darius, she's far from pushing fifty. More like thirties."

Darius's eyebrows shot up. "Really? Is she fine?"

He stroked his chin. "We might have to make another visit soon."

Gabriel recalled Serenity's beautiful face and sexy body. "Yeah. So are her three friends who were there. Anyway, let's get down to business." He decided to hold off on telling them about the grocery store encounter or the mixed vibes she'd given him at dinner. "The new recruiting company needs a system to scan résumés, track applicants…" he said, reading the notes he'd taken during the initial meeting.

Brent nodded. "Right now they're doing everything old-school—by fax or mail—and if an applicant wants to know where they are in the process, it's a phone call, which is taking up a lot of the employees' time. Is this something you and Darius can fit in with building the Luxura Jewels online store?" Brent handled the business side of their business, along with their administrative assistant, while Gabriel and Darius did the actual development of the various systems.

"I think we can get it done," Darius said. "I'm just about finished with the mobile app, so that'll free up some time. Gabe and I will get together to work out the details and timeline."

"Sounds good."

They discussed the next things on their list. Gabriel worried it would be difficult to maintain the workflow long distance and already missed being able to just walk twenty feet to Darius's or Brent's office. However, by the end of the meeting, he felt confident they would be able to continue their weekly staff meetings without any interruptions.

Darius held up a finger. "Gabe, I'll text you later to set up a time to talk."

He nodded. The three men talked a few minutes longer, made plans for next week's meeting, and ended the call.

For the next several hours, Gabriel got lost in coding. When he looked up again, the sun had begun to set. He was tempted to just grab a protein bar and water to stave off the hunger and continue working, but he was supposed to be learning balance. Reluctantly, he shut down everything and went to heat up his dinner.

The weather had cooled some, but it was still warm enough to enjoy his meal outside on the patio in the backyard with his favorite jazz playlist and the mystery thriller his sister had left for him. The patio was much smaller than his next-door neighbor's, and large enough only for a table and four cushioned chairs, but it would fit his needs just fine. Maybe the temporary change in locale would turn out to be what he needed to reduce his stress level. If he could just straighten things out with his new neighbor.

* * *

Serenity rushed into Ms. Ida's and searched for Natasha.

"Hey, Serenity."

"Hi, Ms. Bernice."

"Natasha's on the left near the back. You want your usual Caesar salad with shrimp?"

"Yes, ma'am." She wove her way through the restaurant and slid into the booth across from her friend. "Hey, girl. Sorry I'm late. The office was beyond busy this morning. Did you order already?"

"I've only been here five minutes, and yes, I ordered. I come here so much, Ms. Bernice already knows what I want," Natasha added with a laugh.

"I know. I love being able to eat someone else's food for a change."

"So, what's up with you and Gabriel?"

Serenity stared at Natasha. "Okay, that was out of left field, and I don't know what you mean." She should have known something was up when Natasha wanted to change their typical Friday lunch date to Wednesday.

Natasha leaned forward. "You just met the man, and you were pretty frosty during dinner, especially with that crack about the corn being dry."

Her friend knew her well and didn't miss anything. "He's the same guy from the grocery store." And every time he'd seen her since then, he'd waved as if nothing had happened. She wondered why he was trying to be nice all of a sudden. He hadn't even apologized.

"Ha! I knew it. But that still doesn't tell me why you were all upset. He seems to be a nice guy, based on the conversation, so I can't imagine he was purposely trying to be rude. And he even complimented you on how good the corn tasted."

"Whose side are you on anyway?" Natasha didn't say anything, just waited. Serenity let out a sigh. "Yes, he complimented the corn, but right after, he asked about putting bacon in it, as if how I'd prepared it wasn't good enough."

"I see. Serenity, Gabriel is not Lloyd, and I don't think he meant it that way."

Just the mention of her ex put a bad taste in Serenity's mouth. "Maybe not, but it felt the same." Over the year or so they'd dated, somehow it became less about them building a loving relationship and more about her cooking and playing hostess to his many parties and how she could have always done something a little better. Three months after their one-year anniversary, she'd had enough and ended it. "You're probably right." Had she automatically lumped Gabriel in with her ex when his comments could have been totally innocent? Reluctantly, she admitted to herself that might have been the case. *I need to apologize.*

"I talked to Andrea last night. She asked how dinner went. I told her it was fine. You might want to straighten things out with her brother before she calls, since you did kind of promise to help him out."

Serenity had totally forgotten about that promise. Now she really felt bad. The server brought their food to the table. "Thanks." She picked up her fork and stabbed at the salad, but her appetite had waned. After forcing down half her food, she asked the server to box up the rest.

Natasha glanced at her watch. "I've got to get

back. There are a couple of houses coming up for sale, so I need to do a walk-through, then schedule a photographer for the listing."

"So do I. We're back-to-back this afternoon." There were four doctors in the practice, and when they all worked, it made for a hectic pace. They left money for the bill and a tip on the table and waved to Ms. Bernice and a few of the patrons they passed on the way out. Outside, she gave her friend a strong hug. "Thanks for keeping me on the straight and narrow. You're absolutely right about Gabriel, and I'm going to apologize."

"I'm glad. Since we did lunch today, how about we meet for ice cream on Friday during lunch?"

"I can always make time for homemade ice cream from Splendid Scoops." Laughing, the two women went their separate ways.

The waiting room was already half-full when Serenity got back to the doctor's office. She washed her hands, stashed her salad in the staff refrigerator, and pulled the first chart. Two hours later, she called back her final patient for the day. "How are you, Mrs. Satterfield?" she asked, closing the examination room door.

"Can't complain. The Good Lord let me see another day, so I'm blessed." She took a seat in one of the chairs.

Serenity took the woman's vitals and input them into the digital file.

"How's Andrea liking her new job?"

"She said she's enjoying it so far."

"That's good. Della's sure gonna miss that girl, but she's glad to have her grandson here. Have you met him yet?"

"Yes."

Mrs. Satterfield chuckled. "Della said every time he comes to visit, he's gone before she can blink good."

"Mrs. Satterfield, have you had any problems with your medication, or do you have any other concerns since your last visit?" Serenity had to cut the woman off; otherwise, she'd be there for the next hour, telling everybody's business.

"Oh, no. Everything's going fine. As much as I like my fried chicken, I've been baking it like Dr. Jacobs said."

Serenity smiled and finished typing the information, then logged off. "Dr. Jacobs will be in shortly."

"Thanks, baby."

Serenity closed the door behind herself and laughed softly.

"Mrs. Satterfield spilling tea again?" Starr, her fellow nurse, asked.

"How did you guess?"

"It takes only two minutes to do vitals and get updated health information. You were in there for more than five minutes. Must be the arrival of Ms. Della's grandson, like everyone else has been talking about today."

Serenity whirled around and lifted a brow. "I didn't realize he was such a hot topic."

Starr shrugged. "From what I understand, he's a fine chocolate specimen, and that definitely makes for news in this little town." She winked and sashayed off down the hall.

The mention of Gabriel made her think about what she would do to apologize. Putting him out of her mind for now, Serenity finished her tasks and prepared to leave. By the time she got home, she decided she'd make some of her special brownies and take them over.

She changed clothes, cranked up the music, and headed to the kitchen. Twenty minutes later, the rich scent of chocolate filled the space. While the brownies baked, she sat at the table, ate the rest of her salad from lunch, and read a few pages from her favorite author's latest mystery novel.

Serenity had just gotten into the story when the timer went off. She replaced her bookmark, took out the brownies, and placed them on a rack to cool. She inhaled. *Perfect*. It would take an hour or so before she could package them, so that gave her more time to read.

Once the brownies reached room temperature, she cut four generous portions and put them into a plastic container. "Just apologize, give him the peace offering, and leave. Simple." Steeling herself, Serenity left to make the delivery. She found him on his knees in the yard with his back to her.

"Her name is Serenity, but I haven't seen one thing *serene* about her," he was saying, obviously talking to someone on the phone. "More like uptight and irritating. And I don't even know what I—"

"Is that right?" She placed her hand on her hip and glared at him.

Gabriel spun around and came to his feet. "Serenity. Hey."

"Uptight and irritating? Well, I don't know why your mother named you *Gabriel* because you're *no* angel!" She was so angry, she threw the container at him.

"Ow!" He muttered a curse and rubbed the spot on his head where the container had hit him.

She shot him another lethal glare and stormed off.

"Serenity. Wait."

Ignoring him, she slammed her door. *So much for calling a truce.*

CHAPTER 4

Gabriel stood in his yard, stunned. *She actually threw something at me!*

"Uh, Gabe, you all right, man?"

He'd completely forgotten about being on the phone with Darius. "Yeah. Fine." As if to make him out to be a liar, the spot on his temple where the container hit him throbbed.

"Was that Serenity yelling?"

"Yes. She overheard my comment and threw a container of something at me." He searched for the offending object and spotted it in the bushes about two feet away.

Darius burst out laughing. "Obviously, she hit her mark. Oh, man, you're gonna make me hurt myself laughing at you."

Gabriel didn't see anything remotely funny. Okay, he *had* called her uptight and irritating, but he didn't see how that translated to having an object hurled his way. The woman must have pitched on some baseball team because her speed and accuracy were dead-on. The pain in his head could attest to that.

"Brent and I are going to have to make a trip back out there to meet this woman," Darius said, still chuckling.

"Whatever. I'll call you later." He ended the call and strode across the lawn to Serenity's house. He rang the bell three times before she answered with fire in her dark-brown eyes.

"I don't have anything to say to you, Gabriel. So go home." Serenity closed the door.

This day had gone progressively downhill. First there had been a problem with a part of the program he'd been designing, and now he had a starring role in something akin to *Neighbor Wars*. To make matters worse, even anger didn't detract from Serenity's beauty or lessen his surprising attraction to her. This was *not* helping his stress levels one bit. Gabriel blew out a long breath and walked back to his yard. He bent and picked up the container. He could smell the chocolate without even opening it.

Inside, he washed his hands and removed the top. *Brownies?* He broke a piece off one of the thick cake-like sweets and popped it into his mouth. It tasted so good, his taste buds wanted to break-dance. Before he knew it, he'd eaten two of the four large brownies in the box and had to force himself not to devour the rest.

Gabriel needed to apologize or do whatever it took

to get Serenity to talk to him. One, he didn't like being at odds with her, and two, he needed more of those brownies—or at least the recipe. He checked the time and toyed with trying to get a few more minutes of work done but nixed the idea because he was supposed to be at Nana's for dinner in an hour. "Might as well go over early."

That turned out to be a good idea, and he ended up fixing a couple of light switches while Nana cooked. "All done, Nana. Is there anything else you want done while I'm here?"

"Not right now," she said, not looking up from peeling yams. She finished the last one, then washed her hands.

He watched her add the ingredients and smiled, remembering the times during the holidays when the kitchen would be filled with laughter and conversation between the ladies in the family.

"What are you smiling about?"

Gabriel never did understand how she could see him without looking. "Just thinking about all those years you, Mom, and Andrea used to kick us out of the kitchen so you could discuss *women things*."

She paused. "I miss my baby so much. Those were some good times." As if reading his thoughts, she added, "And I'm okay talking about her and your dad. It's the good memories that get me through."

He had only recently gotten to the point of smiling first, instead of feeling pain, when remembering his parents. "Can I help with anything?"

"You cook now?" Nana asked, giving him a side-long glance.

Gabriel laughed. "I've been cooking a long time. Eating out every night is expensive."

"Check the barbecue chicken and macaroni and cheese. While the candied yams are cooking, I'll make the hot-water cornbread. The cabbage is already done."

Leaning down, he kissed her cheek. "I love you, Nana. I'm looking forward to the best food I've eaten since Christmas."

She blushed and giggled like a schoolgirl. "Oh, go on with you, boy."

Even though the house was more than fifty years old, the kitchen had been enlarged and updated with a double oven and a center island. He opened the top oven, peeled back the foil on the chicken, and stuck a fork in to test for doneness. The meat almost slid off the bone. He brushed on the waiting sauce and slid the pan back in. The mac and cheese was brown, bubbly, and ready to eat.

Twenty minutes later, Nana said the blessing, then Gabriel dug in. The hot-water cornbread was crunchy on the outside and melt-in-your-mouth tender on the inside. Aside from Nana and his mother, he hadn't found one person who could make it this way.

"How are you adjusting?"

"Not being able to go out for food or entertainment after eight takes some getting used to, but I'm getting there. What about you? Have you ever thought about moving?"

"Absolutely not. Why would I pick up and leave the place where I know everybody to go to some random city where I don't know anyone? I like it here."

He nodded and wondered if getting his grandmother to come around to his thinking would be a losing battle.

"Have you talked to Serenity since Saturday?"

"I wouldn't say we've talked, just waved in passing." And yelled. And almost got his head knocked off.

"Oh. Well, I'm sure you'll get to know her now that you'll be here more than a day," she teased. "That girl has a heart of gold. Always doing something nice for somebody. Last month, when I had a touch of the flu, she brought me over some chicken soup. Fixed me right up."

Now, that *I'd like to see.* Then he remembered the brownies. That was a nice gesture, and it had sort of been his fault that they almost ended up in the flower bed. "I'm sure I will." Gabriel continued to eat and contemplate how in the world he and Serenity would patch up their differences. Obviously, his grandmother expected it, and he couldn't keep lying. *What if one of the neighbors saw the argument?* He took a big gulp of iced tea. No, if someone saw, Nana would've met him at the door with a million questions. He relaxed. "How've you been feeling?" he asked, changing the subject.

"Other than the aches that come along with getting old, pretty good. I have a checkup with the doctor next week."

"Let me know what time and I'll go with you."

"You don't need to go."

"I know. I want to. Gotta make sure my favorite Nana is all good." He leaned over and kissed her temple.

She patted his cheek. "I can see you're going to be as bad as your sister. It's Thursday at eleven o'clock," she added with a shake of her head.

Laughing, they finished eating. Gabriel stood. "I'll clean up the kitchen before I leave."

"Thanks, honey. Make sure to fix you a plate to take home. There's plenty. I'm going to put my feet up and watch that cutie Shemar Moore on *S.W.A.T.*"

Chuckling, he cleared the table. His gaze followed her departure and took in everything. Though her steps were slower, she'd maintained her tall, trim frame and still moved with a grace and agility that belied her near eighty years. Spending time with her made him realize just how much he'd missed her and wished he could go back in time and extend all those visits when he had dropped in and out in less than forty-eight hours. Family was precious, and he intended to take advantage of every moment with her.

After washing the dishes, he found Nana in her favorite recliner, eyes glued to the television screen. Knowing she didn't want to be interrupted, particularly during the action scene, he took a seat on the sofa and waited until the next commercial to say his goodbyes. "Thanks for dinner." He held up the bag. "Next time I'm cooking."

Nana's eyes lit in surprise. "You're welcome, and I'm looking forward to it."

"I'll come by Saturday morning to do the yard," he said as they walked to the front door. Gabriel had noticed the slightly overgrown grass on his way in earlier. She had always maintained a manicured lawn.

"Ooh, I'd appreciate that. The young man who's been doing it hasn't come around in two weeks." She kissed his cheek. "Be careful."

"I will."

"I'll see you later, Gabriel. Let me get back before the commercial's over. The good part is coming up."

He chuckled. "Night, Nana." He loped down the driveway to his car.

"Tell Serenity hello and to let me know when she's having the next dinner get-together."

Instead of answering, he threw up a wave. He was the last person Serenity wanted to see.

* * *

Two days later, as he sat writing codes, Gabriel still hadn't come up with a way to approach Serenity. It was the first time in a long while that a woman had invaded his mind during the workday, and no matter how hard he tried, he couldn't stop thinking about her. He'd contemplated going next door and attempting to smooth things over, but memories of the anger and hurt he'd seen in her eyes had kept him away. The anger he could deal with, but the hurt didn't sit well

with him. Never had he let a situation go this long
without a resolution, and he decided that today, one
way or another, he was going to deal with it…starting
with an apology.

Realizing that he wasn't going to get any work
done, he shut the program down and leaned back in
his chair. Maybe going for a run would clear his head.
It always helped to get his creative juices flowing
again. However, he had no idea where to go, as he
hadn't taken time to check out the town to see where
the parks or trails were located. Gabriel drummed his
fingers on the desk. On second thought, he'd head
back down to the town's center. *Ice cream from Splendid
Scoops is calling my name.* The foodie in him was eager
to find out if the ice cream lived up to its name.

He found parking on the same street as before
and headed in the direction of the shop. The noon
hour seemed to be a little more crowded than when
he'd come earlier in the week. With all the businesses
located within walking distance, he figured it would
be far more efficient to grab lunch, pastries, or dessert
in the middle of the day, instead of going home. If the
restaurants near his office back home had food like
what he'd eaten at Ms. Ida's, he would be there every
day. Of course, that also meant he'd have to kick his
workout regimen into high gear.

With the mid-June temperatures hovering near
eighty degrees, it seemed as though everyone else had
the same idea as him. He saw three people enter the
ice cream shop as he approached and just as many

leave. Serenity and Natasha were among the latter group. When Serenity saw him, her eyes widened in surprise.

"Good afternoon, ladies. I see we all had the same idea."

"Hi, Gabriel," Natasha said. "If this is your first time, you'll be back."

"It is, and if it's as good as advertised, you're absolutely right." Gabriel shifted his gaze to Serenity, who, until this point, had acted as if he were invisible. "What about you, Serenity? Any flavors you think are best for a newbie?"

"You can't go wrong with any flavor you choose because they all taste delicious." Serenity briefly looked up at him before focusing on her ice cream again.

"I'll keep that in mind," he murmured. "I won't hold you ladies. But, Serenity, I wanted to thank you again for dinner. Oh, and the brownies were some of the best I've ever eaten." The amused expression on Natasha's face made Gabriel suspect that Serenity hadn't filled her in on the brownie episode.

Natasha waved a hand. "Aren't they to die for? And those chocolate chips just take them over the top." She pretended to swoon.

Smiling, he said, "I completely agree."

"Are you coming to dinner tomorrow?"

Gabriel had no idea what Natasha was up to, but he decided to play along. "I haven't been invited." The glare Serenity shot her friend made him chuckle inwardly. She most likely had no intention of inviting him anywhere ever again, but the one thing he noticed about her that first evening was that she was the consummate hostess. As much as she wished him elsewhere, her prim and proper way wouldn't allow it.

"You're welcome to join us. It'll be at the same time," Serenity said, proving his point. "Your grandmother is welcome, too."

He smiled. "Great. Thanks. Serenity, let me know if there's anything you'd like me to bring. I'll see you tomorrow."

"Tomorrow."

"Bye, Gabriel," Natasha said.

He could see Serenity fussing as they walked away. *Things are getting interesting.*

* * *

"I should ban you from dinner," Serenity told Natasha when she opened the door to her Saturday evening.

"What?"

"Don't act all innocent. I still can't believe you invited Gabriel over after what I told you he said."

Natasha followed Serenity to the kitchen. "Actually, you're the one who invited him. I only asked if he was coming."

She rolled her eyes. "I don't even know how you kept a straight face with that lie," she muttered. Normally, they didn't do dinner on back-to-back weekends, but they had changed the date to accommodate Terri's schedule.

"Ooh, these strawberries are huge. What are you going to do with them?"

"I'm going to dip them in chocolate. They've been soaked in whiskey and champagne."

Natasha rubbed her hands together and grinned. "I can't wait."

Serenity laughed at her friend's exuberance. "I made a couple of each a few minutes ago to test." She took a saucer out of the refrigerator, offered one to Natasha and took the other one. Trying new recipes and flavors had always been one of Serenity's favorite things, and the kicked-up chocolate-dipped berries fell perfectly into that category. She'd dipped the champagne-infused ones in milk chocolate and the whiskey-infused ones in dark chocolate, but she planned to do the full batch using a variety of milk, white, and dark chocolate. "Okay. The taste test. Champagne first." She bit into it and chewed slowly.

"Oh my goodness," Natasha said around a mouthful. "This. Is. So. *Freakin'*. Good!" Her eyes slid closed as she moaned and took another bite. "Girl, I think I'm going to have to pay you to make a few of these as gifts for my clients when they close on a property." She reached for the second one. "You really should think about selling these, especially around Valentine's Day or for bridal showers."

She smiled. "They are good, and they came out better than I expected. That whiskey is a little potent, though."

"This is a grown folks' dessert. What's for dinner?"

"Pan-seared lamb rib chops, roasted potatoes, and sautéed green beans with bacon."

"Yum. And bacon really does make everything much better," Natasha said with a laugh.

Her comment brought to mind Gabriel saying the same thing. Automatically, Serenity's mind went back to what had happened on Wednesday, when he'd accused her of being uptight and irritating. She felt really bad about hitting him with the container, though, especially since she'd never been one to resort to violence for any reason. But how was she going to get through dinner pretending she wasn't still bothered by what she had overheard? And did he really see her that way? She told herself she didn't care, but deep down she knew she was lying. Shaking off thoughts of her neighbor, she said, "The potatoes are already in the oven, and I'll put the rolls in once everybody arrives. What do you think about neutrals for the table setting today?"

Natasha angled her head thoughtfully. "I like it. I brought greenery and a couple of glass candleholders to use with ivory floating candles. Your dark-tan table runner and ivory china with the gold rim would work perfectly—simple and elegant." She pushed off the counter where she had been leaning and walked toward the cabinet where Serenity kept her table linens.

Serenity went about preparing the rest of the meal and dipping the berries. She made sure to keep them separate just in case someone had a preference for a specific alcohol.

Dana and Terri arrived a short while later, and the kitchen became filled with conversation, laughter, and stories from the week.

"I had a patient ask me out on a date," Terri started. "When I told him I was married, he said 'What your husband doesn't know won't hurt him. I won't tell if you don't.' I was too done."

They all laughed.

Dana shook her head. "At least you didn't have some nut get upset because a *woman* had worked on his car and then had the nerve to demand that a *man* recheck it to make sure it was done right." She sipped her wine.

"I would've loved to see his face when your dad told him you were the one in charge," Serenity said, doubled over in laughter.

"Girl, it was priceless, especially when he turned over the engine and it purred like it had just come off the factory line." She toasted them with her glass, and they howled.

In the midst of the next story, the doorbell rang.

"That must be your fine next door neighbor," Terri said. "If I had known he was coming, I would've tried to convince Jon to come." Terri's husband worked as an attorney and always declined the dinner invitation, citing not wanting to be the only man.

Serenity hopped down from the stool. "If Gabriel comes again, I'll be sure to let you know." Although he probably didn't want to be around a lot of women, either, she thought as she made her way to the front to let him in. That was fine by her. The less she saw of him, the better. By the time she got there, a slight flutter of butterflies danced in her belly. Pasting a smile on her face and hoping it looked genuine, she opened the door. "Hey, Gabriel. Come on in." She had to give it to him—the man did look good in jeans and a pullover black silk tee. *And he smells good, too.* The light scent of citrus and wood wafted into her nostrils as he entered.

"Hey." Gabriel handed her a bouquet of flowers. "These are for you."

"Thank you. They're gorgeous. Where's your grandmother?"

"She and some ladies went to Napa to take one of those wine train tours."

Serenity smiled. "I need to have her social calendar. We're all in the kitchen."

He placed a staying hand on her arm when she turned. "Can I talk to you for a minute?"

She looked up at his serious features. "Sure."

He hesitated a moment before speaking. "I want to apologize for my comments. They were way out of line. Also, I truly didn't mean anything by what I said in the store. I was only joking and making conversation."

Serenity sighed inwardly. His sincerity touched her in a way she hadn't expected. "Apology accepted. And I'm sorry, too…for the incident in the store and for the corn remark at dinner. Oh, and for…you know…throwing the container…" She cleared her throat. That had definitely not been her best moment.

A slow smile made its way across his lips. "No

harm done. And since I got to eat every last brownie—which were amazing, by the way—let's just forget about it and start again. I'd really like to get to know you." He stuck out his hand. "Friends?"

She grasped his hand and smiled. "Yeah. Friends." Just like the first time they'd met, he didn't let go of her hand. And the way he was staring at her made her pulse skip. *Ooo-kay. What is that?* She smoothly pulled her hand back. "Um...dinner is almost...I just have to cook the meat and stick the rolls in the oven." Finally, she tore her gaze away from his.

"Lead the way," he murmured.

In the kitchen, Gabriel greeted her friends, then poured himself a glass of wine. Even as he contributed to the conversation, Serenity could feel his gaze on her when she placed the pan of rolls into the oven.

A couple of minutes later, he wandered over while she heated the olive oil in a skillet and picked up the bottle. "Hmm...buttery and sweet. Does this mean it's butter flavored?"

"No. The flavor comes from the type of olive. They do have some flavored oils that I love. The lemon and lime are my favorites for seafood and vinaigrettes. The difference with this brand is that the fruit is pressed with the olives instead of being infused later, and it's delicious." She placed the lamb in the hot oil and cooked it for a few minutes on each side before placing it on a serving platter.

"This smells great. I can help you take the food out." Gabriel set his wineglass on the island.

"That would be great. Thanks. You can wash your hands in the bathroom right down the hall." He walked out, and all three of her friends gave her a thumbs-up as they smothered giggles. She ignored them, took the rolls out, and dumped them into the bread bowl. By the time she finished filling all the serving dishes, Gabriel had returned.

He picked up the platters holding the meat and the potatoes and took them outside.

Dana sidled up next to Serenity. "A man that offers to help in the kitchen without being asked…yes, yes, *yes*. You think he has any friends?"

Chuckling, Serenity bumped her playfully. "Girl, bye. Take these green beans outside."

"I'm just sayin'."

Serenity shook her head and looked at Natasha and Terri. "I don't want to hear one word. Just bring the wine and bread." Terri mimicked zipping her lips, picked up the rolls and butter, and sashayed out to the deck. Natasha followed suit with the wine. Both, thankfully, kept their comments to themselves. Serenity picked up her wineglass, as well as Gabriel's, and joined her guests. Dinner turned out to be a relaxed affair, with Serenity not having to be on guard and worrying about what Gabriel thought of her.

"Gabriel, you've been here a week now. What do you think about the town?" Terri asked.

"It's small," he answered. "And it's hard getting used to the quiet and everything shutting down well before midnight."

Serenity nodded. "I thought the same thing when I first moved here—no fast food or being able to jump in the car to go out for a late-night snack. But the Bay Area isn't too far, and Napa Valley is even closer. So, I get my city fix that way."

"I'll have to keep that in mind. Are there any parks or running trails around?"

"Plenty," Natasha said. "And all within five miles. Seaside Meadows Park is a great one for running, and it's near the lake, so the view is spectacular."

Gabriel nodded as he chewed a piece of the lamb. "I'll have to check it out. Serenity, once again, this meal is incredible. I'm definitely going to have to pick up some of the olive oil."

"Thank you." His praise should not have warmed her heart, but it did. They fell silent for a few minutes, but every time she looked Gabriel's way, his eyes were waiting.

"Okay." Dana held up a rib chop. "Am I the only one who's tired of trying to eat this thing with a knife and fork?"

"I was thinking the same thing," Gabriel said, "but I didn't want to come up in here and act like I didn't have any home training."

Serenity burst out laughing. "Nobody said you had to cut it with a knife. Just pick it up and bite it." She picked up one from her plate and bit into it. "See? Easy."

His eyes sparkled with mirth and he followed suit, taking off nearly all the meat on the small chop in one bite.

Smiling, they all enjoyed the tender pieces of meat sans utensils and continued to converse while finishing the meal.

"Oh, wait. This is my *song*." Natasha raised her arms in the air and started singing along to Mary J. Blige's "Just Fine."

It took only a moment for the infectious rhythm to have the other women joining in, including Serenity. They belted out the lyrics as if they were seated front row at a concert, and Gabriel simply nodded in time with the beat and smiled. Serenity wished she knew what was going through his head, but these were her girls, and they always had fun when they got together.

When the song ended, Gabriel clapped. "You ladies ought to take this show on the road. I have to say it's nice getting a meal and entertainment all in one place." He lifted his glass in salute.

Serenity fanned herself and stood. "I'll bring out dessert." She was gone and back in a flash with the berries and set the two plates in the center of the table. "These are kicked up with champagne and whiskey," she said, pointing to each dish as she spoke. She could never leave them plain and had drizzled white chocolate on the milk-chocolate- and dark-chocolate-dipped ones, the opposite on the white, and had done a few half-white and half-milk. Natasha quickly snatched up one from each plate, while Dana and Terri chose strawberries infused with champagne.

"Where did you get these?" Gabriel asked, reaching for one infused with whiskey.

"I made them." She held his gaze as he bit into the sweet treat and tried not to think about the sexy way his lips closed around the fruit.

He groaned and reached for another one. "I think this is the best dipped strawberry I've ever eaten. I can easily get addicted to these."

The way he stared at Serenity made her think he was talking about more than just the strawberries. *Friends. That's it. Nothing more.*

CHAPTER 5

Gabriel arrived at his grandmother's house and pulled into the driveway thirty minutes before her appointment. She opened the front door as he stepped out of the car.

"Morning, Gabriel. Can you park in front of the house? We're taking my car."

"Hey, Nana. Sure." He climbed back in and did as she asked. He met her at the top of the driveway and placed a kiss on her cheek. "If you give me your keys, I'll go ahead and pull the car out." She still drove the same Buick from twenty years ago.

Nana eyed him. "No need." She pressed the remote in her hand. The garage opened, and she went to the driver's side.

His heart started pounding. Surely she didn't plan on driving. Gabriel hadn't driven with her since he was a kid, and he recalled her being an extra-careful driver. But she was much younger then and her reaction time faster. Although he knew she'd been getting around town on her own, he'd still feel more comfortable being behind the wheel. And he wanted to get there on time. "Ah, Nana—"

"Are you coming? I need to stop by Flora's and pick up some collards, green beans, and tomatoes first."

Sighing, Gabriel walked around to the passenger side and got in. "Do you have enough time? Maybe we should go after your appointment." He buckled his seat belt.

She started the engine, backed down the driveway, and hit the button to close the garage. "It'll only take fifteen minutes to do both. She doesn't live that far."

She pulled off in a burst of speed that had him clutching the armrest. "Aren't you driving a little fast, Nana?"

"This is how I always drive, and I'm not going that fast. Relax." Nana started humming along to the song on the radio. She blew her horn and waved at an older couple walking down the street. "It's good to see them out and about. They've both been sick. I'm going to have to take them some dinner."

Gabriel didn't utter a word. He couldn't. She whipped around a corner so fast, it pressed him against the car door. He hadn't prayed in a long while, but today he offered up a steady litany, in hopes that they would arrive at their destination in one piece. Less than five minutes later, she slowed and turned onto the gravel driveway of a farm-style house with a wraparound porch, and his heart rate started to slow.

He spotted a huge colorful garden off to one side with a light-brown-skinned woman wearing a calf-length lounging dress and a colorful wrap on her head pulling weeds.

Nana got out. "Hey, Flora."

"Hey, Della. I've got your box on the porch. We have so much growing this year, I can't get rid of it fast enough."

Gabriel finally felt steady enough to get out of the car and approach the women.

Nana beckoned him forward. "Flora, this is my grandson, Gabriel. He's taking Andrea's place in watching over me like a mother hen. Gabriel, this is Flora King. We go all the way back to primary school."

A smile creased the woman's weathered face, and she waved a hand. "Nice to meet you, Gabriel. And don't mind your grandma. We old ladies think we can still do everything we did when we were young and don't like to admit we need help, but it's nice to see grandchildren who care."

"It's nice to meet you, too, ma'am."

"Handsome and polite. I might need to introduce you to my two grandsons. Neither of them can spell 'manners.' *Hmph*." She rolled her eyes. "Let me get this box."

He chuckled. "If you show me where the box is, I'll get it." He followed her up the steps and lifted the large box overflowing with vegetables she indicated. Two others sat next to it, and he assumed they were being given away as well.

After loading the box into the trunk, Gabriel braced himself for another mad dash to the doctor's office. When they arrived, Nana breezed in and gave her name to the receptionist, while Gabriel dropped into the nearest chair and wondered if *he* was the one in need of a doctor.

She sat next to him, smiled serenely, and patted his knee. "I want to walk down to the bakery and get a piece of peach cobbler after we leave."

"Okay, but I'm driving back."

She pursed her lips and scowled at him but didn't reply. It took only a few minutes for her to be called in.

He leaned his head back, closed his eyes, and took a couple of deep breaths, trying to calm his nerves.

"Gabriel."

His eyes popped open, and he came to his feet quickly. "Serenity, hey." Today she wore a pair of purple scrubs and had swept her braids up in a bun, giving him an unobstructed view of her beautiful face.

Serenity frowned. "Are you okay? You look a little...I don't know."

"Still shaken up after riding here with Nana. The woman drove like she was trying to qualify for a spot in the Indy 500. My blood pressure is probably through the roof," he added with a shake of his head.

She laughed softly. "Do we need to get you in to see the doctor?"

Gabriel scrubbed a hand down his face. "Maybe." Seeing her smile brought back memories of the fun he'd had at the last dinner. The relaxed and playful side she'd shown intrigued him more than he cared to admit, and as he'd told her, he really wanted to get to know her. More than that, he sensed a growing attraction he was helpless to stop. However, he dismissed any thoughts of him and Serenity becoming more than friends. He didn't plan to stay and shouldn't start anything he couldn't finish. To distract himself, he asked, "Is Nana okay?"

"She's fine. It's just her annual checkup. I'm sure she'll fill you in."

"I doubt it," he said.

"I'll let Dr. Jacobs know you'd like to talk to him."

He blew out a relieved breath. "That would be great. Thanks, Serenity."

She gave his hand a reassuring squeeze. "Anytime." She crossed the room, stopping to comfort a fussy baby before disappearing through the door.

Gabriel had been wrong. She'd been given the perfect name, and it was that calm, serene quality that called to him. Her touch had been meant for comfort, but his body interpreted it much differently. *Friends only*, he reminded himself as he took out his phone to check and respond to emails, send a text to Darius to let him know the first system test ran well, and make notes to himself about the interactive video game he wanted to design for children.

"Mr. Cunningham?"

His head came up. A smiling, middle-aged woman stood near the door. "Yes."

"You can come on back."

Pocketing his phone, he stood and followed her to the examination room where his grandmother and the doctor—who looked to be about the same age as Nana—sat laughing about something.

At Gabriel's entrance, the man stood and extended his hand. "I'm Dr. Jacobs. I've heard a lot about you, Gabriel."

Gabriel shot Nana a quick glance. "Nice to meet you. I hope nothing too bad."

"Not at all," the doctor said warmly. "Have a seat. I understand you have some questions."

He lowered himself into the chair next to Nana. "Not questions really. Just want to know how she's doing."

"She's doing quite well. I adjusted her blood pressure medication last time because her pressure was a little low, but now it's in the normal range, so I'm pleased."

He let out the breath he'd been holding. Her high blood pressure had been the cause of the stroke, and it gave him a measure of relief to know that the levels had decreased. "So am I. Is there anything she needs to be doing or something I should be aware of?"

"We've worked on changing her diet to include less fried foods, and she has started walking a few times a week. She's doing a great job."

"I told you I was okay," Nana said, eyeing both men.

Dr. Jacobs smiled. "I'll see you in three months, Della."

Gabriel stood and helped Nana up. "Thanks, Doctor."

The older man patted Gabriel on his shoulder. "Anytime, son."

Nana slung her purse on her shoulder. "I'll see you later, Howard. Tell Ada I'll call her about the Tahoe trip."

"Will do. Take care." He escorted them out to the front, spoke with the receptionist, then went back down the hall.

It dawned on Gabriel that her next appointment would coincide with the time frame he had planned to be back in Atlanta. Then he thought about her having to find another doctor. She seemed to have a familiarity and rapport with Dr. Jacobs. When he'd broached the subject over dinner, Nana had all but shut him down. It seemed bringing her around to his viewpoint would require far more persuasion than he'd anticipated.

* * *

Friday afternoon, Serenity finished her last chart and packed up to leave. The office closed at four, and that gave her plenty of daylight to still get some things done.

"Hi, Ms. Wheeler."

She turned and smiled. "Hi, Brianna. How are your ears?" The six-year-old had come in to follow up on an ear infection.

"Dr. Thomas said all the bad stuff is gone," she

answered with a huge grin. "I'm having a tea party on Saturday. Wanna come?"

"I'm sure Ms. Wheeler has other things to do," her mother cut in.

Serenity squatted down in front of the little girl. "I'd love to come. I used to have tea parties with my mom when I was little."

"Yay! Kaylee and Tanya are coming, too."

"What are we having?"

Brianna gave Serenity an incredulous look. "It's a tea party. We're having *tea*." She glanced up at her mother as if she couldn't believe what she'd just heard and shook her head.

Serenity couldn't do anything but laugh. "I meant what are we having to eat with the tea?"

She thought for a minute, then shrugged. "I don't know. Mommy, what kind of food are you supposed to eat at a tea party?"

"You can have little sandwiches, some fruit, and dessert."

Brianna nodded. "Ooh, okay."

Serenity stood. "I tell you what. I'll bring the food. I know the perfect cookie to go with tea. They're called vanilla crisps, and they taste so good."

"Serenity, you don't have to do that. This child will have you baking all kinds of things if you let her."

"Pam, it's no trouble at all. What time is the party?"

"I was thinking from noon until about one."

Brianna bounced up and down. "And you have to wear a dress and a hat."

"Oh, I have the perfect hat," Serenity said. Or at least she would once she found one when she went shopping on the way home.

Pam took Brianna's hand. "Come on, girl. Serenity, whatever you wear will be fine." Shaking her head, she led her exuberant daughter out.

Still smiling, Serenity said her goodbyes.

Instead of going straight to the grocery store, she walked a block to Back Porch Boutique. It took only ten minutes to find a navy hat, complete with a bow to match her navy and white striped dress. She retraced her steps, hopped in her car, and drove over to Vineyard Foods.

Inside, Serenity got everything on her list, along with some extra lunch meat and bread for the sandwiches. It had been a long time since she'd gone to a tea party and she was almost as excited as Brianna. Maybe, for the next supper club, she'd do a tea party. *Yep, a tea party.* The wheels in her mind started turning, and she mentally debated on menu options. On her way to the register, she called out and returned greetings. Not for the first time, she realized how much she enjoyed living here.

She checked out, loaded the car, and headed home. The guy from the landscaping company was supposed to be coming to do the yard at five thirty, and she had just enough time to meet him. As soon as she pulled into her driveway, she saw Gabriel sweeping up grass and bobbing his head to what she assumed was music coming through the earbuds in his ears. He wore a tank top and shorts, and she sat watching the way the muscles in his arms bunched and flexed with every movement. As if sensing her scrutiny, he turned and smiled. Serenity felt her cheeks warm with embarrassment and quickly pulled into the garage and got out of the car.

The man must think I'm crazy, sitting in the car staring at him like I don't have good sense. Except it made perfect sense because the man's body was an absolute work of art. Not to mention, he had a smile that reminded her of pure sunshine, and whenever he looked at her with those beautiful eyes, her heart skipped a beat. She felt the heat between them but was determined to ignore it. Putting her mind back where it belonged, she popped the trunk and grabbed two bags.

Gabriel closed the distance between them, yanked out an earbud, then took out his phone and paused his music. "Hey, Serenity. Need some help?"

"Hi. I'd love some help. Thanks." He grabbed the other five bags easily and followed her in through the garage entrance. She quickened her steps to the kitchen counter and dumped the bags to catch her ringing cell. "Hello." Serenity listened to the excuse the landscaper gave and felt her anger rise. She disconnected and tossed the phone on the counter. "*Ugh!* Why can't people just do what they say?"

"Um…where do you want these?"

She'd forgotten about Gabriel. "I'm sorry. You can just set them on the island."

He carefully set them down, then came back to where she stood. "Is everything okay?"

"Yeah. Just the lawn care company canceling again. This is the second time this month. Pretty soon I'm going to need a hatchet to cut the grass."

Gabriel rubbed her arm. "I'll take care of it."

Her surprised gaze met his. "Oh, I can't ask you to do that, but thank you so much for offering."

"You didn't ask. I offered, and it's no problem. My mower is still out, and it'll only take about an hour or so."

"Thanks, Gabriel. You're a lifesaver. I can pay you." First his concern for his grandmother and now his offer to help bring in her groceries and mow her lawn. She didn't even have to think about the number of times her ex had offered to do either of those things. He hadn't. Ever. Gabriel seemed to be of a different mind, and the more she got to know him, the more she found to like. A girl could easily fall for a man like him.

Gabriel raised a brow. "I'm not taking any money from you. While I'm here, you won't have to worry about whether they cancel or not. I've got it. No charge. That's what neighbors and friends do."

He tossed her a wink and strolled out, leaving Serenity with her mouth hanging open. She laughed to herself and began putting her groceries away. He reminded her of the way her father treated her mother—jumping in to help without being asked. It had nothing to do with the fact that her mom couldn't handle the task, because she could. As her mother had told her once, it was just nice that she didn't have to all the time.

Serenity stacked the cans in the pantry and went still. *While I'm here* ... Did that mean he didn't plan to stay long? All the more reason to ignore the attraction that seemed to grow more intense each time she saw him. Besides, she already knew the score—one heartbreak was enough to last her a lifetime.

After she finished, she folded her reusable grocery bags and took them back to her car. She had a habit of forgetting them and, more than once, ended up having to buy more. She couldn't resist a peek at Gabriel. He was more than halfway done. Because her house was on the corner, the yard extended around the side. The size of the front and back yards were selling points for her. But the large kitchen and master bedroom with its sitting area had sealed the deal. Watching him a moment longer, she had to admit that he'd done a far better job than the landscaping company. A thought came to her. He wouldn't take money, but she'd bet he wouldn't turn down food.

She had planned to make a teriyaki chicken stir-fry over rice and always cooked enough for leftovers. Tapping on the counter, she debated on a dessert, then remembered him saying how much he'd enjoyed the brownies. Serenity turned on her music, and as always, it didn't take long for her to get lost in both. So much so that she was startled when she got a glimpse of him through her periphery. *He's doing the backyard, too?* She refocused on cooking. *That's what friends and neighbors do.*

"Knock, knock." Gabriel came in through the garage.

"Hey."

"All done. I already set the garbage can at the curb." Gabriel wiped the sweat from his forehead with the back of his hand.

"Thank you. I can't tell you how much I appreciate this. Have you had dinner yet?"

"No."

"Good. You said you wouldn't take money. How about joining me for dinner? It's the least I can do."

"Now, *that's* an offer I can't refuse."

"Yeah, I didn't think you would." They shared a smile.

His laughter filled the kitchen. "Mind if I go take a quick shower first?"

"Nope. Everything will be ready by the time you get back. You don't have to knock. Just come on in."

"Okay. I won't be long." He blessed her with one of those sexy smiles that made his eyes sparkle, and then he was gone.

He really is a nice guy. Serenity stood there for a minute longer, her smile still in place, before going back to the stove.

She had just spooned the stir-fry onto a bed of steaming rice when he walked back in. "Wow, that was fast."

"It doesn't take long for a man to jump in and out

of a shower. And I was even faster because I knew I'd be getting some great food. What do you need me to do?"

"If you can grab that pitcher of lemonade from the refrigerator and the glasses, that'll be great." Once again, she compared him to her ex. Whenever they'd hosted a party, he'd conveniently made himself unavailable while she did everything from cooking and setting the table to bringing out the platters of food. *The jerk.* Serenity couldn't believe she'd stayed with him as long as she had. "Do you want to eat in here or out back?"

"Out back, if it's not too cool for you," Gabriel said. "I think the temps have dropped a bit."

"Let's see." She came over and opened the sliding glass door. It had cooled some, but not enough to be uncomfortable. "This will be fine." She scanned her yard. "Oh my. This looks like the eighteenth green on one of those golf courses." He'd mowed the lawn diagonally, and it seemed to make the grass look greener and lusher.

"I'm glad you like it."

While he took care of the drinks, she brought out the plates, silverware, and bowl holding their dinner. "Wait. I need to get the candles." The sun had begun its descent, and it would be dark soon. She hurried back inside, grabbed the first ones she saw, along with a lighter and the portable speaker, and returned to the table. After lighting the candles, she jumped slightly when Gabriel eased behind her and helped her with her chair. "Thank you."

Gabriel rounded the table and took the seat opposite her. "This is nice."

In hindsight, the candles and soft music made for a romantic atmosphere she hadn't counted on. "It is."

"Ladies first." He gestured for her to fill her plate before filling his own. After the first bite, his eyes slid closed briefly, and a look of pure enjoyment came over his face. "I have to tell you, Ms. Wheeler, you may never get rid of me if you keep feeding me all this delicious food. This tastes better than any restaurant. Did you go to culinary school?"

"The culinary schools of Agnes Wheeler and Minnie Lee Jefferson," Serenity said with a grin. "My grandmothers. I was fascinated by how they could make cakes, rolls, and just about everything without looking at a recipe." She laughed softly. "Of course, much later I learned they'd memorized those precious recipes that had been handed down through generations." She forked up a bite.

"And have you memorized all of them, too?"

Serenity leaned forward and whispered conspiratorially, "Maybe."

Gabriel threw his head back and roared with laughter. "You are something else. In case you haven't noticed, I love good food. My boys tease me because whenever we take a trip, the first thing I do is check out the restaurants."

"So, you're a foodie, huh?"

"A little bit."

"I'd think you'd be the one to do culinary school."

"I thought about taking a couple of classes, but I love designing programs." He braced his forearms on the table. "There's something about being able to create a program or game that gives me a rush. When I was younger, I lived to play video games with my buddies. Only, I wanted to know how the developers could create the many different levels based on the choice of the game player. I became obsessed to the point that I decided to follow that path in college."

His passion excited Serenity, and the melodic sound of his deep voice soothed her. She could listen to him all day. "It's amazing to be able to find a career you love."

"It is. But you've done the same. I can see why you chose nursing. You're caring, compassionate, and I saw how you went out of your way to comfort a baby in the waiting room. I know I'd be in good hands if you were my nurse."

"That's the best compliment I've ever gotten. Thank you," she said softly. They fell silent for a few minutes and continued eating, both seemingly lost in their own thoughts. The sun had dipped below the horizon, leaving a clear black velvet sky dotted with stars and the light from the moon. Contemporary jazz competed with nature's song.

Gabriel took a sip of his drink. "There's one thing I'm curious about."

"What's that?"

"How did you start the whole dinner thing you do?"

She dabbed the corners of her mouth with the

napkin, then smoothed it in her lap. "I'd put my love of cooking on the shelf for a good six months, and after moving here, I figured it was time to dust my pans off again." She kept the reason to herself for now. "I decided to invite my girlfriends over, including your sister, and we had so much fun, I did it again. It kind of snowballed from there and became a regular thing. Andrea even gave it a name—Serenity's Supper Club."

Gabriel shook his head. "Leave it to Drea to come up with a name. I'll admit, it is kind of catchy. Good company, good music, great food—it has all the qualities of an old-school supper club."

Serenity laughed. "That's exactly what she said. It must be that sibling thing."

"Or something."

She pointed to his empty plate. "There's plenty if you'd like more."

"Nah, I'm good. I ate a double portion the first go-around."

"I hope you left room for dessert." She wiggled her eyebrows.

"I'm definitely going to have to work out more hanging around you. Otherwise you're going to have to roll me out of here."

"It's all about moderation." She stood. "I'll be right back." When she placed the small plate of brownies on the table, he groaned.

"You're killing me, woman. There's no way I can even *think* about moderation with these brownies."

He got the biggest one and took a hefty bite. "I could eat just these for the rest of my life." Gabriel grasped her hand. "Serenity, you are one helluva cook. I'll mow your lawn and do anything else you want if it means I can have this as payment." Holding her gaze, he placed a soft kiss on the back of her hand. He devoured the rest of the brownie in two bites and reached for another one.

The warmth of his strong hand in hers and the feel of his lips on her skin sent a flurry of sensations through her. *Breathe, girl. I am not going to fall for this man.*

CHAPTER 6

Saturday morning, Gabriel sat on the terrace attached to his bedroom, still thinking about his dinner with Serenity. He couldn't recall the last time he'd enjoyed a woman's company so much, and it hadn't even been a real date. Although, sitting across from her with lit candles and the moonlight as a backdrop had provided an intimacy he hadn't realized he was missing. The last three women he had gone out with had had him itching to leave within the first half hour. But last night he'd talked and laughed with Serenity for a good four hours, and not once did he sense the restlessness that usually crept up. Just the opposite. He'd wanted to stay all night listening to her sultry voice and had to force himself to leave.

Holding her soft hand, though initially not intentional, had him fantasizing about touching her, caressing her, kissing her. That gave him pause. They'd agreed on friendship, but what he was beginning to feel went beyond that limit, and he didn't quite know what he should do about it. The one thing he did know was that he wanted a repeat of last night. He didn't think she was seeing anyone. Surely he would have noticed a man hanging around. And if she were his lady, she certainly wouldn't be entertaining another man, new neighbor or not.

A thought occurred to him. He didn't even have her phone number. With her being next door and them always running into each other, it had never crossed his mind. Gabriel would be correcting that oversight the next time he saw her. Okay, so that made two things on his to-do list. He wanted to take her out, but someplace other than Ms. Ida's. He planned to go running at the park Natasha suggested, and afterward, he would see what else the quaint town had to offer.

Gabriel heard his phone ringing and went back inside to answer it.

"Brent, it's nine thirty on a Saturday morning," he said when he connected.

Brent laughed. "We figured we'd catch you before you got started for the day."

He lifted a brow. "We?"

"Yep," Darius and Glenn said.

"Uh-oh. Did something happen?" It wasn't unusual for Brent and Darius to conference call him, but rarely did all three of his friends hop on a call.

"That's what we're calling to find out. I told them about the run-in you had with your neighbor, and we wanted to get the scoop on round two."

"It wasn't that serious that you had to be the town crier, Darius." He should have known.

"No, but it was funny as hell. You guys should've heard her. Man, I would've given anything to see that. What was in the container anyway?"

"Brownies." And he had four more in the kitchen waiting for him. That brought a smile to his face.

Glenn chuckled. "Well, have you gotten anything else thrown at your head since then?"

"No. We're past that and decided to be friends. We had dinner together last night." Gabriel wanted to snatch the words back as soon as they were out of his mouth. That's all his friends needed to hear. They'd been trying to hook him up with one woman after another to "help" him get over his heartbreak. This would be all the ammunition they needed.

"Dinner, as in the get-together thing like before?"

"Just the two of us. And before you clowns start, she invited me to dinner because I mowed her lawn. The company she hired no-showed on her twice." He crossed the room to the terrace and reclaimed his lounger.

"Aw, look at you out there being all neighborly," Brent said. "How long were you over there?"

"Why?"

"Just answer the question."

Gabriel sighed. Reason number twenty-five to keep personal business *personal*. "A few hours," he finally mumbled.

"Well, that settles it. I do believe it's time for another trip out West, gentlemen," Darius said.

"Agreed," Brent said.

Glenn, always the level-headed one, said, "Sounds like she was just returning the favor."

"Thank you, Glenn. At least one person has some sense. That's all it was. Besides, there's no reason to start anything with Serenity when I don't plan on being here long." Gabriel said the words but knew they weren't completely truthful. He did want to start something with Serenity. Just what, he didn't know.

Darius snorted. "Nah, bro. Nice try, but we know you. You're feeling this woman."

Why do I even bother? "And if I am?" Like Darius said, they knew Gabriel. Knew how devastated he'd been by his ex's betrayal and how he'd used work as a cover-up, a substitute for what was missing in his personal life. Though he no longer thought of it that way, the long working hours filled the void whenever loneliness came calling. Yes, he'd finally put that chapter behind him, and the pain no longer consumed him day and night, but his version of dating now didn't involve anything remotely close to an emotional entanglement. Dinner: check. Movie: check. Sex: maybe. Love: absolutely not. But if he were being honest with himself, Serenity did stir something inside him. And not all of it was physical, which would typically send him running in the opposite direction. Why wasn't he running this time? *Maybe because I know I won't be here long.*

"Then it's a good thing, and I hope it works out with her."

"Darius, I don't know how you and Brent are deep into my business when the two of you don't even have your own relationship issues straightened out."

Darius laughed. "Hey, I told you I'm looking for that one woman, but if I don't keep dating, how am I supposed to find her? It's not like she's going to appear out of thin air and announce she's my one."

"He's got a point," Brent chimed in. "At least we do date. You, on the other hand, have gone out what…four, five times in the past two years?"

Gabriel didn't appreciate having his love life or lack of one analyzed so early in the morning. "Did y'all call for something else? If not, can we be done with this conversation?"

"Sure, but we're still making that trip. And before you start again," Darius said, "we're not coming to interfere with your love life. We rarely get out to the West Coast and want to check out San Francisco, Oakland, and maybe even Napa. And since you're there now, it gives us a reason to fly out."

He had been to the Bay Area only a couple of times years ago, and it would be cool to visit again. "Sounds like a plan. Let me know when you're coming and we can make it a weekend."

"You all will have to count me out of this one," Glenn said. "I don't think Toya wants to hang out for a guys' weekend. Once you three stop playing around and get married, we can take a group vacation."

"On that note, I've got to go," Gabriel said with a chuckle.

Brent's laughter came through the line. "Yeah. Gabe, we'll let you know when we're coming and will probably have it worked out by the time we meet next week."

"Sounds good. Later." Gabriel disconnected and smiled. He relished the friendship with his boys, even if they got on his nerves sometimes.

Swinging his legs over the side of the lounger, he stood and checked the weather on his phone. Seventy degrees was perfect for running.

The drive to Seaside Meadows Park took less than ten minutes. Natasha hadn't lied. The beauty of the area took his breath away—flowers blooming in every color, majestic tree-lined trails, and a tranquil lake perfect for just about anything. He saw a few couples strolling along the paths hand in hand and imagined bringing Serenity here.

Gabriel took a few minutes to stretch, set his watch for three miles, then started a slow jog. He kept the easy pace for the first few minutes, then gradually increased his speed. While he ran, he thought of new ideas to deal with the technical issue he'd been having with one aspect of his program and how he was going to convince his grandmother to leave her home. But mostly, his mind kept straying to Serenity and why she had captured his attention the way she had.

His watch buzzed, letting him know he'd reached his goal. He reversed his course and, instead of jogging back, opted to walk and take in the scenery. At the end of the trail, he detoured to the lake and stood at the water's edge, enjoying the slight breeze and the gentle ripples across the surface. Gabriel inhaled deeply, allowing the sweet air to fill his lungs, and exhaled slowly. After a few minutes more, he made his way back to the car and drove home. This time he took a different route and came upon another business district, this one with a bank, a few more shops, and an upscale steakhouse. A smile curved his lips. He noted the name and street for future reference.

When he arrived home, he saw Serenity coming out her front door with a large tote. She had on a blue and white patterned dress that stopped at her knees, strappy navy sandals that added several inches to her petite frame, and a matching hat. *She is stunning.* He climbed out of the car and closed the distance between them. "Good afternoon. You look beautiful."

Serenity gave him a bright smile. "Thank you. I'm on my way to a tea party."

His brows knitted together. "Women still have those?"

She shrugged. "I have no idea. This one is with a group of six-year-olds. One of my patients invited me, and there's no way I could turn down an invitation to a party. I've known Brianna since she was born."

"Wow. You are brave." Her declaration was one more piece of evidence of her caring and compassionate personality. "Well, I don't want to make you late. Have a great time."

"I intend to," she said with a laugh and slid in behind the wheel.

The movement made her dress slide up, exposing a few inches of her smooth thighs. Gabriel tried to ignore the jolt that went to his groin and closed the door. He threw up a wave as she drove off. As Brent had put it, Gabriel was definitely *feeling* her. And despite the fact that his time in California would be short, he wanted to feel more.

* * *

"Hi, Serenity. Please, come in," Brianna's mom said. "You look so gorgeous."

"Thanks. So do you."

Pam smoothed a hand down her yellow sundress. "You know, Brianna picked it out when we went shopping a couple of weeks ago and insisted I wear it for the tea party." She shook her head.

Serenity grinned. "Hey, she has good taste."

Smiling, Pam called out, "Brianna, guess who's here?"

The pounding of feet sounded on the hardwood floors, followed by a loud squeal.

"Ms. Wheeler! You came!"

"Of course I came." Brianna's excitement warmed Serenity's heart, and she barely had time to brace herself before Brianna launched herself at Serenity, nearly knocking her over in her heels. Serenity hugged the little girl, whom she'd bonded with from birth. Serenity had been in Firefly Lake only three weeks and was still trying to get over her heartbreak when Pam and her husband showed up in the ER with Pam in labor. She had rushed out with a wheelchair, but the impatient child ended up being delivered right there in the back seat, and it was the most beautiful thing that Serenity had been part of in her entire career. As a result, she'd been invited to every birthday party and a few other celebrations, and Serenity felt as if she was an aunt of sorts. She disentangled herself from Brianna. "Let me see your pretty dress and hat."

Brianna did a little pose and turned around slowly, to give the full effect of the pink dress. The pink ruffled socks and white patent leather T-strap shoes reminded Serenity of her own childhood. Then Brianna patted her pink hat adorned with small pink and white flowers.

"I love it. And you girls look beautiful, too," she said to Tanya and Kaylee. The two girls beamed and did their own version of a fashion show. She held up the tote. "I've got food."

A chorus of *yay*s went up.

Pam held up a hand. "Okay, girls, let's go out back and see what Ms. Wheeler has for lunch." They took off running. "Walk, ladies."

Serenity chuckled and followed Pam through the house to the backyard, where she had set an elegant table for six. "This is lovely."

"Thank you. Do you need plates for the sandwiches and cookies?"

"No. I brought everything." She started unpacking the tote and arranging the food on the fine white crystal china she'd brought and placed silver tongs on each one. She'd chosen the simple tableware to match whatever pattern Pam was using.

Moments later, a woman she recognized as Pam's younger sister—whom Brianna had been named after—arrived wearing a bright tangerine dress and matching hat. The color complemented her almond-colored skin to perfection.

"Auntie Bri is here!" She passed out air kisses and took a seat at the now full table. "Brianna, did you make these delicious-looking sandwiches and cookies?"

"No, Auntie Bri," she answered with a giggle. "Ms. Wheeler did. She said we're supposed to have food with the tea."

Bri leaned close to her niece. "She's right, and I'm glad because I'm starving." She smiled at Serenity. "It's always good to see you, Serenity."

"Same here."

"Can we have the tea party now?" Brianna asked.

Bri patted her hand. "Sure thing, baby girl."

They filled plates while Pam poured chamomile tea. Serenity enjoyed watching the girls sip their tea daintily. The innocent laughter transported her back to the times she'd spent with her mother, sister, and grandmothers doing the same thing. Some traditions were worth keeping and passing along, and she knew she would do the same if she ever had daughters. An image of Gabriel cradling a baby flashed in her head, and she choked on her tea. All eyes shifted her way. "Sorry. I think the tea went down the wrong way." She dabbed her mouth and gave them a quick, reassuring smile.

"Ms. Wheeler, you should try to swallow your tea the right way then," Kaylee said sagely.

It took everything in her to keep a straight face. Pam and Bri were trying as well. "You're absolutely right. Let's see if I can do it the correct way." Serenity took a careful sip.

All three girls' eyes lit up, and Brianna said, "She did it."

This time the adults all laughed. Hard. She managed to finish the remainder of her tea without mishap.

"Oh, honey, these cookies are fabulous," Pam said. "They're not too sweet and are almost like a tea cake. Just perfect."

Bri held up one. "I totally agree. Please tell me you can share this recipe."

Serenity smiled. "Of course. I'll write it down before I leave." While she did possess a few prized secret family recipes, the one for vanilla crisps didn't fall into that category. Obviously, the girls enjoyed them, too, if the way they crammed the pieces into their mouths was any indication.

When it came time to leave, Pam declined assistance with the cleanup. The girls were happily playing on a swing set on the other side of the large backyard. "You made all the food, so you are most definitely not going to be washing dishes. I'll wash your plates up real quick, so you don't have to do it when you get home."

Before Serenity could protest, the woman picked up the plates and strode off.

Bri leaned over and whispered, "She's always been bossy."

"No, I haven't," Pam said over her shoulder and disappeared into the kitchen.

Bri shook her head. "And she can hear everything within a two-mile radius. I think it's a mama thing because my mother is the same way. But I wouldn't know."

"So is mine, and neither do I." They both laughed. Once again that previous image floated through her mind, and she didn't understand why. She'd known Gabriel less than three weeks, and it wasn't as if they had some romantic relationship going on. They had barely decided to become friends.

True, but you're attracted to the man, a mocking inner voice reminded her. But that didn't mean she wanted to have his babies. Without warning, the line about wanting to have a guy's baby from that old rap song by Salt-N-Pepa, "Whatta Man," popped into her head. Just as fast as it entered, Serenity quickly dismissed it. At thirty-four, she had all but given up hope of having her own family. She was quickly approaching the high-risk category and had no prospects in sight for marriage. Not that she wanted to open herself to heartbreak again. No, she would have to be content with being an aunt. It was one more thing she had allowed her ex to steal from her. Everything had to be done on his timetable: marriage, children—

everything. It hadn't mattered that she'd wanted those things. Pam's voice drew her out of her thoughts.

"Here you go, Serenity." Pam handed her the two clean plates.

"Thanks, Pam." She stood and placed the tote bag on the table. "Before I go, I have a little tea party favor for everyone." She withdrew five small decorative boxes tied with ribbon. "There are a few vanilla crisps."

Bri snatched hers. "Bless you."

"Oh, I almost forgot. I promised to write down the recipe."

"Just text it to me," Bri said and pulled out her cell. "What's your number?"

She recited it, and Bri called her. Serenity already had Pam's number. She typed it in and sent the recipe to both women. "On the directions where it says to flour your pan, I know you'll be tempted to use a nonstick spray, but don't. I tried it and found that the cookies tend to burn."

Pam shook her head. "A true old-school recipe. Thanks so much for coming. You've been an angel from the day we met." She gave Serenity a tight hug.

Her emotions welled up. "It's been a joy watching her grow." She waved to the girls, and they skipped over. Serenity bent and hugged Brianna. "Thank you so much for inviting me to your tea party. I had the best time."

"You're welcome, and thank you for bringing all the food. Ham and cheese is my favorite."

She embraced the other two girls. "Tell your moms I said hello."

"Okay," they chorused.

Serenity said her final goodbyes and left. The first thing she did when she got home was kick off her shoes. The hat had come off the moment she hit the car, reminding her why she never wore them. Those things were hot. She ran her hands through her braids and noted she needed to schedule an appointment to get them redone. She had started wearing them two years ago, after tiring of weekly salon appointments, relaxers, and bad hair days. Sure, it was an all-day affair, but only once every two months, and she could go from business to casual to elegant in a matter of minutes. Of course, she normally left her hair down for about a week or two in between getting new braids, but with the weather warming up, she didn't want to deal with it for the moment. Also, Vonda had such a soft touch and had perfected the art of braiding without causing so much stress on her natural hair, Serenity felt she'd be okay to skip it this once.

She changed into shorts and a T-shirt, then called the salon. Her stylist didn't have an appointment available for three weeks.

"I know you can't get in here during the week, so I tell you what, I'll come to your house on Sunday."

Serenity's disappointment turned to delight. "Tomorrow? I love you, girl! And I'll cook."

Vonda let out a little whoop. "Yes, honey. Will ten work? It'll take about six or seven hours if you want something similar to what we did before."

"Yes, it will, and I'm thinking about keeping it the same, and maybe doing the braids a little bigger. I appreciate you." It would take her a good three or four hours to take it down, then wash and deep condition her hair tonight.

"Hmph. And I appreciate that good food I know I'm going to get. See you tomorrow."

Laughing, she ended the call. It rang again almost immediately, and she smiled upon seeing Natasha's name on the display. "Hey, Tasha."

"Hey, girl. Open up. I'm at the door."

She jumped up and made her way to the front door. "On my way."

As soon as Serenity opened the door, Natasha said, "So, what's up with Gabriel cutting your grass? I thought Top Lawn did your yard."

Serenity just shook her head and stepped aside to let her friend enter. "I thought so too, but all of a sudden, they keep canceling five minutes before they're supposed to be here." They walked back to the family room and sat on opposite ends of the sofa. "Gabriel happened to overhear the call and he was already outside doing his own, so he offered to help me out. 'Just being neighborly' is how he put it."

"Aw, that is nice, but it doesn't explain why the brother was at your house until late," Natasha said, trying to smother a laugh.

Serenity's mouth fell open.

She lifted a brow. "You know folks here don't

have nothing else to do except be in somebody else's business. So spill it. I might as well get the truth."

Chuckling, Serenity fell back against the sofa. "That is the one thing I still haven't gotten used to." Natasha didn't comment, just waved a hand. She sighed. "I invited him to dinner to repay him for helping me out. That. Is. All."

"Did he kiss you?"

Serenity felt her eyes widen. *"No."*

"But you wanted him to," Natasha said in singsong.

"What are you talking about? We've barely gotten past the point of I-can't-stand-you. The man is definitely not thinking about kissing me." *Woo, I told that lie with a straight face.* She knew he'd wanted to kiss her. She'd seen it in his eyes, especially after he'd kissed her hand. Serenity absently rubbed the spot where his lips had been, then caught herself. "Anyway, were you on your way somewhere?"

"Naw, girl. I came strictly to be nosy." She fell out laughing.

Serenity joined her laughter. "You are such a nut." But she didn't know what she'd do without her friendship.

It took a minute for Natasha to calm down. She fanned herself. "Okay, my sister. How about you tell me the truth? I saw the way he was staring at you during dinner. He's interested. Are you going to push him away like you've done every other guy for the past six years?"

"Just go for the jugular, then," she grumbled,

folding her arms. She closed her eyes and tried to put her thoughts into words. "He's nicer than I ever imagined. We talked for hours last night about everything and anything." She opened her eyes and rolled her head in Natasha's direction. "After spending time with him, I truly believe he didn't mean anything negative when he made those food comments. It was me hearing Lloyd's criticisms all over again. It's hard not to like Gabriel," she added softly.

"Serenity, there's nothing wrong with the two of you developing a relationship, if that's what you both want."

"Says the woman who's turned down at least five guys this year."

Natasha gave her a wistful smile. "Yeah, well. I blew my chance with the perfect guy, so we'll see what happens down the road. But that's beside the point."

"He said something the other day that makes me think he doesn't plan to live here permanently."

She shrugged. "You never know."

Maybe not, but Serenity did know she wouldn't put her heart on the line to find out.

CHAPTER 7

I love your hair." Gabriel reached up and fingered one of Serenity's newly done braids. "I didn't know hairstylists made house visits." He'd arrived home as the woman was leaving, and he couldn't resist coming over.

"She usually doesn't, but because I rarely have a day off during the week and her Saturdays are always booked solid for weeks in advance, she made an exception. I threw in lunch, so…" Serenity shrugged.

"The food would've gotten me, too. Does everyone in town know how well you cook?"

She shook her head. "They know I bake, but that's about it. A couple of years ago, I contributed three cakes for the Fourth of July celebration fundraiser. Before the evening ended, the women in charge asked me to do it again. Speaking of the Fourth, you should plan to join the festivities."

"I just may do that. Oh, I wanted to give you my number in case you needed something."

"Funny, I thought about the same thing. I told Andrea I'd be available to help you and totally dropped the ball. Let me run inside and get my phone. Or better yet, you can just come in."

Gabriel debated for a few seconds. "I should probably wait out here. Nana's on her way over, and I don't want to miss her."

Serenity smiled. "Good thinking. I don't want to get in trouble with Ms. Della."

His eyes were glued to her shapely backside in her snug shorts as she walked away. The woman looked good from every angle. The sound of a car approaching caught his attention, and he saw his grandmother park in front of his house. Pushing away from the porch column, he went to meet her. "Hey, Nana," he said, opening her car door and helping her out.

"Hi, honey." She wrapped him up in a hug. "You waiting for Serenity?"

"Yes. She went inside to get something." Gabriel didn't think she needed to know they were exchanging phone numbers.

"Good. Flora sent her a box. Can you get it out of the back seat?"

He went around to the passenger side and retrieved a box of fresh vegetables and fruit twice the size of the one the woman had packed for Nana.

"I told her Serenity would put it to good use." Nana closed the door and followed him over to where Serenity was just coming out of the house. "Hey, Serenity."

"Hi, Ms. Della. We missed you at dinner last week. How was the wine train?" The women embraced.

"We had such a good time. You really need to go."

"I keep saying I will, but I haven't gotten around to it."

Gabriel listened to them talk about wine tasting and good food, thinking maybe he could interest Serenity in taking the daylong trip with him. He'd never been to Napa and knew he would enjoy seeing it with her. A touch on his arm cut into his musings. "I'm sorry. What did you say?"

"Are you going to stand here staring off into space all day?" Nana asked, her hand on her hip. "Take the box on in for her."

Out of his periphery, he saw Serenity fighting hard not to laugh. She climbed the steps and held the door open. He let Nana go in first and moved to the side to let Serenity pass.

"Better start paying attention," Serenity whispered with a chuckle.

"Just tell me where to put this box." He tried to keep a straight face but failed.

"Bring it on back to the kitchen."

Gabriel left Nana in the living room and followed Serenity. After placing the box where she indicated, he dug his phone out of his pocket and handed it to her. "Input your number and I'll call you, so you'll have mine." She added her information to his contacts and handed it back. He hit the call button, let it ring once before disconnecting.

"Wow, I can't believe Ms. Flora sent all this."

He leaned over as Serenity dug below the bunches of greens to unearth tomatoes, strawberries, green beans, and a few other goodies. Her head came up and their faces were mere inches apart. Neither moved for several charged seconds. He leaned a fraction of an inch closer, wanting to find out if her lips tasted as sweet as the desserts she made. Then he remembered Nana was in the living room and thought better of it. "I'd better go."

"Y-yes. You don't want to keep Ms. Della waiting."

"May I call you later?"

She nodded.

Unable to resist, he brushed his lips across her cheek, pivoted, and put one reluctant foot in front of the other to get away from temptation. She was slow to follow, and he could tell that she had been just as affected as he was by the moment.

"Thanks for bringing the goodie box, Ms. Della. I'll call Ms. Flora later to thank her, too."

"You're welcome. Ready, Gabriel?" Nana divided a knowing glance between him and Serenity, then smiled.

Uh-oh. "Yes."

"He's cooking dinner for me tonight," she told Serenity. "First time."

"Ooh, that sounds fun. You'll have to tell me how it turns out."

Nana reached up and caressed his cheek. "He'll do fine. Did I tell you the time he—"

Gabriel felt his cheeks warm. He needed to nip this conversation in the bud. "Come on, Nana. See you later, Serenity." He hustled her out before she could finish whatever embarrassing story she planned to tell.

Back at his house, she went on a self-guided tour and returned to the kitchen. "You have far less furniture than your sister. I guess that's a man thing."

Laughter spilled out of him. "Do you want to relax and watch television while I cook?"

Nana pulled out one of the chairs. "Nope. I'm going to sit here and keep you company. What are we having?"

"Roasted beef tenderloin with a garlic butter sauce, mashed potatoes, and sautéed spinach." He'd ordered a bottle of the buttery and sweet olive oil Serenity had and wanted to try it out.

She lifted a brow. "You're going all out, huh?"

"Of course. I have to pull out all the stops for my favorite lady." He wrapped his arms around her and kissed her temple.

"Mm hmm." She rolled her eyes, but she was smiling.

Gabriel preheated the oven, then seasoned the meat. He planned to pan sear it to get that crispy outside and lock in the juices, then finish it in the oven. He'd already cut up the potatoes and had them sitting in cold water. All he had to do was turn on the burner. He heated the skillet, added the oil and meat.

"I heard you cut Serenity's grass last week."

"Yes," he said slowly. "The guys who were supposed to do it canceled at the last minute."

"Did you put salt in the water with the potatoes?"

"Yes. It's not my first time cooking, Nana," he added with a laugh.

"And that you didn't leave her house until the next morning," she said, picking up on the previous conversation.

He spun around so fast he almost dropped the tongs in his hand. "Whoa. Wait, wait. *What?*" He shook his head in stunned disbelief.

"Now, I know you're grown, but she's a sweet girl and—"

It took him a moment to find his voice. "Nana, I did *not* spend the night with Serenity. We had dinner together, yes, but she slept at her house and I slept here. Where did you hear that?"

"Adele called me."

"Who is Adele?"

"She lives in the middle of the block." She pointed toward the front.

Gabriel quickly turned the meat. He was so outdone, he didn't know what to say. He'd heard that small-town folks were nosy, but goodness. Did they just sit around with binoculars, checking out everything happening on the block? He reined in the irritation that rose swiftly and tried to keep his voice neutral. "Nana, I would appreciate it if you'd tell Adele, and anybody else, that none of what they heard is true. I was just doing what a good neighbor would do."

"Okay. But she is a sweet girl."

"Yes, she is." He focused on making sure the food didn't burn.

"You like her, don't you?"

He turned his head and glimpsed her pleased expression over his shoulder. "I think she's a great person. But I just met her, so I don't really know much about her." Yet he found himself wanting to know everything there was to know about Serenity Wheeler, from her favorite color to what made her laugh. "Have you talked to Drea?"

"She called me earlier in the week. Said they're keeping her busy, but she's happy. Lord knows I miss my baby, but it was time for her to live her life."

Outside of a text, he hadn't talked to his sister in over a week. She told him she was trying to keep her word and not bug him. He teased her about the frequency, but deep down he didn't mind. He slid the skillet into the oven and sat next to Nana.

Giving him a soft smile, she said, "You need to live yours, too, baby."

"I am." He paused to look at her. "Speaking of that, what do you think about moving to Atlanta with me?"

"My life is here, Gabriel. My friends, my church family, everything. I know you and your sister think you need to watch over me, but I'm fine. When the Good Lord decides it's time for me to see Him, it'll be time, and I'm going to be buried here right next to your grandfather. I understand that you want to go back to Atlanta—it's your home—and you're free to do that. I just want you and your sister to come and visit every now and again."

Gabriel bowed his head and listened to her words, torn between going back to the life he had and his obligation to his family. Andrea was enjoying her job, and he couldn't ask her to give up her newfound freedom. She'd earned it. Then there was Serenity. Did he really want to leave without getting to know her?

* * *

Almost a week later, Serenity still couldn't get the near kiss out of her mind. More than once, she'd fantasized about what might've happened if Ms. Della hadn't been there. *No, I know exactly what would have happened. A kiss would have happened.*

"Earth to Serenity." Terri snapped her fingers in front of Serenity's face.

She jumped. "Huh?"

Terri frowned. "Are you okay?"

"Yeah," she said, waving her off. "Just thinking about something. It's nothing. What did you say?" Natasha and Dana also wore concerned expressions.

"I asked if you were baking again for the Fourth."

"Yes, but I haven't decided what to make yet." Serenity liked to change her offerings, instead of making the same thing year after year.

Dana tapped on the table. "I know what you should make—more of those boozed-up berries."

"I second that," Natasha said. "Your grandmother's pound cake is a good option, too. But after you give people a taste of that, they're going to be hounding you day in and day out for more."

Serenity shook her head. "In that case, I might skip it. I don't have time to do baking full-time."

"*No* is a complete answer," Dana said emphatically. "I say make the cake and don't worry about the requests. There are always so many cakes, people probably won't even know who baked what."

"True." So far she'd done apple pies and peach cobblers. "What about three different desserts—berries, pound cake, and brownies?" Immediately, her thoughts went back to the look of pure pleasure on Gabriel's face as he ate the brownies. The soft kiss on her hand and the resulting sensations.

"Ooh, yes. I think that's perfect. For the first time, I have that day off, and I'll be buying some of each," Terri said.

"Is Jonathan coming with you?"

Her smile faltered. "I don't know. Lately he's been working more hours, and we haven't done anything fun in the past month." She tilted the wineglass to her lips and drained the contents.

Serenity grasped her hand. "I'm so sorry. Hopefully, it's just temporary."

"I hope so. I didn't mean to drag the party down."

"Girl, please," Natasha said. "We're all having men problems. At least you've found your Prince Charming and didn't let him get away. Everything will work out."

Dana lifted her glass and touched the side of Natasha's. "At least you don't have to worry about brothers being mad because I can fix a car better than they can and accuse you of not being *ladylike*." She rolled her eyes.

Serenity shook her head. Dana was probably the most refined in the group. A classically trained pianist, she'd played in concerts all over the country while in college and for a while after. Although she no longer played professionally, she still offered private lessons. "I say forget all those losers. You'll find the one who'll appreciate the diamond you are."

"See, that's why I come over here. I can get the best cooking in town and the encouragement I need." Dana gave Serenity's hand a gentle squeeze. "You're the jewel. I say we toast Natasha for convincing Serenity to relocate here."

They touched glasses and broke out in a fit of laughter. The mood lifted, and the women continued to converse, interspersed with moments of singing and dancing. Usually, her friends stayed around to help clean up after their dinners, but tonight, for one reason or another, they all had to leave a little early. Serenity hugged each woman at the door and, with promises to talk early the next week, they said good night.

She went back outside to make sure they'd brought in all the dishes. Seeing none, she doused the candles and locked the sliding glass door. In the middle of putting away the leftover food, her cell chimed with a text. She wiped her hands and read the message from

Gabriel: *Are you up for company? Just for a little while?* Her heart rate sped up. She did a full minute of "should I or should I not?" before replying: *Come on over.* She nervously ran a hand over her loose braids and checked her top to make sure she hadn't spilled anything on it. Two minutes later, the doorbell rang.

Taking a deep breath, she let Gabriel in. "Hey."

"Hey."

They stood there a long moment staring at each other. Serenity shook herself. "Um…I'm in the kitchen."

"Are you cooking this late?" Gabriel asked.

"It's only nine, and I've cooked much later than this, but no, I'm cleaning up."

He scanned the counter and stove. "Supper club?"

"How did you guess?"

"There are way too many dishes for just one person." He came over to where she stood. "What do you want me to do? With the two of us, we can finish faster."

Once again, he'd surprised Serenity with his offer. "How about you rinse the dishes and put them into the dishwasher while I put away the rest of the food?"

"Sounds like a plan."

They worked in companionable silence, but she heard him humming to the music. After she completed her task, she ran water in the sink to wash the pots. Without her asking, he picked up a towel and dried them as she rinsed each one. She smiled up at him. "How did your dinner with Ms. Della go?"

"I didn't burn anything if that's what you're asking. She didn't have any complaints and said I could cook for her again, so I guess I passed," he added with a grin. "Did you have a busy week?"

"It feels like every week is a busy one, but the first part of summer always is, with everyone bringing their children in for checkups. It'll drop off some until school starts back up. Then we'll be inundated with high schoolers needing physicals for the various sports." She put away the pots while he wiped down the counters. He'd been right. She finished in half the time it would have taken her alone. "Would you like a glass of wine?"

"Please."

She poured one for him and refilled her glass. "We can relax in here," Serenity said as she led him to the family room. She took a seat on the sofa, and he lowered himself next to her, leaving less than a foot between them. To distract herself from her nervousness, she reached over, grabbed two coasters, and placed them on the coffee table in front of them. "I know it's Saturday, but do you tend to work on the weekends?"

Gabriel shifted to face her and draped his arm on the back of the sofa. "I did do a few hours today, but according to my buddies, I need balance in my life, so I forced myself to quit."

"And do you need balance?"

He swirled the contents of his glass. "Probably. Definitely."

She angled her head and studied him. "With your career, I can see how easy it would be to get caught up working at all hours of the day and night. All it takes is the click of a switch and your office is there. I have set hours, so it's not a problem. What you need to do is set your work hours and stick to them." Before moving, Serenity had started taking on extra shifts, trying to position herself to be ready when a nurse manager job became available. But she ended up close to burnout and had to take off nearly a month to recover. She'd had to learn the hard way that her health was more important than prestige.

"You're probably right. I was supposed to be taking a vacation—well, a *forced* vacation—but instead I negotiated a deal to decrease my time for the next few weeks, and then I'll see how it goes. The crazy thing is I've actually cut back on my work hours and have been able to get more done."

"It could be that because you're rested, your brain can be more productive."

Gabriel leaned closer. "Is that your professional opinion, Ms. Wheeler?"

His nearness was playing havoc with her senses, and she took a huge gulp of her wine. "Um...both professional and personal. I've been where you are, and it's not worth it."

He tilted the glass to his lips and didn't comment immediately, as if he were deep in thought. Finally, he asked, "What made you decide to move here? Andrea said you used to live in San Diego. I'd think the opportunities for professional growth, not to mention the salary, would be much better there."

"I needed a change."

"But this is a drastic change from living in a big city. I'm not sure I could stay here past a few months. Couldn't you have transferred to another hospital, LA, or some other similar place?"

"I had a bad breakup, and I wanted some distance." She paused and thought about how hard it had become to do her job with all the whispering and looks of pity she received once everyone found out she and Lloyd had parted ways. She'd actually started to feel somewhat insecure in the job she loved and knew it was best she leave and have a fresh start. "He was a doctor at the hospital where I worked as an ER nurse. At first it was great, but then it went steadily downhill. I wasn't ambitious enough. I should've taken advantage of this or that. My food was good, but I could've always done something to improve on whatever dish," Serenity said bitterly. "Not to mention everything was always about him and *his* schedule. In the end, my only role was playing a glorified hostess to his many social gatherings."

She finished her wine and set the glass down with a thud. *Well, just tell him everything, girl.* Serenity hadn't intended to share the details of her past relationship with Gabriel. It had to be that extra glass of wine that had her feeling all mellow and spilling her guts.

"I don't even know what to say, but I understand. I guess we went to the same school of heartbreak," he added with a mock salute. "At least you didn't have to deal with having someone you love make a play for your best friend while cheating with two other guys. She said she wanted to keep her options open."

Now *she* was at a loss for words. The pain she heard in his voice made her hurt for him. If the few things he'd done for Serenity were any indication of how he'd behave in a real relationship, a woman would have to be out of her mind to cheat on him. If her ex had offered to help her set a table or wash one dish, even half of the time, she might have stayed and given him a chance. But Gabriel went out of his way to do things for her, and she didn't have to ask. Without thinking about her actions, she cupped his cheek. "I'm sorry, Gabriel. It's her loss."

Gabriel stared at her for what seemed like forever, his breathing increased, before lowering his head and touching his lips to hers tentatively, as if seeking permission. "May I?"

The spark that lit from the brief contact rendered her speechless, and she could only nod. This time when their lips met, the spark turned into a flame. The kiss was gentle but infused with a passion and need she hadn't felt in a long time, if ever. His tongue delved in and out of her mouth with a slow finesse that melted her on the spot. *Good thing I'm already sitting down.* With that thought, the sensual haze around her brain cleared and she went still. She'd told herself she wasn't going to get caught up in another man.

Apparently, Gabriel felt the same because he shot

up off the sofa. "I'm sorry…I…I should probably go."
He scrubbed a hand over his head. "Serenity…"

Serenity slowly came to her feet, still shaken by
the intensity of his kiss. "It's okay. You're right. We
should probably call it a night."

He nodded, walked halfway across the room, and
turned back. He stood there for a few seconds, as if
battling between what one wanted to do versus what
one should do. After another moment, he murmured,
"Good night," then turned and strode out.

As soon as she heard the front door close, she
collapsed on the sofa, let out a loud groan, and banged
her hand against her head softly. "What are you
doing, Serenity? Friends. Neighbors. The end. No
kisses. No nothing." Except now she had no idea how
to keep her emotions from getting involved.

CHAPTER 8

Friday, Gabriel sat on his terrace. It had become his favorite place to think and unwind. Only today, relaxation was nowhere to be found. He'd been pre-occupied with thoughts of Serenity and the explosive kiss they'd shared all week. One minute they were having a "Heartbreak Hotel" moment, the next his lips were fused to hers and he was kissing her with an intensity that still stunned him. Every rational thought had gone right out the window. The cozy conversation, the wine, the closeness—he'd been fine with all of it. Until she touched him. *I'm sorry, Gabriel. It's her loss.* Even now the sweetness and sincerity in her voice made his heart do crazy things. It was as if she'd known how much he'd been hurt, could feel the pain and emotional turmoil his ex's betrayal had caused. That's what pushed him over the edge.

The heartache he'd buried and thought he'd gotten over began to surface. Gabriel closed his eyes in an attempt to force it back down. Somehow, saying the words aloud that night had dredged up every excruciating moment of that time. He took a few deep breaths and let them out slowly. The tightness in his chest eased.

He hadn't been the only one who'd experienced a painful breakup. He shook his head, thinking about what Serenity had shared about her ex. Her reaction to his innocent comments about her food now made sense. In her mind, even though it hadn't been Gabriel's intent, he had criticized her just as the other man had done.

But now he had a dilemma. Though he'd seen her over the past week and was no less polite and friendly, he'd kept his distance. Gabriel hadn't outright told her he was leaving, but he had mentioned that he most likely wouldn't stay past a few months. It didn't make sense for them to embark on some sort of relationship that had no chance of going anywhere. The best thing would be to go back to their original friends-only agreement. He had to laugh. It sounded good in theory, but now that he had kissed her, it only made him want to do it again. And again.

His phone buzzed, and he read the text from Brent saying that their plane had landed. Gabriel had offered to drive to the Bay to pick them up, but both Brent and Darius had said they would rather rent a car. Hopefully, their arrival would provide the distraction he needed to keep his head on straight.

Placing his laptop on his lap, he stuck in his earbuds, cranked up the music, and went to work. He didn't know how much time had passed when the insistent buzzing of his phone startled him. He paused the music and connected. "Are you guys here?"

"Yeah."

Gabriel saved his work as he talked. "Be right there." On his way to the front, he stopped by the office to leave the laptop.

"You must've been working," Brent said as soon as he walked in. "I called you twice."

"Had the music up and didn't hear the phone. How was the drive?"

Darius dropped down on the sofa and placed his duffel on the floor. "Long. Traffic was a little heavier than last time." He yawned and stretched. "I'm starving. Please tell me there's a restaurant nearby."

Gabriel chuckled. "There are a few." He outright laughed at the twin looks of horror on his friends' faces. He glanced down at his watch. He figured since it was only five thirty, they should be able to get ahead of the dinner rush. "Let's go."

Serenity was getting out of her car when they stepped out onto the walk. "Hey, Serenity."

"Hey."

He headed in her direction, and she met him halfway. It took every ounce of his control not to kiss her. "I want you to meet my friends." He waved them over. "Serenity, this is Brent and Darius. Guys, Serenity."

Brent nodded. "Nice meeting you."

"It's nice to finally meet you," Darius said. "I heard you have a helluva throwing arm."

Gabriel shot him a dark glare. "Ignore him."

Serenity giggled. "Yeah, well, we're past that now. How long are you guys staying?"

"Just the weekend," Gabriel answered, stifling the urge to knock the smug grin off Darius's face. "We're going to get something to eat." It was on the tip of his tongue to invite her, but that didn't fall under the category of keeping his distance.

"Have a good time. See you later, Gabriel." She sauntered back to her house.

"Definitely not pushing fifty," Darius said with a low whistle.

They piled into Gabriel's car, and he took a scenic route that passed the park where he jogged regularly and one of the older neighborhoods.

"Man, this really is one of those old, small towns." Brent shook his head. "Are there any jazz clubs, or bars, or something that would pass for entertainment?"

"I haven't seen any, but Napa is about half an hour away, and they have some there." He found parking halfway down the block on Main Street and walked back to the family-style restaurant that had become one of his favorites.

Darius still wore a skeptical expression as they stopped in front of the restaurant. "Seriously, man? Ms. Ida's?" He groaned.

Gabriel clapped him on the back. "The food is good. Trust me."

"Hey, Gabriel," Ms. Bernice said. "Takeout?"

"Hi, Ms. Bernice. Not this time."

A smile covered her face. "Well, follow me." She led them to a table near the far wall and handed them menus. "You two new in town?"

"Ah, just visiting," Brent answered.

"I hope you enjoy your stay. Let me know if you have any questions."

Smiling, Gabriel thanked her.

Darius opened his menu. "You must come here often, if she knows you by name."

"Nope. I've only been here three times. You know that saying about everybody knowing everybody in small towns? Believe me, it's true."

"This place has everything," Brent said with surprise. "I don't even know where to start."

The three men pored over the menu, going back and forth over choices before deciding to share a seafood family supper with fried catfish and shrimp and sides of macaroni and cheese, green beans with potatoes, baked beans, and cornbread.

After placing their order, Darius folded his arms on the table. "How's it going with you and your neighbor?"

"Complicated."

Brent grinned. "Don't tell me she's back to throwing things at your head."

"Hardly. She's...I really like her." He didn't know how to describe what he felt because he didn't understand it himself. "We've spent some time together talking, and it's like we've been friends forever." The easy rapport he and Serenity shared still amazed him. The server placed glasses of iced tea in front of each man and departed.

"Sounds like things between you two are heating up."

"I can't let it go there." *Again*.

"Don't tell me she's dating someone else," Darius said.

"No. But I don't think she's looking, either. Besides, I told you I'm not planning on staying here."

"And your grandmother is cool with moving?"

Dilemma number three. "Hardly. She shut me down cold."

Brent and Darius shared a look, and Brent said, "So, you're going to commute back and forth or something? And if so, it shouldn't be a problem having a relationship with Serenity."

Gabriel blew out a long breath. "I have no idea. But whatever I decide to do, I don't want to get too deep with her—or anyone, for that matter."

"It's a little late for that, given the way you were looking at Serenity."

He frowned at Brent and opened his mouth to say something, but the server returned with their meal. After the young man walked away, Gabriel said, "I wasn't looking at her in any way."

"Mm-hmm," Darius said, filling his plate. "She's gorgeous, and if she's as nice as you say, you're in big trouble, my brother." He paused. "But I'm willing to bet you've already gotten yourself into a little trouble.

She might be just the woman you need, so don't over-think it or try to compare her to you-know-who."

Yeah. Trouble. But he wouldn't give Darius the satisfaction of admitting it. And Serenity could never be Christine. The woman had never offered to cook, and when he suggested they spend an evening in and make dinner together, she'd looked at him as if he'd lost his mind. Her idea of "eating in" meant eating *in* a restaurant. The more expensive, the better. He added generous portions of food to his plate and changed the subject. After the three men had started their company, they'd decided whenever they hung out together, work topics would be off-limits. In the past, Gabriel had difficulties shutting down work mode. However, tonight, as they laughed and talked, deadlines and projects never crossed his mind.

"Okay, I have to admit, the food was off the chain," Brent said after leaving the restaurant. "It tasted like somebody's mama was in the kitchen."

Gabriel nodded. "I said the same thing the first time I came. And since D considers himself an ice cream connoisseur, we have one more stop to make." He gestured to the shop across the street.

"I am seriously going to hurt myself," Darius muttered when they entered the ice cream parlor. "Homemade...like three dozen choices."

Almost ten minutes later, Brent threw up his hands. "How long are you going to stand there staring at the menu? It hasn't changed since we walked in the door. You're worse than a five-year-old in a candy shop."

Darius closed his eyes after sampling another flavor. "You cannot rush this kind of process. You have to select the right combination of flavors to create the perfect taste in the bowl."

"Or you can just get scoops of all the flavors you want *separately* and we can leave," Gabriel drawled. Darius had tasted more than half the listed flavors so far and didn't appear to be any closer to making a decision. Had Gabriel known this would happen, he would've skipped it altogether. More people had crowded into the space, and his friend was oblivious to the fact that he was holding up the line. Thankfully, he and Brent hadn't ordered yet. Otherwise, their ice cream would have already melted. It took Darius another couple of minutes to make his selection, and Gabriel and Brent quickly chose theirs. "Remind me to never go to an ice cream shop with you again."

Darius merely smiled.

At the house later, they sat outside on Gabriel's back deck talking.

"This quiet takes some getting used to. I don't know how you can deal with this." Brent stood and stared up in the sky. "Although, without all the buildings, you can see just about every star." He reclaimed his seat. "Are we doing San Francisco tomorrow?"

Gabriel leaned back in his chair. "I was thinking about checking out one of the lakes here, then heading up that way. We can leave around ten."

"Sounds like a plan, but right now I need to find

a bed," Darius said around a yawn. "I know it's only nine, but my body is still on East Coast time."

"I hear you. I think I'm going to turn in, too." Brent stood. "See you in the morning."

"Night." The temperatures had dipped and the cool night air swept over him, but Gabriel opted to stay out for a while longer. His gaze strayed to the fence separating his and Serenity's homes. He didn't see a light, and he wondered if she was still up. It had been hard to stay away, and he was tired of fighting it. Pulling out his phone, he scrolled to her name and hit the call button. He had no idea what he would say, but he wanted to hear her voice.

"Hello."

"Hey, neighbor. Did I wake you?"

Serenity's soft laughter flowed through the line. "This early? What are you doing calling me instead of entertaining your friends?"

"They're still on Atlanta time, so they went to bed. What are you doing?"

"Having a me-time night. I took a long bubble bath with candles and gave myself a facial. I try to do it at least once a month."

Gabriel didn't hear anything after *bubble bath*. A vision of her lounging naked in the tub surrounded by bubbles spiked his arousal. He imagined trailing his hands over every inch of her body and—

"Gabriel!"

"What?"

"Are you okay? I called your name three times,

and I asked if you guys had any special plans for tomorrow."

"I'm good," he said. "Yeah, we're going to San Francisco."

"Ooh, are you going to Pier 39?"

"I figure we will."

"If I give you some money, can you bring me back some chocolate? The store there is the only place I can find good white chocolate that doesn't taste like vanilla plastic. I try to get down there every few months, but I haven't had the chance and I'm running low."

He chuckled. "Text me the name of the store and what you want and I'll get it." He'd bring her back anything she asked for.

"What time are you leaving? I can either drop the money off tonight or in the morning, whichever is easiest for you."

Gabriel wanted to tell her neither time would be *easier* because the moment she walked into his line of sight, he would want an instant replay. "Don't worry about the money. As long as you let me sample whatever you plan to make, we'll call it even." She didn't respond for so long, he thought they'd gotten disconnected. "Serenity, you still there?"

"I'm here. Just not sure what to say. Why are you doing all these things? I mean we're not even..." She trailed off.

Good question. He had never gone out of his way like this for a woman he wasn't dating, but for some reason he enjoyed seeing her smile. "We said we were friends, and I'm just honoring the spirit of that friendship."

"You're doing more than that, and I appreciate it."

They seemed to be talking about everything except the kiss. He wanted to bring it up, find out how she felt about it, but decided it should be something done face-to-face, so he'd table it for now. "I'll let you get back to your *me time*, and don't forget to send me the information."

"I won't. You guys be careful, and have a good time."

"We will. Good night."

"Sweet dreams."

Smiling, Gabriel went inside.

The next morning, Gabriel, Brent, and Darius strolled around Crystalwood Lake. It was located about fifteen miles outside of town in an undeveloped area, and though they saw a handful of boats in the lake, they didn't see one other person. At a far end, they spotted a partially hidden archway and went to explore.

"Talk about being out in the boonies," Darius cracked. A minute later, they passed through another archway. A small, almost invisible sign read Brookshaw Cove. "I take it back. Wow."

Gabriel just stared. They had entered a small inlet with crystal-clear blue-green water and a path of golden sand. A smile curved his lips. He'd just found the perfect date spot.

* * *

A few days later, Serenity dropped her desserts off at the donation table and went to meet her friends. They had decided to come early to the Fourth of July celebration to make sure they were able to purchase their choice of desserts. For the past two years, they didn't arrive until almost time for the fireworks, and by that time just about everything was gone. She spotted her friends on a blanket under a large shade tree and headed in that direction.

"Hi, Serenity. Did you make another peach cobbler this year?" a woman asked as Serenity passed.

"Not this year, but I did a couple of cakes."

"Aw, I was waiting all year to get a piece of that cobbler. That's the only reason I'm out here in this heat this early," she added with a laugh.

"Maybe next year." She waved and continued to her destination. Only she got stopped four more times by people asking her what she'd made and wanting her to give them advice about one ailment or another.

"For a minute I thought I was going to have to come and rescue you," Natasha said when Serenity finally made it. "That's what happens when everybody loves you."

"Or something. I don't know why people always ask me about diagnosing some issue. I keep reminding them I'm not a doctor."

"Maybe not, but your bedside manner is way better than any of those doctors you work with," Dana said.

"Whatever. Where's Terri?"

Natasha gestured. "With Jon."

"I'm so glad he came. They look like they're having a good time." She had been worried about her friend's marriage and hoped this meant they were back on track.

Dana stood. "Now that you're here, you can save our spot while we load up on your desserts. What kind of container did you use? I don't want to end up with one of those dry cakes somebody else made. Did you make the strawberries, too?"

Serenity shoved her playfully. "Quit talking about folks' cakes. And yes." Thanks to Gabriel, she had enough chocolate to last for a while. She described her containers and told them where she had placed them.

"You want me to bring you something back?"

"No. I left a couple of pieces at home for later."

"Okay. We'll be back."

Serenity made herself comfortable and surveyed the large crowd. People stood around talking and children ran and played. On the far edge of the park, several grills were being manned and held everything from ribs and chicken to corn and vegetable kabobs. She waved at a few people, then stifled a groan when she saw Cole Richards heading her way. She'd made the mistake of going out with him once two years ago, and every couple of months he came up with a new reason they would make the perfect couple. He reminded her too much of Lloyd, so nothing he said would move her or change her position.

"Well, if it isn't the most beautiful woman in

town." Whereas everyone else had worn shorts, tees, and tennis shoes or sandals, Cole had on dress slacks, a polo, and expensive loafers.

As hard as she tried, she couldn't stop the eye roll.

"I can't let you sit here all alone," he continued as if she'd invited him to stay.

"She's not alone," Dana said, eyeing him, hand on her hip. "You mind?"

Serenity could've kissed her. She glanced over her shoulder, and her pulse skipped when she saw Gabriel standing there with her friends. He looked so good in his black shorts and a gray tee that molded to his wide, muscular chest.

Cole stepped aside and looked Gabriel up and down. "Do I know you?"

Gabriel lifted a brow. "No." He sat down next to Serenity. "Hey."

"Hey, yourself."

Realizing that he had been summarily dismissed, Cole stalked off without another word.

Natasha dropped down on the other side of the blanket. "Pompous jerk."

Gabriel chuckled. "Y'all are some cold sisters. Remind me never to get on your bad side."

Serenity gave him an incredulous look. "*Us?* What about that terse one-word reply you gave? I do have to say the look on his face when he realized you weren't going to give him any more information was priceless, though."

He shrugged. "Have you all eaten yet? Or are you planning to have dessert first?"

Natasha broke off a small piece of pound cake and popped it into her mouth. "We're going to get something to eat in a few minutes. We just wanted to make sure we got some of Serenity's desserts before they're gone."

Gabriel stood. "I'd better do the same." He held his hand out to Serenity. "Want to show me which ones are yours?"

Doing her best to ignore the smiles on Dana's and Natasha's faces, Serenity placed her hand in his and allowed him to help her up. She immediately let go once she was on her feet. One, she didn't want to give anyone anything to talk about, and two, touching him went beyond the boundaries of friendship she was trying hard to maintain.

"Is it always this crowded?" Gabriel asked as they walked toward the dessert table.

"It has been since I moved here. Is your grand-mother here?"

"Yes. I left her and Ms. Flora playing bingo."

She laughed softly. "Those women are serious about their bingo. They play every week at the community center."

"That's what she told me. I thought it was just fun and games until she told me there's money involved. She said the reason I didn't know was that it's grown folks' business. She is something else," he added with a shake of his head.

Serenity pointed out her desserts on the table and waited while he purchased two each of the pound cake and strawberries and four of the six remaining brownies. On the way back, she said, "Four brownies?"

"Hey, I was trying to be nice leaving those two." He held her gaze. "They're my weakness."

Have mercy! He stared at her as he had that night, forcing her to remember the timbre of his voice, the tender touch of his lips. She took a step and nearly tripped.

Gabriel slid an arm around her waist to steady her. "You okay?"

She nodded and prayed no one else noticed. Blessedly, she made it back without further mishap. A smile spread across her face when she saw that Terri and Jon had joined them. She hugged them both and introduced Gabriel to Jon.

The two men hit it off, and the group spent the remainder of the day laughing and eating. Eventually, the conversation turned to cooking.

"I can barely boil water," Jon confessed. "So I can't say anything about somebody's skills."

Dana laughed. "What about you, Gabriel? Can you throw down in a kitchen?"

"I can do a little somethin' somethin'."

Natasha and Serenity shared a look before Natasha said, "Think you hang with our girl?"

A mischievous grin spread across Gabriel's mouth. "Maybe."

Dana and Natasha hollered.

"I say they should do a cook-off, best side dish," Dana said with a squeal, clapping her hands.

Natasha high-fived her. "Yes, girl! Let's do it."

Serenity held up a hand. "Hold on a minute. How are y'all going to just volunteer us to cook? And exactly how is this going to work?"

Dana shrugged. "Simple. He comes to the supper club this weekend, and we vote on which dish tastes the best. Y'all can work out the prize. Now we just need to decide which dish."

Serenity's mouth fell open. *Prize?* Her gaze flew to Gabriel's. He didn't seem to be bothered in the least, and it had her speculating on what he would want if he won.

"What about candied yams?" Natasha wiggled her eyebrows.

"Works for me." She felt confident she could easily win. Even if he did cook, she doubted his candied yams would top hers.

Gabriel stuck out his hand. "I'm in."

"Y'all are a mess," Terri said. "I can't believe how quickly you roped them into this food battle."

They agreed on Saturday for the next dinner, since both Terri and Jon would be available. Serenity would still prepare the meal, as always, but she and Gabriel would each cook their version of the side dish.

As night fell, everyone found spots to view the fireworks. The committee had really outdone themselves with the amazing display of colors bursting across the sky.

Serenity leaned over and whispered to Gabriel, "What do you think?"

"They're spectacular." He reached between them and covered her hand with his, then quickly pulled back. "I...Um...sorry."

Her breath hitched. She smiled and gave his hand a gentle squeeze. He trained his eyes back on the sky. She took a cautious glance around to see if anyone was watching them, not wanting to be the subject of any gossip, but everyone was focused on the show. Serenity started to withdraw her hand but changed her mind. She knew they wouldn't ever be more than friends, but just for tonight she could pretend.

CHAPTER 9

Gabriel stood in his kitchen, slicing yams, on Saturday afternoon. He had watched his mom make the dish plenty of times, and Nana had just cooked them a couple of weeks ago. He lined up the sugar, nutmeg, cinnamon, and vanilla extract on the counter and added them to the pot one at a time. At the last minute, he remembered the dash of salt and butter. He poured in the water and set the pot on the stove to cook.

Serenity told him she still hadn't decided on a prize, but he'd finally come up with one: another kiss. Which meant he *had to* win. A short time later, the sweet scent of the yams filled the kitchen. *Yep, just like Mom's.*

While waiting for them to finish, he cleaned the few dishes and returned the text from his sister, telling him how much she missed her friends, especially their dinners.

Andrea: *That's just wrong telling me you're going over to Serenity's for dinner.* 😞

Gabriel: *I'll try not to have a good time. Will that make it better?*

Andrea: *No! Lol. Tell everyone I said hello. Love you.*

Gabriel: *Will do. Love you, too.*

He rose to check the potatoes. They were nice and tender. He got a clean fork from the drawer and dug out a small piece. *Mmm, it smells good.* He blew on it to cool, then carefully put it in his mouth. *"Ugh!"* Gabriel coughed and his eyes started to water. What had he done wrong? *Cinnamon.* Way too much cinnamon. And he didn't have enough time to go to the store for more yams and redo the dish. He thought for a moment, glanced at the clock, then took off, phone to his ear.

Gabriel made it home with about twenty minutes to spare. He turned on the oven, hurriedly dumped candied yams into a casserole dish, and slid it in to warm. By the time he changed clothes, the food was hot.

The women were all there when he arrived, as was Terri's husband, Jon. Gabriel joined them at the table, where he saw that Serenity had outdone herself again with a pork tenderloin and roasted asparagus to accompany the two dishes of candied yams.

Serenity's dark eyes sparkled, and her smile lit up the room. "I know what I want as my prize, and I can't wait to win."

He smiled down at her and folded his arms. "And what might that be?"

"Oh, you'll find out after you *lose*."

"You can't just leave me hanging."

"Okay, fine. I want…to go on a Napa Valley wine train tour like the one your grandmother was talking about. I'm going to enjoy myself *soooo* much." She laughed and sashayed off with an extra switch in her hips.

Gabriel stood there mesmerized. It dawned on him, whether he won or lost, he'd still get to spend time with her. And as he'd told himself a few days ago, he was tired of fighting his feelings.

"Okay, okay, gather around, ladies and gentlemen," Natasha said. "Here are the rules. This is going to be a blind test. Serenity and Gabriel will put portions of their yams on plates for everyone and line them up on the counter labeled *A* and *B*. We'll wait in the family room until you two are done."

"Instead of labeling them, how about using two different patterned saucers?" Serenity asked

"That works. Call us when you're ready. We'll taste each, then just bring the entire dish out to the table with the rest of the food so we can really enjoy it." Natasha shooed everyone out.

Gabriel couldn't believe how serious they were about this. A part of him felt guilty. However, he did plan to tell Serenity the truth before leaving. He turned to Serenity. "Ready to get this party started?"

She handed him five navy-colored saucers and kept the gray ones. "The question is are *you* ready?"

He just chuckled. It took only a couple of minutes to spoon the portions onto the plates. After they were lined up along the island, she went to call everyone in. Spirited debates about flavor, sweetness, and balance of spices ensued as they went back and forth. Reflecting on what she'd gone through with her ex, he had to wonder whether that played a part in the way Serenity now stood off to the side nervously biting her lip and wringing her hands. For him this challenge had been nothing more than a way to have a little fun with a group of people he'd begun to think of as friends. It obviously meant more to her, and the vulnerability he saw tore at his insides.

The group huddled together for a few more minutes, then Natasha held up a blue plate. "We have a winner! But I have to tell you it was so close. The blue one edged the gray one out by this much." She put her thumb and index finger very close together.

"Then we'll declare it a tie," Gabriel said.

"I can go with that," Dana chimed in. "Now can we eat?" Laughter filled the kitchen.

Serenity playfully bumped Dana. "The asparagus has another five minutes, but everything else is ready to go."

While everyone carried the various dishes out, Gabriel hung back with Serenity.

"Well, since it wasn't really a tie and you won, what do you want?" Serenity asked, leaning against the counter with her arms folded and a mock pout.

Gabriel closed the distance between them and placed his hands on the counter, effectively pinning her in. He bent close to her and whispered, "What I want, more than anything, is to share another amazing kiss with you." Her eyes widened, and a soft gasp escaped. "However, I have a confession to make."

"What?"

"The yams I made are still in a pot on my stove because the amount of cinnamon in them is enough to choke you or send somebody to the hospital. These"—he gestured toward his casserole dish—"belong to Ms. Ida."

Serenity stared at him for a full minute before she burst out laughing.

A wry smile curved his lips. "You think we can keep this little faux pas between us? And since you're the true winner, we'll take your trip whenever you're ready."

She made a show of thinking. "Well…since you did own up to cheating and I'm going to get my prize, and I'm feeling generous today…I guess so."

Moving closer and leaving mere inches between their bodies, he asked, "Does that generosity and the fact that I told the truth mean I can still get the kiss?"

"Um…everybody's waiting for us."

Gabriel sent an unhurried glance over his shoulder to her friends seated on the deck, then checked the timer on the oven and brought his gaze back to her. "They're fine and there's still one minute left on the oven. Plenty of time. So?" Serenity peeked around him. From where they stood in the kitchen, the partial wall blocked them from view.

"Yes," she whispered.

She'd barely finished saying the word before he captured her mouth in his, needing to kiss her as much as he needed to breathe. He slowly, thoroughly explored every inch of her mouth, twining his tongue around hers and feeling the slight tremble in her body. Then it was his turn to shudder when she slid her hands up his chest, wound them around his neck, and arched her body against his. He groaned and pulled her closer. Somewhere in the recesses of his mind, he heard the oven timer going off. Reluctantly, he lifted his head. "Time's up," he whispered against her lips.

Serenity moaned. Her eyes fluttered open. "What?"

"The oven timer. I don't think you want burned asparagus."

"Oh, shoot." She ducked under his arm and rushed over to turn off the timer and remove the tray. She let out a sigh of relief. "You're way too much trouble in the kitchen."

Gabriel placed a hand over his heart. "Who, me? I'm an angel."

She rolled her eyes and snorted. "Whatever." She placed the asparagus on a plate. "What are we doing here, Gabriel? I thought we agreed to be friends. But this…" She waved a hand as if it were an explanation itself.

He knew what she was asking, but he didn't exactly have an answer, either. "We are. And this isn't anything I'd planned. How about we talk later?"

Serenity nodded. "All right. Can you get the pitcher of iced tea out of the refrigerator?"

He did as she asked and followed her to the back

deck. Throughout the meal, he contributed to the conversation but continued to mull over what Serenity had asked. He couldn't deny how he liked being with her, but a relationship wasn't on his radar. Or so he kept telling himself. Only there was something about this woman that made it hard to remember his vow.

Afterward, they all pitched in to clean up, which turned out to be a good thing because it took less than thirty minutes to get everything cleared up and put away.

As Terri and Jon were leaving, Jon shook Gabriel's hand. "Man, let me know when you're cooking something else. I'll be happy to taste test."

Laughing, Gabriel said, "Will do." He shot Serenity a wink.

A few minutes later, Serenity and Gabriel were alone. He could only hope their conversation ended where he wanted, which was... well, he had no idea.

* * *

Serenity kept wiping a spot that had been cleaned long ago. It had been difficult getting through dinner and not thinking about the kiss that had literally made her weak.

Gabriel gently eased the towel from her hand, tossed it on the counter, and led her to her family room. They sat next to each other for a moment without speaking.

Serenity clasped her hands together in her lap and lowered her head. "Gabriel, you are... a great guy, but

I don't think I'm ready to open myself up to be hurt again. I don't know if I'll ever be ready. I've finally gotten my life to a place where I'm happy, and I can't mess that up."

"And I don't want to mess that up, either. But something is happening between us, and it'll be hard to go back to being just friends. Or am I out here by myself?"

"No, you aren't," she said, her voice barely audible. "But there's something else." She lifted her eyes to meet his. "You're not planning to stay, are you?"

"I'd like to tell you yes, but since I've already told one lie for the day…" Gabriel shrugged.

She tried to hold back a smile. "Yeah, you might not want to press your luck. My generosity only goes so far." Even though this was a serious discussion, he'd still managed to put her at ease and make her laugh. It was one more thing on a growing list she found to like about him.

"But, honestly, I can't say right now. When Andrea asked me to move here, I had it in my mind to hang out for three or four months and convince Nana to go back to Atlanta with me. Nana doesn't want to leave, but my plans haven't changed."

"Then what do we do?"

"Do all the things we've been doing and let the future take care of itself. We don't have to label it anything—we can be just two people who enjoy each other's company."

Serenity rubbed her hands up and down her thighs.

"Can we keep it light—no commitments, no ties? Just two people enjoying each other's company," she added, tossing his words back at him. The short time he planned to stay would be a plus, and in her mind it was a win-win for both of them, since neither wanted an emotional involvement. She wasn't one to fall in love quickly, and that worked in her favor, as well.

"If that's what you want. Absolutely."

"Then, okay."

Gabriel slanted his mouth over hers, once again robbing her of her senses.

"Deal. Now, I'd like to take you out on a real date. We could do the wine train later."

"I'd like that. Do you mind if we don't go to any of the restaurants in town? I want to keep my business *my* business as long as possible."

He chuckled. "It might be a little late for that. Apparently, someone named Adele called Nana because she saw me mowing your lawn and said that I didn't leave your house until the next morning."

"*Whaaaat?* Are you kidding me?" Serenity shot up from the sofa. "Ooh, that woman is always sticking her nose in somebody's business. One of these days she's gonna get it chopped off." She paced in front of him, muttering about small towns and people minding their own business.

Standing, he placed his hands on her shoulders. "We know the truth, and I would never do anything to disrespect you or give anyone a reason to think you're not the amazing woman you are. And as far as the date, I think I can handle that. What are you doing next Saturday or Sunday around noon?"

"My sister is going to be in Sacramento for a conference, and I told her I'd drive up and spend a few hours with her before she flies out Saturday evening. But I can do Sunday."

"I didn't know you had a sister. Is she older or younger?"

"Chandra is eighteen months older and loves to remind anyone who'll stand still long enough to listen." She dropped back down on the sofa and gestured for Gabriel to do the same. "She's been married for four years, but they don't have any children yet, much to my mother's disappointment." Her mother had also been asking when Serenity was going to find a "nice man" to marry, but she kept that part to herself.

Gabriel stretched out his long legs and crossed them at the ankle. "May I ask you a personal question?"

"I'm thirty-four," Serenity said, figuring that's what he wanted to know.

He smiled. "Two years younger than me."

"So, basically, you're closer to forty than not," she teased.

"Basically. Are you saying I'm too old for you?"

"I'm not saying anything at all." *If those kisses are any indication, he's just the right age for whatever I need.* The thought popped into her head unbidden, shocking her. Thinking it better to shift her attention elsewhere, she said, "Then again..." She leaned forward, scrutinized him, and pointed to his head. "Is that a gray hair I see? You get one, it snowballs from there. Maybe you *are* a little old." Before she could draw her next breath, he scooped her up onto his lap and covered her mouth in a hot, demanding kiss. His tongue swirled around hers with a finesse that made her lose track of all time and place.

"Still think I'm too old?"

She wasn't thinking at all. *I am in so much trouble.* "No comment."

Gabriel's low rumble vibrated through her. "It's getting late." He stood with her in his arms and carried her to the front door. Setting her on her feet, he placed a lingering kiss on her lips. "I don't want Adele accusing us of having another sleepover." He opened the door and stepped out onto the porch.

Serenity rolled her eyes. She was a grown woman and could do what she wanted. But having people gossip about her was a reminder of the hospital drama that had plagued her in the months following her breakup, and it still made her uncomfortable. Serenity wasn't eager for a repeat. However, she did appreciate him wanting to protect her reputation. She scanned the woman's house. "The lights are on in her front room. I'd be willing to bet she's sitting right there at the big picture window spying on everybody on the block."

"Then I probably shouldn't kiss you again."

"Yeah, probably not." For more reasons than one. She didn't think she could handle any more of his kisses. "I'll see you later."

"Good night."

Serenity watched Gabriel lope down the steps and stroll across the grass. As he mounted the steps to his house, he turned back and discreetly pointed to Adele's house. Serenity shifted her gaze to where he'd indicated and, sure enough, she saw the woman's curtains slightly pulled back. Gabriel lifted his hand and waved to Adele. The curtain dropped. Laughter poured out of Serenity. She closed her door, ran back to the kitchen where she'd left her phone, and sent Gabriel a text: *I bet she won't tell anyone about that!* 😊

A moment later, he replied: *Lol! I couldn't resist.*

She flipped the lights off on the deck and in the kitchen and headed for the shower, her smile still in place.

Serenity had just gotten dressed when her phone rang. *Speaking of Chandra.* "Your ears must've been burning. I was just talking about you," she said when she answered.

Chandra snorted. "I hope it was all the good stuff. And why were you talking about me?"

"Of course it was the good stuff, girl. I keep all the bad stuff to myself so I can use it as blackmail."

"You just ain't right." They both laughed. "So, you never answered the question."

Serenity had hoped Chandra wouldn't notice, but she should've known better. Nothing got past the psychologist. "I was just telling my neighbor I'm coming to meet you next weekend."

"Oh. How is Andrea?"

"She's good. She was promoted to regional manager

and relocated to Seattle almost a month ago. She got her older brother to move here to watch over their grandmother."

"How much older?"

Here we go. "He's a few years older than her…thirties."

"Hmm. And he looks like…?" When it took too long for Serenity to answer, she said, "Maybe I should be coming to Firefly Lake, instead. We definitely need to talk, little sister."

"Oh, please. There's nothing to talk about."

"Serenity, spill it."

Serenity hesitated briefly, then said, "Okay. Gabriel Cunningham is fine, with a sexy body to match."

"Mmm…sounds like he has a body women would love to run their hands all over," Chandra murmured.

"I wouldn't know." Not the entire truth. She *had* run her hands over his chest and had, admittedly, after feeling his hard thighs beneath her as he held her in his lap, fantasized about doing the same to the rest of his body.

"But you could," Chandra countered.

"*Anyway*, he's a really nice guy."

"And you like him."

"Yes, I like him. He makes it hard not to, but I'm not trying to put my heart out there again. You remember how it was with Lloyd. My self-esteem took a beating, and I don't want to go through that again."

"Who says you will? Honey, you aren't the first woman to experience a broken heart, but if you put yourself on a shelf, thinking that'll protect you, you're going to end up alone and left with a lot of what-ifs. I don't want that for you. I'm not saying this guy is the one, but someone is going to come along who is worthy of your heart, and you'll have to decide whether you want to take the risk."

She heard every word Chandra said. Everyone else—her mother, Natasha, even her father—had said the same thing, but Serenity didn't believe she would ever be able to give herself or her heart to another man.

CHAPTER 10

Gabriel increased his pace, the slip-slap of his running shoes hitting the pavement with a steady rhythm. The midmorning run was just what he needed to clear his mind. He'd been in town a little over a month and had done only minimal work. He didn't want to admit that Glenn had been right about his needing some downtime. But now he was ready to get back into the groove. He had a call with Darius scheduled so they could go over the specifics of the new app they were developing. This would be a project for themselves, which they hoped to market once completed.

He hit the curve and decreased his speed to a slow jog. Since it was a Thursday, he pretty much had the trail to himself. A shortcut he'd discovered last time led him to a small waterfall, and he continued his stride until he reached the lake. Once there, he stopped for a moment to catch his breath, then walked back to his car.

Gabriel had enough time to shower and grab a quick bite to eat before calling Darius.

"What's up, G?" Darius said when he picked up. "I'm thinking we should switch to video, so we can screenshare. I have a few things I want to show you."

"Works for me. You want to send the invite, or do you want me to do it?"

"Just sent it."

"Okay." He ended the call, opened the email, and hit the "join meeting" link. For the next two hours, they discussed what they wanted to include on the note-taking app. "Are we talking something where multiple people can take notes, share them, or add to them, all from their phone or tablet?"

"Yes, and the ability to use it on a desktop, as well. Think about how easy it'll be if people could access their notes across all platforms."

Gabriel read the document Darius had up. "Even better." They went on to discuss having a variety of fonts, highlighting, folders. By the time he looked up again, four hours had passed. But they'd made good progress and would be able to start writing the initial codes. "I can't believe we talked this long."

Darius nodded. "The only time we get caught up like this is when we're designing our own programs," he said with a chuckle. He ended the screenshare. "Now that we're done with this, what's up with you and Serenity? I hope you took our advice."

Because they had always kept each other's confidence, Gabriel was comfortable sharing the decision he and Serenity had made. "We decided to date for as long as I'm here, but to keep it light…no commitments. And before you say anything, it's what she wanted. She's been hurt before."

"Welcome to the club. You sure it's a good idea, though? I can see this going sideways if one of you changes your mind."

"It won't," he said emphatically. Because of their histories, he felt it wouldn't be an issue for them to keep their emotions out of the equation. He had finally met a woman who wanted the same thing he did out of a relationship, and he planned to enjoy it to the fullest.

"If you say so. Well, it's after six, and I'm supposed to be meeting someone for dinner in an hour."

"A potential Mrs. Right?"

"We'll see."

"Keep me posted and let me know if I need to dust off my tux."

Darius chuckled. "At the rate we're going, by the time you, me, and Brent get married, we'll have to buy new ones because the old ones will have disintegrated."

Gabriel laughed. "You're probably right. Later." Still chuckling, he cut the connection.

He'd promised Nana he'd do her yard, so he put on his shoes, loaded up his mower, and drove over.

"Come on in, Gabriel," Nana called when he knocked on her screen door.

He found her exactly where he'd expected—

watching reruns of *Law & Order*, one of her favorite shows. "Hey, Nana. I'm going to start on the yard."

"After you get done, go on in the kitchen and fix you a plate. I made some spaghetti. All you need to do is toast the bread."

Gabriel smiled. "Thanks, Nana." Between her and Serenity, he was kept well fed. That reminded him, he hadn't decided what to have for his picnic date with Serenity. He toyed with picking up something from Ms. Ida's, but he wanted to make up for the candied yam fiasco. He waved at one of Nana's neighbors as he started up the lawn mower. Her yard was twice the size of his and took twice the time.

"You sure have Della's yard looking good."

He paused in sweeping. The same woman he'd waved at earlier, who looked to be around the same age as Nana, came toward him, leaning heavily on a cane. "Thank you."

"I haven't seen you before. Are you one of Top Lawn Care's new employees? They canceled my appointment, and I need to make another one."

"No, ma'am. I'm just helping my grandmother."

She frowned and studied him critically. "You're Della's grandson?"

He'd just said that. "Yes, ma'am."

"Gabriel, you're not done yet?" Nana called from the porch. "Oh, hey, Inez."

"Hey, Della." The woman started in the direction of the porch. "Why didn't I know your grandson was here?"

"Was I supposed to take an ad out in the paper to let everybody know he's here? He came to visit me. Wasn't nobody else's business."

Gabriel took that as his cue and eased his way to the other end of the yard. His Nana was a trip. She didn't want anyone in her business, but she had no problems getting deep into his. He finished sweeping up the grass, rinsed off his mower, and dried it. Hopefully, the afternoon heat would dry it completely by the time he was ready to leave. Seeing the neighbor still talking to Nana on the porch, he decided to go through the side door and enter the house through the garage to avoid being caught up in whatever conversation they were having. He'd just sat down to eat when Nana came in.

"Whew, that woman can talk your ear off. Made me miss the good part. I wanted to see if Detective Green caught that man who killed his wife, and she was out there asking me all these questions about when you came to town." Nana shook her head and grunted. "Then she had the nerve to ask me about getting you to do her lawn, too."

Alarmed, Gabriel froze with his fork halfway to his mouth. He didn't mind doing Nana's yard, or even Serenity's, but he had no intention of adding someone else's to the mix. Next thing he knew, there would be a domino effect, and he'd be on the hook for the whole town. "Uh…"

She waved him off. "Don't worry. I told her you had a job and didn't have time to be doing her lawn.

That woman has three boys and four or five grandsons. Most of them live here. I told her she needed to get one of those lazy children of hers to do it. Don't make no sense not helping their mama out when they know good and well their father can't do it."

"Did you eat yet?" he asked, cutting into her tirade. If he didn't interrupt, she'd end up going on forever. At least she hadn't mentioned getting a call from his neighborhood spy, so his waving had worked. As Serenity had put it, Adele didn't run and tell that. He smiled inwardly.

"No. Let me fix my plate."

"I already buttered your bread and left the oven on."

"Thanks, baby. You want some tea? It's not too sweet, though. Howard wants me to decrease my sugar intake."

Howard? Gabriel searched his mind for who the man might be, then remembered it being Dr. Jacobs's first name. "That's fine, but I can get it." He rose from the table, filled two glasses from the pitcher in the refrigerator and placed them on the table. He sat and continued to eat.

Nana brought her plate to the table. "It's nice sharing dinner with someone. We need to do this more often."

"You know I love your cooking, so that's definitely not a problem." He didn't realize how much he'd come to enjoy being around her, too.

"What about Sunday?"

"Actually, Serenity and I are going to check out one

or two of the lakes around here. I'm still learning my way around, and I heard they were nice spots. She was nice enough to agree to show me around," he rushed to add when he saw her curious expression.

"That girl always goes out of her way to do something nice for others. She's going to make some man a wonderful wife one day."

The thought of Serenity being married to someone else gave him momentary pause. Not that it should matter, since he had no designs on her. But still… "I'm sure she will."

"You two should think about having a picnic. Seaside Meadows Park is a great spot for that. And there's a beautiful lake there. In fact, your grandfather and I used to have our picnics there all the time." Nana laughed softly, as if recalling one of those special moments. "That's how I got him. Made him some fried chicken, baked beans, corn on the cob, and my homemade biscuits on our very first date. He said it was the best food he'd ever eaten and told me right then and there I was going to be his wife."

Gabriel smiled, watching her blush like a schoolgirl.

She pointed her fork his way. "If you find that one special young lady, don't let that blessing pass you by."

He didn't know how to answer, so he ignored the comment. But the way she looked at him made him think she had someone specific in mind. "You never told me that story before. I guess Grandpa was serious. How long did it take for you guys to get married?"

"A month. And after fifty-five years, he was still the love of my life and I was his. Ooh, I miss that man..." She smiled wistfully and forked up some spaghetti.

What she described had been the same thing he'd seen with his parents. They'd met in college—his father a senior and his mother a junior—and had gotten married right after she graduated. Gabriel was born nine months later. Even after more than two decades of marriage, he recalled moments of them stealing kisses, laughing about some intimate secret, or just sitting quietly together with contented smiles. In a way it had been a blessing that they'd died together. Apparently, his grandparents had shared the same kind of love. But somehow Gabriel had gotten it wrong. None of his relationships had ever mirrored that kind of deep, passionate love Nana had described. Some parts of him envied that experience, but he had come to accept that, for him, some things, or *blessings*, weren't meant to be.

* * *

Serenity walked into the Embassy Suites in downtown Sacramento late Saturday morning and searched the lobby for her sister. She and Chandra spotted each other at the same time. The two women let out screams of excitement and ran toward each other, gaining the attention of more than a few people, but Serenity didn't care. She hadn't seen her big sister in months and had missed her tremendously.

"Oh, I'm so glad to see you, Serenity." Chandra and Serenity hugged, rocked, and cried, then hugged some more.

When they finally stepped apart, Serenity wiped her eyes. "Girl, I've missed you so much." While both women had similar skin color and features, Chandra had inherited their mother's trim five-feet-six-inch height, while Serenity's curvy body barely reached five three. "How was the conference?"

"Not too bad. Some of these folks need to learn how to present, though, with those long, drawn-out boring lectures. I almost fell asleep in a couple of them."

Serenity laughed. "I know what you mean. I'm not looking forward to mine." She had to keep up with the continuing education requirements for nursing to maintain her license. "Do you want to grab something to eat in one of the hotel restaurants?"

"No. I know it's blazing outside, but I wanted to check out Old Sacramento right across the street, and the brochure mentions lots of choices." The city's July temperatures were projected to hit the century mark later in the day.

"That's fine. Good thing I decided to wear my tennis shoes."

"You could've worn my extra pair if you hadn't," Chandra said as they headed for the exit. They crossed the wide street and meandered through the quaint area, stopping to check out restaurant menus and the various shops lining the cobblestone streets.

Serenity had come to Sacramento a few times but

hadn't yet had a chance to visit Old Sac. "I like this."

Chandra snorted. "Of course you would. It kind of reminds me of your little town, except here you can drive five miles and find civilization."

She playfully bumped her sister. "Quit hating on my town. I love it there. And the Bay Area isn't too far."

"The key words being *too far*," Chandra said with a laugh.

"*Whateva*. Where are we eating?" They walked around to Front Street and saw the *Delta King*, a paddlewheel riverboat. "How about eating with a view of the river?"

"I'm game."

The riverboat's restaurant only served dinner, so they ate at the bar and grill located in the boat's forward section. They had a panoramic view of the river, and despite the heat, a slight breeze blew off the water. Over a meal of clam chowder, crab cakes, and salad, they caught up on everything that happened since their last conversation.

"Did Mom tell you she and Dad are taking a trip to DC?"

"No. But I'm so excited for them. She's been wanting to visit the National Museum of African American History and Culture since it opened."

"I know. I wish Mark and I could go with them, but when I brought it up, Mom told me we were welcome to take the trip on our own because theirs was a trip for two."

A surprised giggle escaped Serenity. "I guess she told you." Their parents had always made a practice of taking vacations with just the two of them. When she and Chandra were growing up, Serenity had memories of them going on weekend excursions while she and her sister stayed with their grandparents. "It's really cool that they're still so much in love after all this time."

"Girl, those are marriage *goals*."

"At least one of us can reach that goal," she said wryly, taking a bite of her crab cake.

Chandra waved her fork dismissively. "You'll get there. You might already be there if you hadn't had to deal with Lloyd's conceited ass." She gave Serenity's hand a sympathetic squeeze. "I'm sorry. You know my mouth gets ahead of my brain every now and again."

Serenity pushed her salad around on her plate. "I know. But you're right. Sometimes I try to recall what attracted me to him, and for the life of me, I can't figure it out." All her girlfriends back home had been excited that a doctor had set his sights on Serenity. With his tall good looks and intelligence, theirs was a match made in heaven. Except it hadn't been. She'd be the first to admit that there had been some good times in the beginning, but in hindsight, the things she valued most, like having quiet dinners at home and spending time just talking or watching a movie together, weren't on his list of favorites. He preferred dining at exclusive restaurants, attending the

symphony, and having networking parties. She liked
to do those things too, but only in moderation.

"Well, like Grandma always said, that's why you
date—to find out what kind of person he is *before*
saying 'I do,'" Chandra said around a mouthful
of food.

She smiled. "Thank goodness for that." She shuddered to think what her life would be like had she
hung in there, as a few of her friends had suggested.
The women had tried to convince Serenity that things
would change once they got married. But Serenity
subscribed to Maya Angelou's saying about believing
what a person shows you. *What has Gabriel shown you?*
that annoying inner voice asked. But she didn't think
she'd known him long enough to determine whether
what he'd shown her were his true colors. *Liar!*

Chandra braced her elbows on the table and rested
her chin on her hands. "Since we're on the subject
of men, tell me more about this new neighbor of
yours."

Serenity lifted her shoulder in a careless shrug.
"There's not much to tell outside of what you already
know."

"No? So, you haven't spoken to him or seen him
once since we talked last week? It doesn't sound very
neighborly."

"You know I can't stand you right now, Miss
Psychologist," Serenity said with a mock pout.

Chandra laughed softly. "What? I'm just asking a
simple question."

"Yeah, right." She knew she wouldn't be able to deflect the conversation like she could with her friends. Chandra would risk missing her flight to get the information she wanted. "Yes, I talked to him. He asked me out on a date for tomorrow."

"Hallelujah!" Chandra clapped a hand over her mouth and took a discreet glance around the half-full grill. "My bad."

Serenity shook her head. "You act like I haven't gone out on a date since I left San Diego." So what if she could count the number of times on one hand, or that they were more like lunch hangouts with an acquaintance? The point remained that she *had* gone out.

"If my memory serves me right, you're the one who said you didn't want to waste your time and energy going out with a man, knowing it wouldn't lead anywhere. But that's neither here nor there. Right now I'm interested in … What did you tell me his name was again?" She tapped her finger against her chin. "Oh, I remember. Gabriel Cunningham. I want to know all about Gabriel and this upcoming date." Chandra grinned and bounced impatiently in her chair.

"Can we finish eating first and talk while sitting on one of those benches? I'd rather not have an entire restaurant in my business."

"Well, hurry up, then, girl." She dug into the remaining food on her plate with gusto.

"I don't know what I'm going to do with you." Serenity speared a tomato with her fork and popped it into her mouth.

Once they'd finished, Chandra all but snatched the bill, paid it, then rushed Serenity off the boat and down the wood-planked walkway to a bench facing the water.

"I don't even recall you being this excited when you first started dating Mark."

Chandra wiggled her eyebrows. "That's because you didn't see me behind closed doors."

Serenity closed her ears. "Ugh. TMI, Chandra. *TMI*."

"Oh, girl, please. We used to bathe together, so tell that to somebody else. Now, where is he taking you?" She frowned. "Wait. Does Firefly Lake even have an upscale restaurant or somewhere to take a date?"

"Ha ha. Funny. Yes, we do. But I have no idea where we're going. He didn't say."

Chandra shifted her body to face Serenity. "Let me get this straight. Gabriel asked you out, you said yes and didn't ask where you were going?"

Serenity realized with a start that her sister was right. But then her brain had been in a sensual fog from his kisses. Other than his assurance it would be out of the public eye, it had never even crossed her mind to ask. Her sister burst out laughing. "What's so funny?"

"Honey, Gabriel must be some kind of man because the Serenity I know would have asked for the date, time, dress code, weather forecast, and every other little detail. Exactly what were you two doing when he asked?"

"We were talking after the supper club dinner once everyone had gone. And as you so rudely pointed out, it's not like we have a lot of options. But I did ask if we could go someplace with a little privacy. You know how people talk, and the last thing I want is for anyone to start thinking there's more to our relationship than there is." She told her about the two incidents with Adele. "The last time nearly killed me, and my self-confidence took a nosedive. I started to question not only my cooking skills but also my competency as a nurse. I can't go through that again." Just the thought made Serenity shudder.

"Good for Gabriel. Had it been me, I might've marched down to her house and told her to mind her own business. As far as what happened with *he who shall remain nameless*, you survived and are stronger because of it. But you can't lock yourself away, Sis. You deserve to have the love of a good man, and deep down inside I know you still want it."

Serenity opened her mouth to refute her sister's statement, then closed it. Chandra was right. A small part of Serenity wanted what her sister, parents, and grandparents had, but a larger part of her was afraid to put her heart on the line again.

"It's okay to be afraid," Chandra said perceptively. "Love always carries a risk, but trust me when I tell you it's the most beautiful thing with the *right* person. Whether that's Gabriel or someone else, time will tell."

"I hate it when you're so wise."

Chandra laughed. "Older, wiser...yep, that's me." She bumped Serenity's shoulder playfully. "Now, back to this date tomorrow, I'm curious about where he's going to find a spot with any level of privacy unless you leave town."

"I have no idea, but he said we'd save the Napa trip for later." The moment the words left her mouth, Serenity wanted to call them back.

"Hold up. Napa trip?"

She told Chandra all about the competition and how Gabriel had won by cheating.

"What's he going to get as his prize? Because, technically, you both won."

Why do I have such a nosy sister? "He already got his prize at the dinner."

Chandra lifted a brow. "Which was?"

Serenity squirmed in her seat and gazed out onto the water. "A kiss," she mumbled.

"Aw, sookie sookie. Gabriel came to win."

Serenity snapped her head around. "Win what?"

Chandra hugged Serenity's shoulders. "Your heart, dear sister."

Her gaze went back to the water. "My heart is not part of the bargain."

CHAPTER 11

By Sunday morning, Serenity was a basket case. She'd barely slept a wink, speculating on where Gabriel planned to take her. More than once she had picked up her phone to send a text asking, but she chickened out each time. She had no idea why she felt so nervous. It was just a lunch date, not to mention, she and Gabriel had shared more than a few meals together. She snatched her phone up again, and before she could lose her nerve, sent the last text, which was still waiting in draft. Several minutes passed before he replied: *Just somewhere to have a quiet lunch. Dress casually and wear sneakers.*

"That's it?" She waited to see if he was going to say more, but the phone stayed silent. *Maybe I ought to go see Adele. If anybody knows, it's her.* Willing herself to relax, she checked the temperatures, then selected a pair of black shorts and paired it with a sleeveless purple top. Not a huge fan of makeup, she put on her standard light coating of mascara and some lip color.

At the last minute, she decided to switch out her purse for a mini crossbody, one just large enough to carry the necessities.

Gabriel rang her doorbell at exactly noon, and all the calm Serenity had worked hard to restore flew right out the window the moment she opened the door. He looked devastatingly handsome in a black tee that reminded her just how well defined his upper body was and dark-tan shorts.

Gabriel's gaze made a slow tour down her body and up again. "Hey, beautiful. Ready?"

"Hi. Yep." She stepped out onto the porch and locked the door. Belatedly, it dawned on her that leaving in broad daylight didn't help keep the busybodies out of her business.

He must have sensed her apprehension because he said, "I don't think we have to worry about Adele. Apparently, that wave did the trick, or at least it made her step back because, just as you predicted, she didn't say one word to Nana."

"That's good to know." But she couldn't stop herself from doing a hasty perusal up and down the block. Because it was Sunday, a good number of the people were in church at this hour, which worked in their favor. Gabriel helped her into his SUV, then rounded the fender and got in on the driver's side. "This is the first time I've been in your car."

Gabriel cocked his head to the side. "Hmm, you're right." He started the engine and pulled off. "But it won't be the last."

Serenity didn't have a comeback for that one, so she leaned against the seat and made herself comfortable. India Arie singing about a steady love flowed through the speakers from one of the satellite radio stations. *Of all songs.* A few minutes later, Gabriel turned onto a road leading out of town, and her curiosity mounted. "Are we going to the Bay?"

He slanted her a brief glance. "Nope."

She eyed him, but just like the text, he offered no other information. She had never ventured out this way before, and as they drove, she began to see fewer houses and more hills and trees. *Where is this man taking me?* After another fifteen minutes or so, they came upon a sign that read CRYSTALWOOD LAKE. Gabriel turned into the small lot and parked at the far end. He came around and helped her out of the car. Only two other vehicles were there, and Serenity saw maybe four or five people milling around. In the distance, the water shimmered like crystals beneath the sun, and she wondered if that had anything to do with the name. "I've lived here for six years and never knew this place existed. How in the world did you find it?"

Gabriel leaned against the side of the car and folded his arms. "When Brent and Darius were here, we found it while exploring the town. I thought it would be a beautiful place for a picnic."

"It's gorgeous, but you need food for a picnic, and I didn't see anything other than a gas station a few miles back."

He straightened and, using the remote, popped the

trunk. When he closed it again, he held a large picnic basket and a blanket. "I do have food."

Serenity didn't know what to make of a man who planned a private picnic for a first date. He entwined their fingers and led them down a concrete path. He passed several good shaded spots, but he kept going until he stopped at an archway.

"Be careful going through here. The first couple of steps are a little uneven."

She peered through the opening before fully stepping onto the cobblestone entry. A few feet in, the rocks gave way to a paved path. She didn't see any place for them to sit.

"We're going to a spot just beyond the other archway ahead," Gabriel said, gesturing in that direction.

When they finally made it to their destination, Serenity froze and could only stare. She walked across the golden sand closer to the clear blue-green water just to be sure her eyes weren't deceiving her. It looked like they'd stumbled on some private tropical island for two.

"What do you think?"

"I don't believe it. This is the most amazing thing I've ever seen." She whirled around to face him. Emotions she shouldn't be feeling engulfed her. "Thank you for this."

The corner of his mouth inched up in a smile. "You're welcome." He set the basket down to spread out the blanket, then gestured for her to sit.

Serenity leaned over to look in the basket as he opened it. "I know I don't smell fried chicken."

"Yes, you do." Gabriel waved the container past her nose.

Her stomach grumbled in response. "Did you get that from Ms. Ida's?" She'd had the chicken there a few times and it was some of the best she had eaten.

"Not this time," he said with a little laugh. "I wanted to make up for the whole candied yams thing, so I cooked this time—*everything* except the rolls."

He'd said he could cook, but after the last time, she was a little nervous about trying his food. If it didn't taste good, she didn't want to hurt his feelings, especially since he'd gone through all the trouble to make the picnic special. "Um…you weren't lying about being able to cook, were you?"

He laughed harder. "I promise I can cook. I'm still perfecting some dishes, but I went with a menu that I'm comfortable with."

"Okay," she said, still somewhat skeptical. "What are we having with it?"

"Potato salad and corn on the cob." He unearthed the rest of the food, plates, utensils, and drinks.

Serenity held up a hand. "Wait a minute. Now, you know it's bad enough to mess up picnic staples like fried chicken, but it is downright sacrilegious to screw up the potato salad. What's the first thing everybody asks when they go to a picnic?"

"Who made the potato salad? I know." Gabriel leaned over and gave her a soft kiss. "Do you want to fix yours first, or should I while you're still deciding?"

"No, no, I'll go first." He watched her, seemingly

amused as opposed to being upset, as she selected a wing, an ear of corn, a small scoop of potato salad, and a roll. She loved these particular rolls, so if nothing else, she could fill up on bread.

In contrast, he packed his plate with two pieces of chicken and a mound of potato salad. "I have bottles of iced tea and lemonade."

"The lemonade, please."

He opened the bottle and handed it to her, along with a napkin and a fork.

She glanced down at her plate. Thinking she should work up to the chicken and potato salad, Serenity started with a few bites of the roll and corn. Knowing she couldn't hold off any longer, she bit into the fragrant wing. The flavors exploded on her tongue, and before she could stop it, a moan escaped. "Oh, Gabriel, I am so sorry for dissing you. This chicken is…" She took another bite and chewed. Her eyes slid closed, and she wanted to hum like babies did when eating something that tasted good. "This chicken is beyond amazing."

"Thanks. I told you it wouldn't be too bad. My feelings should be hurt, but I'm going to let you slide this time, since I did kind of put the doubt there in the first place."

Serenity finished the wing so fast, she would swear someone else stole half. She reached into the container for another piece, a thigh. After a few bites, she worked up enough courage to try the potato salad. She forked up a little bit and tentatively put it in her mouth. It was so good, this time she actually swooned. "Did your grandmother help you make this?"

"I can assure you Nana did not help me."

She glanced all around her and behind him.

He gave her a strange look. "What are you doing?"

"Checking to see if I'm being punked." His food tasted as good as her mama's and grandmother's. She narrowed her eyes at him. "Are you sure you messed up those candied yams?"

Gabriel roared with laughter. "Baby, trust me when I tell you, you did *not* want to taste those yams. You know I love good food, so I learned how to cook some of my favorites well. This meal is at the top of my list. It took me a while to get it just right, but now I can make the potato salad without measuring. And yeah, I was definitely one of those people asking because you can't eat everybody's potato salad."

Still trying to process the endearment, it took her a few seconds to respond. "You've got that right." When he went for a second helping, she snatched the spoon from him. "Let me get some more before you eat it all."

"Oh, so now you want to be eating up all my food."

"Mm-hmm, and now that I know you can indeed cook, I may need to sample something else in your repertoire."

"Movie night. My house next weekend. I'll cook," he said before she could continue.

Serenity blinked. *I should've seen that one coming.* "Okay," she said slowly.

Gabriel tilted the bottle of iced tea to his lips and took a long drink. "Any particular movie you'd like to see?"

She thought for a moment. "Does it have to be something new?"

"It can be anything you want, old or new."

"The Shawshank Redemption."

His mouth dropped. "How did you know that's one of my favorite movies? I had to buy a new copy because I watched it so much, I wore the disc out. Apparently, we have a lot in common."

Too much—food, music, and now movies. And how could she forget the fact that for their first two dates, the things he'd planned were things she enjoyed most in a relationship. But they didn't have a relationship, she reminded herself. Serenity shifted her focus to the water and finished eating.

"Do you want anything else?"

"No, thank you. I'm so full, you might have to roll me back to the car."

Gabriel started repacking the basket. "That's a good thing."

She let out a little snort. "How is that a good thing?"

Holding her gaze, he said softly, "Because it means you enjoyed it, and that was my goal." He placed a lingering kiss on her lips.

I. Can. Not. Fall. For. This. Man. To distract herself from her thoughts, she helped him clean up.

"How about we walk off some of this food?"

"That's a good idea." Serenity pointed to the basket. "What should we do with the basket?"

"I think it'll be fine to leave it. We can have the dessert I brought when we get back."

"Sounds good." They started a slow stroll down the curved path parallel to the water in companionable silence, stopping every so often to watch the waves. They retraced their steps, and when they'd made it almost back to the blanket, she noticed how the golden color of the sand seemed brighter. "Look at the color of the sand." A thought came to her. "You know what it reminds me of?"

"No, what?"

Serenity hooked her arm in his and started belting out the chorus of "Ease on Down the Road" from *The Wiz*, complete with the dance.

Gabriel doubled over in laughter. When he finally calmed down, he swept Serenity into his arms. "You are something else. This is the most fun I've had in a long time."

Time seemed to slow as their laughter faded. Something flickered in his intense gaze that sent a tremor down her spine. Suddenly, the air around them thickened with sexual tension. "Gabriel," she whispered as his head descended. The kiss started off sweet and tender but changed to demanding and all-consuming in a split second. Without breaking the seal of their mouths, he somehow lowered them both to the blanket.

Gabriel trailed kisses along the column of her neck, her bare shoulder, and the exposed part of her chest while his hands blazed a path up her bare thigh, hip, and around to her breast, setting every molecule in her body on fire. Her hands were just as busy, charting her course across the hard planes of his chest and muscular arms. Somewhere in the recesses of her mind, a voice said she should stop this before things went too far, but it was quickly drowned out by the rising desire between them. She had never been this impulsive with a man, especially one she had known for only a short while, but her body overruled her mind, and she gave herself up to the sweet sensations taking over.

"We should probably stop," Gabriel murmured against her ear as he continued to plant butterfly kisses there.

Her breath came in short gasps, and her heart thumped erratically in her chest. "Yeah, probably." Only she didn't want him to stop. He kissed her once more, then rolled onto his back with his arm thrown over his face. His breathing wasn't any better than hers.

He reached for her hand. "You're a special lady, Serenity."

She didn't respond. She couldn't. They lay together quietly, listening to the sounds of the waves crashing softly against the shore until their passions cooled.

"Ready to head back?"

"Honestly, no. But I'm starting to roast out here, so it might be a good idea. You know, we never got around to dessert."

"I beg to differ."

She rolled her head in his direction and found his

eyes waiting with a look so tender, it almost brought tears to her eyes. *Remember, keep it light, girl.* On second thought, leaving was definitely a good idea.

* * *

Hours later, after Serenity returned from her picnic date with Gabriel, her body still hummed with desire. The man's kisses were something straight out of a fantasy and could rob a woman of her senses in a millisecond, something she had never experienced before. She felt as if she were swimming in uncharted waters without a life jacket. She toyed with calling her sister to talk but decided against it, not wanting to interrupt Chandra and Mark's reunion. Instead, she called Natasha.

"Hey, Tasha. Are you busy?"

"Dana and I are just leaving the nursery. I wanted to pick up a few planters. How did your date go with Gabriel?"

"That's what I'm calling about. If you're going straight home, I can meet you there."

"Is everything okay?" Natasha asked, concern evident in her voice.

"Serenity, we'll be there when you get here," Dana said into the phone.

She smiled. She loved her girls. "Thanks. See you in a bit." She stuck her feet into her shoes, grabbed her purse and keys, and set out. Once there, she parked in the driveway, headed up the walkway, and rang the bell. The door opened almost immediately.

"Come on in, girl." Natasha hugged Serenity and pulled her inside her house, leading her straight to the kitchen, where Dana stood at the counter pouring three glasses of wine.

Dana handed Serenity a glass. "Here. From the way you sounded on the phone, I figured you could use this."

"I can," Serenity said, accepting the glass.

"What's up?"

"He took me on a picnic at Crystalwood Lake."

"I can't remember the last time I was there," Natasha said. "It's so far out, I forgot about it. How in the world did he find it?"

"He and his friends were exploring the town, and he happened upon it. I have to admit, it was the perfect place to have some privacy. We didn't see more than five people the entire time."

"Did you have a good time?"

Serenity didn't know where to begin or how to describe the time she had. "It was…he…"

Dana ran a comforting hand over Serenity's back. "I get it, Sis. Gabriel seems to be one of the good ones."

"He cooked all the food, and oh my goodness, the man's fried chicken and potato salad are *beyond* amazing." He'd given her the rest of the food to take home, including a few of the divine chocolate chip cookies they didn't end up eating. "It was one of those dates that you always wished you could have, but with the man you love. But that's not what this is, and I'm not sure if I should keep hanging out with him in that way."

Natasha sat at the kitchen table. "I don't understand the problem. We all agree that he's a good guy, so why wouldn't you want to spend time with him? And who knows, he could be feeling the same. We always talk about men not putting themselves out there for a woman and expecting her to do all the heavy lifting in a relationship. Now when one comes around willing to do just that, you're backing away. Don't let what Lloyd did keep you from exploring what could be with Gabriel."

She took a sip of her wine. "I hear you, but I still don't think I can let myself get that close to a man again. This thing, or whatever it is with Gabriel," she said, waving a hand, "won't ever be anything more than what we agreed to because he's not staying."

Dana frowned. "What do you mean he's not staying? Andrea said he was moving here to help Ms. Della."

"According to him, he plans to talk her into moving back to Atlanta with him at the end of the summer."

"Wow. And wait a minute. What did you mean by 'what we agreed to'?"

Serenity took a deep breath. She hadn't planned to tell them everything, only she couldn't stop the words from coming. "I told him we could go out sometimes until he leaves."

Natasha chuckled. "I hate to tell you this, but if you keep hanging out with that man, it's going to lead to more than just *hanging out*." She made quote marks in the air.

"Tell me about it," she muttered. Her body tingled with the remembrance of how his mouth and hands had set her body aflame earlier. The afternoon sun beating down on them had nothing on the heat Gabriel could produce in her.

A grin played around the corner of Dana's mouth. "I was hoping *you'd* tell *us* about it. Obviously, Gabriel can do more than plan a good date."

"He kissed me."

"Well, that explains your confusion," Natasha said with a little laugh. "Are you sure you're going to be able to keep hanging out with him without falling for him?"

Dana crossed her arms. "Inquiring minds want to know."

Serenity waved them off. "Of course. He agreed that we'd keep it light. No ties or commitments. Just a couple of friends enjoying each other's company. He doesn't want a relationship any more than I do." She mentally shook her head as she recalled him sharing how his ex-girlfriend made a play for his best friend. She still couldn't imagine why.

"Is he one of those commitment-phobic men?" Natasha asked with a raised eyebrow.

"No." She hesitated. "I'm going to tell you something, but I will hurt the two of you if you breathe one word."

Dana and Natasha stared eagerly.

"He had a bad breakup and isn't willing to put his heart on the line. The woman came on to his best friend and cheated with two other men." She wondered if it had been one of the two men she'd met. Gabriel hadn't said, and Serenity hadn't felt comfortable enough to ask.

Natasha shook her head with disgust. "Again, women always talking about not being able to find a good Black man, but then get one and do the stupid."

"That's why I know I can deal with our relationship staying this way." Talking with her friends had helped her get her head on straight. Serenity knew the score. Anything they shared would be temporary, and she felt confident she could handle a short affair.

CHAPTER 12

Saturday afternoon, Gabriel positioned the double chaise lounge that had been delivered earlier so that it would provide optimal viewing of the mounted flat-screen TV. Aside from his recliner, a small love seat, and an end table, there wasn't any furniture. Andrea had taken the rest. He'd decided he needed something for Serenity to sit on when she arrived later. To say he was looking forward to the dinner and movie night with her would be an understatement. He paused. *What am I doing?* They agreed to keep things light, and at the moment, he couldn't decide whether the impromptu purchase qualified. *I'll be here for another couple of months, so it's not like the lounger won't get any use,* he reasoned. Satisfied, Gabriel went into the kitchen to put the dry rub on the steaks he'd thawed.

As soon as he finished washing his hands, his cell chimed with a text message. He picked it up, read the words, then smiled. Serenity offered to bring dessert.

Gabriel typed back: *I planned to make dessert, but since whatever you make is sure to be a hundred times better, I'm all for it.* He hoped she'd bring the brownies he couldn't get enough of. A quick peek at the time showed he still had a couple of hours before his date, so he grabbed his laptop out of his bedroom and went out to the back deck to work on the note taking app.

Gabriel was so engrossed in his work, it took a moment to register the doorbell ringing. He glanced at the time and jumped up from the lounger, almost knocking the laptop over. Muttering a curse, he caught the device before it hit the ground and rushed to the front.

"Serenity. Hey. Come on in." Gabriel stepped back to let her enter, then placed a brief kiss on her lips.

Serenity smiled. "Got caught up in work again, huh?" she asked teasingly.

He ducked his head sheepishly. "Something like that." It was a good thing he had decided on an easy dinner of steaks, potatoes, and salad. Otherwise, he would've been in trouble. "Let me put this away and I'll meet you in the kitchen." His gaze dropped to the gift bag in her hand. "Brownies?"

"How did I know you'd ask that? Nope, not brownies this time, but there are peaches, sugar, and crust involved."

Gabriel grinned. "Can't wait." He went down the short hallway and deposited the laptop on the nightstand, then headed to the kitchen.

Serenity leaned against the counter. "This kitchen is awfully clean, and I don't smell anything cooking."

"Ha ha. You got jokes," he said, removing the plate holding the steaks from the refrigerator. "For your information, I've already seasoned these steaks. We're having potatoes, salad, and French rolls."

She chuckled. "Mmm, sounds delicious. And whatever seasoning you put on the meat smells so good." She handed him a clear plastic container. "This needs to go into the freezer."

"Please don't tell me this is homemade ice cream."

"Okay, I won't tell you," Serenity said with a smirk.

He waged an inner battle for several seconds, and it took everything inside him for him not to open the container right then. Snatching open the freezer, he set the container on the shelf and closed the door before he was tempted to devour the entire bowl before dinner.

"Let me wash my hands and I'll help."

Gabriel stared at her incredulously. He closed the distance between them and slid his arms around her waist. "Help? Baby, I didn't invite you over to put you to work. Tonight is all for you. The only thing I want you to do is relax." She always went out of her way to do nice things for everyone, including him, so he wanted to do something special for her.

Serenity laid her head against his chest. "I can't tell you how much this means to me, Gabriel."

The feel of her arms tightening around him and her sweet confession stirred something in his chest, leaving Gabriel more than a little shaken. Needing some distance, he released her and gestured to a chair. "Have a seat. Would you like a glass of wine?"

"Yes. Wine sounds nice."

He poured them both a glass and handed her one.

Serenity lifted hers. "To the cook."

Gabriel inclined his head and took a huge sip. He stood there a moment trying to discern what it was about Serenity that drew him. He'd never had a problem keeping his emotions out of any casual relationships. But with her, he seemed to have no control over his growing feelings and had to remind himself that whatever they had would end in a couple of months. "I'll go get the grill started. Want to keep me company?"

"Absolutely." She stood, followed him outside, and sat on one of the patio chairs.

Most people tended to use gas grills, but he preferred using charcoal. There was something about the smoky flavor that couldn't be duplicated. After starting the coals on the grill, Gabriel took a seat next to Serenity, marveling at the peacefulness he felt.

"How are you planning to cook the potatoes?" Serenity asked, cutting into his thoughts.

"I was thinking about drizzling a little of that olive oil you told me about and an herb seasoning, then tossing them on the grill. Why?"

"Ooh, that's going to be so good. I have a few other flavors, too."

He lifted a brow. He hadn't ordered any of the other flavored oils. "Which ones?"

"I can run home real quick and get them, if you like," she added with a smile.

The foodie in him jumped at the thought of trying something new. When she chuckled, he figured the wide grin on his face had shown his excitement. "Yes, please. I'd really like to try them too."

"Sure." Serenity placed her wine on the small table next to her and made a move to stand.

Gabriel leaped to his feet and extended his hand to help her up.

Laughing softly, she shook her head. "A little anxious, are we?"

He shrugged. "What can I say? You know I love good food." He walked her to the front door. "You don't have to knock when you come back. Just come on in."

"Okay. It'll only take me a minute."

He watched the sweet sway of her hips in the blue sundress as she hurried across the lawn and over to her house and felt the stirrings of arousal. *Get a grip, man.* Shaking his head, Gabriel went to check the grill. Seeing that it was almost ready, he went inside to grab the seasoned steaks he'd left on the kitchen counter. He heard the front door close, and seconds later, Serenity strolled into the kitchen carrying a gift bag in one hand and a Ziploc bag containing a slice of what looked like French bread in the other. "That was quick."

Serenity smiled and placed everything on the breakfast table. "If you'll get a plate, I'll pour a bit of each and you can taste them with the bread."

"I wondered about the bread," he said, reaching

for a plate in the cabinet. He stood next to her as she added the different flavored olive oils—lemon, orange, lime, basil, and garlic. "I don't know which one to taste first."

"I felt the same way the first time. Natasha and I had gone up to Apple Hill and stopped by a winery that sold them. I was hooked from the first taste."

After tearing off a small piece of bread, Gabriel dipped it into the garlic oil. "Mmm, good. This would work on the potatoes, as well." Next he tried the basil and couldn't stifle a groan. He took a sip of wine to cleanse his palate and went for the citrus ones. "They're all good, but I think my favorites are the buttery and sweet and the lemon."

"Something else we have in common. Those are mine, too."

The more time they spent together, the more he found to like about her. "I have got to get some of these. How far is Apple Hill from here?" He tried the final oil and agreed that it would definitely complement the roasted potatoes.

She grinned. "You'll be happy to know the actual company is located in Stockton. It's a one-and-a-half-to two-hour drive, or longer, depending on traffic. But you can order them online. The delivery is very fast."

"Let me get the meat and potatoes on the grill, and then you can pull up the website."

Serenity burst out laughing. "Somehow I knew you'd say that. I already have it loaded." She held up her phone.

Smiling, Gabriel grabbed tongs and the steaks, put them on the grill, and was back in a flash to place an order. He'd chosen to use the gold mini creamer potatoes because they were softer and would cook faster. It took him only a couple of minutes to cut them into bite-size pieces, drizzle the oil, and add the sea salt and herbs. He divided them between two pieces of foil and made packets.

She folded her arms and leaned against the counter. "You're pretty handy in the kitchen. Not too many men cook. When you mentioned having potatoes, I expected you to bake them in the microwave."

He slanted her a sidelong glance. "The same can be said for some women. I've known a few who couldn't do more than microwave and order out."

Serenity held up her hands in mock surrender. "You've got me there. I'm just glad you're one of the guys who do cook. I'm enjoying eating food prepared by someone other than myself."

And he was enjoying being the one preparing the food *for* her. In the short time he'd known her, Gabriel realized they liked many of the same things, something he never would have believed given their first introduction. Carrying another pair of tongs, the potatoes, and clean plates, he gestured her toward the sliding glass door.

She reclaimed her seat, sipped her wine, and let out an audible sigh. "Yep. This is the life."

He dropped the packets on the grill, closed the top, and took the lounger next to her. "I agree." For one crazy moment, Gabriel imagined what it would be like sitting with her like this for longer than the summer. While the food cooked, they chatted about everything and nothing. Twenty minutes later, plates loaded, they sat at the table outside as the sun made its descent and the moon rose.

"I don't even know where to start," Serenity said. "Everything looks so good, Gabriel."

"Thanks. Hopefully, it'll pass the taste test."

She rubbed her hands together. "Well, let's see."

He watched as she tentatively ate a bite of the steak.

Pointing her fork Gabriel's way, she shot him a glare. "I think I've been had."

His brows knitted together. "What?"

"That sad story about only being able to cook a few things. This steak is better than any of the ones I've eaten at those high-end restaurants. It literally melted in my mouth." She propped her elbows on the table and rested her head in her hands. "Okay, spill it. I want to know how you did it."

Gabriel laughed so hard, his side ached. "That is the best compliment I've ever been given." He leaned over and gave her a quick kiss. "There's no secret really, other than starting with a quality cut of meat." He'd been more than a little surprised to find the Wagyu rib eyes at a small meat market tucked away right off Main Street. The highly marbled meat gave it its tender, butter-soft richness, and as Serenity said, melt-in-your-mouth goodness. That alone made it worth the expensive cost.

She ate another bite. "I've bought prime cuts from the market, and they *never* turn out like this."

"That's because I bought them from Palmer's Butcher Shop."

"And? I've purchased steaks there, too."

"Wagyu."

Her mouth formed the perfect O. "*Ooo-kay*. So, how are the potatoes?" Serenity gave him a winning smile and wiggled her eyebrows.

Chuckling, he forked up a portion of the potatoes. They had always turned out well before, but this time they were over-the-top good. "All I know is I can't wait for my order to get here." He'd purchased two more of the buttery and sweet and one each of the others.

"Told you." She popped a piece in her mouth. "The citrus-flavored ones are so good on seafood or for making vinaigrettes."

As Gabriel listened, he made a mental shopping list. He'd be purchasing seafood as soon as his package arrived. They finished the meal in companionable silence, interspersed with quiet conversation as smooth R & B music floated through concealed speakers. After they finished their meals, he asked her the question that had been bugging him since he found out she'd been in town only six years. "Was it hard to make the transition from a big city to small-town living?" Although he enjoyed the fresh air and being able to run at nearby lakes, he didn't think he would ever be able to stay indefinitely. He thrived on the fast-paced Atlanta lifestyle.

Serenity ran her hand idly up and down the stem of her wineglass and gave him a wistful smile. "I'll concede that it took some getting used to, but at that time in my life I needed the change, and it turned out to be the best decision." She shrugged. "It's strange, but I don't think I could imagine living anywhere else. The slower pace allows me to catch my breath and indulge in more self-care. Before, I rarely made time to take care of myself. Now I make it a priority."

He studied her for a lengthy moment. Admittedly, she did always seem to have a calmness about her— aside from the two instances when they'd butted heads, for which he'd been partly responsible. Still, he had a hard time picturing himself growing old in a place like this. He could envision visiting more, however, because, despite the circumstances that brought him to town, he wanted to continue seeing her. As friends. The heated kisses they'd previously shared surfaced in his mind. Okay, maybe friends with a few benefits.

"Andrea said you were a city boy through and through, so I'm sure this pace isn't as relaxing for you."

A soft smile tilted the corner of his mouth. "She's right. This is the longest I've stayed, and it hasn't been too bad." Gabriel saluted her with his glass and drained the remainder of his wine. "Meeting you has helped."

"Aw, that's so sweet. Thank you." Serenity paused and raised an eyebrow. "You're not saying that just because you want more brownies?"

He opened his mouth, then closed it. "I...no."

"Mm-hmm, I bet."

"I won't lie and say those brownies aren't addictive, but I enjoy hanging out with you."

"Same here," she said softly. She cleared her throat. "Since we've had time to let that fantastic meal settle, are you ready for dessert?"

"Do you even have to ask?" He rose from the table and collected their plates. Serenity stood, grabbed the glasses, and followed him inside. "You can just place them in the sink. I'll take care of everything later. Right now I want to know what's in the bag."

Serenity shook her head as she slid the container out of the bag and opened the top.

"Peach cobbler!" Without another word, Gabriel reached into a drawer, grabbed a spoon, and dug out a big scoop. The second it hit his mouth, he moaned. He didn't know which he liked more, this or the brownies. "I'm going to have to up my workout regimen around you with all these amazing desserts." They filled their bowls with the cobbler, added the ice cream from the freezer, and then took them back outside. He'd probably gotten far more than he should've, but he couldn't resist. "And this ice cream is better than at Splendid Scoops."

"More flattery?"

"More *truth*. I never lie about food."

She picked up the piece of crust that had fallen and ate it. "It is one of the best I've made recently."

She licked the bits of sugar and cinnamon off her

lips, and the sight prompted Gabriel to swoop down and finish the job. The kiss that he'd meant to be light turned hot and intense in a nanosecond. He cradled her face in his palms as his tongue stroked hers. He trailed kisses along her jaw and throat, then moved back to her mouth. At length, he lifted his head. "Come on. Let's go start the movie."

"I've been waiting all week to see it," Serenity said, doing a little shimmy out of the kitchen. "My favorite part is when the warden tore down that poster. The look on his face was priceless."

"That it was," he agreed, chuckling. After getting comfortable on the spacious lounger and starting the movie, they shared a smile and turned their attention to the screen. Gabriel thought about the woman curled next to him. Every moment of the evening, from the conversation and food to the kiss and relaxed domesticity they shared, had been incredible. A wave of contentment so strong washed over Gabriel that it scared the hell out of him. He was getting in too deep. In that instant, he decided a quick trip home might be a good idea. Sure, he knew he was running from his feelings, but hopefully, the short reprieve would help him regain the distance he needed to keep from falling further for Serenity. Or at least he hoped it would.

* * *

Sunday afternoon, Serenity removed the roasted chicken breasts from the oven and set them aside to cool. She'd made it a practice to meal prep when she worked at the hospital because of her long hours, and even though she now had a consistent daily schedule, the habit remained. Besides, it gave her more time during the week to relax when she came home.

As she added some of the buttery and sweet olive oil to a skillet to sauté some yellow squash, a smile curved her lips. Last night's date with Gabriel had been one she'd never forget. No man had ever cooked for her, and she knew the Wagyu beef had cost him a pretty penny, but he appeared to not mind. In fact, it was just the opposite. He'd gone out of his way to make sure to provide her with a spectacular meal. And the kisses they'd shared both before and after the movie had been out-of-this-world good. She only wished she'd met him before her ex soured her on relationships.

Serenity added the squash, sprinkled Himalayan pink salt and cracked black pepper, gave it a toss, and hurried to answer her ringing phone.

She smiled when she saw Gabriel's name on the display. "Well, hello, neighbor. Are you calling to invite me over for another delicious meal?" She went back to the stove to stir the vegetables.

Gabriel's warm chuckle came through the line. "Good afternoon to you, too. And not this time. Something came up at home, so I'll be headed to Atlanta tonight."

She paused stirring the squash. Her smile faded, and her heart rate kicked up. Not that it should have, since they weren't involved in anything serious. "How long will you be gone?"

"Probably about a week."

"Oh, okay. When you get back, it'll be my turn to cook. Maybe we can have brunch—waffles from scratch with my homemade vanilla maple syrup, or biscuits with some of my famous strawberry jam."

He groaned. "You're killing me, you know that?"

"Hey, just trying to give you an incentive to come back." The words left her mouth before she could stop them, and she wished she could go back and slap a hand over her mouth. It didn't help that Gabriel remained silent for what seemed like forever.

Finally, he said, "I'll be looking forward to it."

"I'm sure you have a million things to do before you leave, so…um…have a safe flight." Serenity figured she should get off the phone before she said something else she shouldn't.

"A few things. I'll call you."

"Sounds good." They spoke a minute longer, then disconnected. She banged her palm lightly against her forehead. "Great, Serenity. Now the man probably thinks you're trying to push for something more serious." She'd gotten way too comfortable with Gabriel over the past several weeks, and she found it harder and harder to keep her guard up. She finished the squash, then set the pan aside so it could cool before she added it to her containers.

Two hours later, with her meals and laundry done, Serenity poured herself a glass of iced tea, picked up her cell, and went to sit on the deck. Leaning back on the lounger, she inhaled deeply and let the breath out slowly. Thoughts of Gabriel immediately came to mind, and no matter how hard she tried to keep them at bay, they kept coming. If she were in the market for a long-term relationship, he'd definitely top the list of what she'd want in a man. He was intelligent, considerate, easy on the eyes, and the best kisser, hands down, that she'd ever had.

She was so lost in her reflections, it took her a moment to realize her phone was ringing. She snatched it up. "Hey, Natasha."

"Hey, girl. Are you busy?"

"Nope. Just chilling. Why?"

"Good. I'll be over in ten minutes to get *all* the details of last night's date."

Serenity let out a little laugh. "There's not that much to tell, so—" She heard a beep and glanced at the phone. "I know she didn't hang up on me," she muttered, staring at the black screen. Shaking her head, she went back inside.

Natasha rang the doorbell in half the time. She hugged Serenity and breezed past her toward the kitchen. "Okay, spill it."

"You know you ain't right hanging up on people," Serenity said, pulling out a small tray filled with cheese, grapes, and strawberries and a bowl of chicken salad from the refrigerator and placing them on the bar. She added baguette slices, poured a glass of tea for her friend, and topped her own glass off, then slid onto the stool next to Natasha.

"Hey, I knew you'd probably give me some excuse

or say it was nothing, and I know better." Natasha topped a piece of bread with the chicken salad and bit into it. She groaned. "You make the best chicken salad. I would've never thought to add the dried cranberries, but it gives it just a hint of sweet that's so, so good." Serenity reached for a slice of cheese, and Natasha waved her hand away. "Talk first, eat second. I want to be able to understand *every* word."

Serenity rolled her eyes. "Whatever, girl." She ate the cheese and bread, making a show of chewing slowly. Natasha eyed her, and Serenity laughed. "Okay, okay," she said after swallowing and taking a sip of tea. "Dinner was amazing. He grilled steaks, made foil-packet herbed potatoes and a salad. That steak was the best I've ever eaten."

"So not only can the man cook, but he grills, too?"

She nodded. "Gabriel bought Wagyu rib eyes."

Natasha choked on her drink. "Wait a minute. Are you telling me that a man who you're dating *loosely*—if that's what you want to call it—cooked you one of the most expensive grades of steaks and expected nothing in return?"

"That's exactly what I'm saying." Serenity helped herself to the chicken salad. "And then we ate the peach cobbler and homemade ice cream I made while watching *The Shawshank Redemption*." Natasha stared at her so long, Serenity shifted in her seat. "What?"

"You like Gabriel, do you?"

"Of course I do. I wouldn't be hanging out with him if I didn't." And those feelings were becoming muddier by the day.

"Is he still planning to leave at the end of next month?"

"As far as I know." She tried not to think about the reasons why his leaving for good bothered her. "Actually, he called earlier and said he had to go back to Atlanta this week. I assume it has to do with his job."

"And you're okay with that?" Natasha asked with a raised eyebrow.

"Why wouldn't I be? We both agreed that whatever this thing is"—she waved a hand for emphasis—"it would end when he left. Nothing has changed."

"Hmm. I wonder," Natasha said, stuffing another piece of bread piled with chicken salad into her mouth.

Serenity sighed. "I won't lie and say he's not a great guy and one I could probably fall for at some point. He is. But I don't want to get serious with anyone at this stage of my life, and I don't know if I'll ever be ready to put my heart on the line again. Gabriel feels the same way, so this works perfectly."

"I hear you, Sis, but what if things do change and you start to feel more?"

She already felt the little stirrings of "more" and firmly shut them down. "They won't." She couldn't allow them to change.

CHAPTER 13

What the hell are you doing here? I thought someone was breaking in and almost called the police."

Gabriel glanced over to the office doorway where Darius stood—phone in hand—glaring. "Good morning to you, too. I'm working. What does it look like I'm doing?"

Darius entered and dropped into the chair across from Gabriel. "When did you get in?"

"Sunday evening."

"It's *Tuesday*, Gabe. Why didn't you tell us you were coming? And you never did answer the question as to why you're here."

Sighing, Gabriel leaned back in the chair. "I thought I'd pop in to check on things at my place, and I figured since you and Brent have been doing all the traveling, I'd do it this time."

Darius folded his arms and angled his head. "You're going to have to do better than that. We meet every week by videoconference, we've been taking care of your condo, and you had your mail forwarded. So, again, what's going on?"

Gabriel should have never stepped foot in the office, and instead worked from home like he originally planned, avoiding this little interrogation. But the part of his workaholic personality that still existed wouldn't let him stay away. Here he had dual monitors and could work on multiple things at once. And he needed a distraction. However, that old adage of out of sight, out of mind wasn't working when it came to Serenity. She invaded his thoughts during the day while he worked and his dreams as he slept. For the past two mornings, he'd awakened aroused and hard, and none of his cold showers had helped. Gabriel eyed Darius, whose expression hadn't changed. "Nothing's going on." He shrugged. "I just wanted to come home for a bit."

"I see. How's your grandmother?"

"Nana's fine. Feisty as ever." And still not budging on moving away from her home. "I have no idea what I'm going to do if I can't change her mind about coming here. Even though her doctor said she's doing well, she's still getting older, and I'm not comfortable leaving her alone. Besides, Drea would kill me if I did."

"Man, you're in a tough spot. If you need to stay a little longer, I'm sure we can work it out." Darius smiled. "Besides, I kind of like having somewhere to visit that I can use as a tax write-off. And you mentioned Serenity having some good-looking friends, so it's a win-win for me."

He shook his head. "Only two of them are single. Terri is married."

"Speaking of Serenity, how are things going between you two?"

"Fine."

Darius threw up his hands. "That's all you're going to say? I know you like her."

"Yes, I like her." *A lot. More than I should.* "We decided to see each other while I'm there. She's not looking to get serious, which works perfectly for me because I'm not, either."

"With the way you were staring at her the day we met, I'm not so sure." He leaned forward. "It doesn't have to be that way, Gabe. There's no reason for you to stop seeing Serenity. People have long-distance relationships all the time, and if Nana decides not to move here, you're going to be stuck in your little town for a while."

"I know," Gabriel murmured. "The town isn't as bad as I previously thought, and I could possibly extend my stay, but I still don't know if I want to live there permanently. I mean, it's so...*small*."

As soon as he finished the thought, a vision of Serenity's beautiful smile flashed in his mind. His simple plan of getting to know her as a neighbor and possibly just a friend had turned into something else entirely. She was kind, considerate, and had a generous heart. Their attraction didn't surprise him. What man wouldn't be attracted to such a beautiful woman? His problem—he liked kissing her too much and couldn't recall the last time he'd enjoyed being with a woman this much. Everything about their relationship seemed…easy. Maybe knowing their liaison had a definite ending made it feel that way. Easy or not, he couldn't afford to get caught up in his emotions. Once had been enough. Yet he couldn't deny that he was happier than he had been in a long while.

Darius chuckled. "I hear you. It would be hard not having all the conveniences of a big city after living here all your life. But you should give some thought to staying."

"We'll see."

"Darius, who are you talking—*Gabe?* What are you doing here? What happened?" Brent rushed into the office, his face lined with concern.

"Nothing happened," Gabriel answered. "I'm just here for the week. To check on things."

Brent arched an eyebrow, giving Gabriel the same look Darius had moments ago, and folded his arms. "Check on things? Because? I mean, with all the technology," he said, waving a hand toward the elaborate computer setup, "I can see why that would be necessary."

Darius let out a short bark of laughter. "Yeah, that's the same thing I said. I think Gabe is falling for a small-town girl and is trying to run away."

Gabriel really wanted to punch his friend. Darius had always been able to read him—and everyone else—and he hated it. His friend was dead-on, but Gabriel wouldn't give him the satisfaction of knowing that. No, he'd cling to his story, no matter how weak it sounded. "There's no need to run from something that hasn't happened." He spun his chair back toward the computer. "If the two of you are done, I have work to do." When neither commented, Gabriel glanced their way. Both Brent and Darius sat staring at him with goofy smiles on their faces. "What?"

"If you want to continue to live in denial-land, that's fine." Brent shrugged. "Since you're here, I'm sure you want to see a little nightlife, so we can meet up at our usual place tonight."

Gabriel agreed readily. "I'm down. It'll be nice to hear something other than the crickets at sunset." And the bar and grill always had a packed house and live music. The perfect thing to keep his mind off Serenity.

That evening Gabriel found out he'd been wrong. Nothing had been able to erase his thoughts of her— not even the laughter, a great band, and delicious food. At one point, a sexy woman strolled over to their table, slipped him her phone number, and leaned down to whisper an offer that left nothing to his imagination. A decade ago he might have taken her up on a night of uninhibited passion, but not tonight. He compared the woman to Serenity and found her lacking in every way. Gabriel didn't mind an assertive woman and one confident about her sexuality, but pressing her body against his and trying to touch him before asking his name turned him off. Completely.

Brent and Darius broke out in laughter as soon as the woman left the table. Brent said, "Man, clearly she was ready to do *anything*. Back in the day, you wouldn't have hesitated. Hell, I might not have, either," he added, his gaze following the woman as she sashayed across the room.

Gabriel saluted Brent with his drink. "Key phrase is *back in the day*. I'm way past jumping into bed with women I don't know." Not that he'd ever made a practice of having one-night stands. He considered himself to be pretty discriminating when it came to who he allowed in his bed.

"What about with one you *do* know?" Darius asked pointedly.

He swirled the dark liquid in his glass and started to pretend he didn't know what Darius was talking about but changed his mind. They'd been friends too long and knew all of each other's secrets. "It probably isn't a good idea since I only plan to be there another month or so, but yeah, I've thought about it." More than once. Each time he kissed and touched her. Every time she unleashed that sultry smile on him. At this point he knew it would be only a matter of time before their desire exploded. The chemistry between them was too strong for either of them to resist.

"There's nothing saying you two can't continue to see each other," Brent said.

Gabriel shot Brent a dark glare. "I don't do long distance." Every one of his friends who tried it had ended up miserable after the relationship crashed and burned. He saw no reason to add his heart to the pile.

Twice more, as Gabriel, Darius, and Brent sat talking and listening to the music, women sauntered over to the table to proposition one or all of them. An hour later they called it a night and parted ways in the parking lot.

Gabriel arrived home a little after ten, early by his past standards. He made his way down the hall to the guest bedroom, where he'd been sleeping, and kicked off his shoes. Dropping down heavily on the bed, he expelled a long breath. He glanced around the spacious room and thought it would be the perfect size for his grandmother. Then again, she was used to living in a single-family home that included a yard where she grew a variety of flowers. Gabriel guessed he'd most likely have to give up the convenience of condo living in favor of a house. *If he could convince Nana to move. No time like the present.* With the three-hour time difference, he knew she wouldn't be asleep.

He dug his phone out of his pocket, scrolled to her name, and hit the call button.

"Hey, Gabriel," Nana said when she answered. "Everything going okay with the job?"

"Hi, Nana, and yes. I'm just checking on you."

Her soft laughter came through the line. "Oh, I'm all right. Just the normal aches and pains that come from getting old."

"You're not that old, Nana. Especially as fast as you were going the last time we went walking," he said with a chuckle. Gabriel made it a practice of joining her for her daily walk at least once a week.

"I've got to keep myself in shape. It keeps Howard off my back and allows me to splurge with my fried foods and desserts every now and again."

He couldn't deny he loved when she splurged, especially when it came to her desserts. He had yet to figure out how she always made that yellow cake with chocolate frosting so light and moist.

"By the way, I ran into Serenity today. You two have been spending quite a bit of time together, huh?"

"Like you said, she's a great person. She's been nice enough to invite me over for dinner a few times." Gabriel decided to keep the kissing to himself.

"Hmph. You could do worse."

"Are you trying to hook me up with Serenity, Nana?"

"I don't have to. According to Adele, you two are doing just fine on your own."

So much for them being discreet. "Hold up a minute. Serenity and I are just friends, and I'm sure she won't appreciate her neighbor spying on her or spreading her business." He fully understood why Serenity had asked to keep their liaison quiet.

"It's not really spying when it's all out in the open. I will say that Serenity would definitely make a wonderful wife."

Wife? "I'm sure she'll make some man a great wife, but I really hadn't planned to stay permanently. Speaking of that, have you given any more thought to moving to Atlanta with me?"

"I've given it all the thought I plan to, and my answer is still the same. So you can stop bringing it up. You still coming back on Sunday?" she asked, changing the subject.

"That's the plan."

"Okay, well, I won't hold you. My show is about to come on."

He didn't bother to ask which one of the many television dramas it was this time. "I'll see you when I get back."

"Love you, baby."

"Love you, too." He ended the call and placed the cell on the nightstand. Gabriel scrubbed a hand down his face. This was not going the way he'd anticipated. He'd naively believed it wouldn't take much persuasion to get Nana on board with his plan. The finality in her voice made him speculate on whether he'd ever be able to change her mind, and when he returned to Atlanta permanently, if he'd be going alone. Would he have to extend his time in Firefly Lake? Could he change his plans and relocate? Gabriel didn't have a clue as to what he should do.

* * *

Wednesday evening, Serenity stood at the counter dipping strawberries and talking to Natasha. It took longer than necessary because her friend kept snagging the berries. "Natasha Baldwin, if you eat one more of these strawberries, you can forget about taking those boozy ones for your clients."

Natasha froze with a berry halfway to her mouth. "Okay, okay. Last one. I've only eaten four regular ones and one champagne-infused strawberry. That's not a lot."

She skewered Natasha with a look. "Mm-hmm, keep talking and eating my berries. I'm supposed to be delivering two dozen to the Women's Society for their luncheon tomorrow." The women's group did lots of philanthropic work in the town and had been around almost since its founding. "I could've been finished by now if *somebody* wasn't sitting over there messing with my process."

"It's your fault. If they didn't taste so good, I wouldn't be stuffing my face." She popped the last piece in her mouth and groaned. "So, so good. I know my clients are going to love them."

She'd been only too happy to help when Natasha mentioned wanting to give the dipped berries as a gift to her clients when they closed on a property. Of course, for Serenity, presentation was everything, and she'd purchased silver boxes with a clear top that could hold four of the sweet treats and added a matching silver ribbon.

Natasha picked up one of the boxes. "I think this is going to be my signature from now on. I just received the custom gift tags with *thank you* written on one side and a replica of my business card on the other." She reached into a tote sitting on the empty stool beside her and retrieved a small box. "Aren't they gorgeous?" she asked, handing one of the cards to Serenity.

Serenity smiled. "Oh my goodness, yes." She ran her hand over the thick, matte velvet black card and flipped it one way, then another. "I love how they feel. You went for the top-of-the-line, girlfriend. The other three real estate agents are going to be so jealous."

"Hey, I'm trying to make a good impression with my clients. I've been thinking more and more about stepping out on my own, and I'm going to need every referral I can get. I'm also considering doing a little interior decorating on the side and finally putting that degree to good use. Being my own boss will allow me time to do both."

"I'm so glad you're finally deciding to follow your dream."

In college, Natasha had spent hours with her head buried in one design catalog after another and talked about moving to Los Angeles to become a designer to the stars. Serenity had been more than a little shocked when her friend decided less than a year after graduation to return to her hometown. Natasha had never shared the full details but mentioned a painful breakup and needing to get away as her reasons. She definitely understood.

"If you need help with anything, let me know."

"Oh, girl, you know I will." Natasha reached for a champagne-infused strawberry that had yet to be dipped and popped it into her mouth. "I know I said I wasn't going to eat another one, but it was sitting there on the plate looking so lonely. When word gets out about how good these are, people all over town are going to be lined up at your door. With the way you cook and bake, maybe you're the one who should be considering a career change." She held up a hand. "Wait. Strike that. If you start cooking for everybody else, that'll mess up our supper club, and I *can't* have that."

She laughed. "Agreed. I love our get-togethers, and I'm not letting anything interfere with that."

"Whew. So…have you talked to Gabriel lately?" Natasha asked, changing the subject abruptly.

"Not since Sunday when he called to let me know he'd made it to Atlanta."

Natasha's eyes widened. "It's been three days. I thought for sure he would've at least called."

Serenity shrugged. "Nope." Even though they'd agreed to keep the relationship light, she found herself missing their talks and quaint dinners, and had been tempted to call more than once. However, she didn't want him to think things were more serious or that she was chasing after him.

"What are you going to do when he leaves permanently? The two of you have grown pretty close."

She shrugged. "Nothing to do. What we have ends when he leaves. It's what we both want—no commitments, no ties." Gabriel leaving had been on her mind a lot lately, and she didn't want to examine why the thought bothered her. "You're into my business, but what about you? When are you going to find your Prince Charming?" Serenity dipped another strawberry into the melted milk chocolate, then set it on the tray with the others.

A wistful smile curved Natasha's lips. "I found him once but let him go." Natasha had confided in Serenity about the breakup with her high school sweetheart.

"Who knows, you just might find another one." Serenity walked over to the refrigerator and removed the tray holding the already finished fruit and set it in front of Natasha. "Since these are yours, you can fill the boxes." She'd covered half in milk chocolate with white chocolate drizzled in thin ribbons over the top, then did the opposite to the other half. She gestured to the shredded black paper that would fill the bottom of the box and several paper liner cups similar to those that surround Reese's Peanut Butter Cups.

Natasha hopped down from her stool. "Okay. Let me wash my hands first."

They were laughing and boxing up the berries when Serenity's doorbell rang. She glanced over at the stove clock. "Who's ringing my bell this late?" It was nearly ten o'clock.

"Only one way to find out," Natasha said, gesturing toward the front. "It might be somebody who heard about these chocolate-dipped strawberries."

Laughing, Serenity shook her head and started toward the front. Her pulse skipped when she looked through the peephole and saw Gabriel standing there. She snatched the door open. "Gabriel! What are you doing here? I thought you weren't coming back until Sunday."

"I changed my mind." Gabriel stepped inside and curved his arm around her waist at the same time his mouth connected with hers.

He kissed her with an urgency she returned. Had it been only four days since she'd felt his lips on hers? Tightening his hold, he continued to plunder her mouth, and her body started to tremble. Through the haze of desire, she heard dishes, remembered she wasn't alone, and jumped back.

He stared down at her curiously. "What's the matter?"

"Nothing. I forgot for a moment that Natasha's here. You want to come into the kitchen?"

"Nah. I don't want to interrupt. I just wanted to see you for a few minutes to let you know I'm back."

Serenity smoothed her hair down. The man's kisses had the ability to rob her of every brain cell. "And you never did answer my question."

"I wrapped things up sooner than I thought." His hand made a slow pass down her back as he nuzzled her neck. "What are you doing this weekend?"

It took a moment for his words to register because she couldn't concentrate with his tongue and lips on her. "Um..." Her head dropped back and her eyes slid closed. "I don't have anything planned. Why?"

Gabriel lifted his head. "I thought we could drive down to Napa on Saturday for your wine train tour, dinner, and anything else you want to do, then come back Sunday."

Serenity waged an inner debate for several seconds. Was he planning for them to share a room, and was *she* ready for whatever happened? Staring up at his handsome face, she answered her own questions with a resounding *yes*. She was ready for everything he wanted to give. "I'd love to go. Do you want me to make the reservations?"

"Nope," he said, dropping a kiss on her nose. "I've got it. I'll call you to let you know the itinerary. Tell Natasha I said hi." He stepped back onto the porch and, after gifting her with one more spine-tingling kiss, loped across the yard to his house.

She closed the door and leaned her head against it for a moment to calm her racing heart. Once she felt in control, she went back to the kitchen. "That was Gabriel. He just stopped by to let me know he was back earlier than expected."

A wide grin spread across Natasha's face. "He could have called. Obviously, that's not the only thing he stopped by to do by the look of your lips."

Serenity's hand involuntarily went to her mouth, and she snatched it back down. Natasha chuckled. "He also wanted to know if I'd be available to go to Napa this weekend as part of a bet I won." She didn't say what the bet was because she'd promised not to divulge his secret about the yams.

"Mm-hmm. With a man like him, it's going to be harder than you think to let him go when he leaves. And, as I said, long distance is still an option."

"If he'd come along before Lloyd, I might've thought about it, but I've finally found my peace, and I'm not too inclined to jeopardize it."

"Who said he'd jeopardize it?"

Serenity shrugged. Her friend had a point. "He

only has another month or so left, and I think I'm just going to leave things as they are." So far he hadn't done anything to upset her balanced life, but she was a realist. She didn't see it lasting past the allotted time and didn't plan to get her hopes up.

CHAPTER 14

Gabriel got up early Saturday morning and drove over to Nana's to cut her grass. It had been over two weeks since he'd last done it, and when he'd called to let her know he was back, she had asked if he had time to stop by on the weekend to handle the chore. Halfway through, he noticed Nana standing on the porch waving at him and cut the power on the mower. "You need something, Nana?" he asked, moving in her direction.

"No, baby. I was just coming to tell you I can cook you some breakfast after you're done. If I had known you were coming this early, I would've had it ready when you got here."

"You don't have to do that. I ate before I came. And Serenity and I are doing the Napa wine train tour today, so I can't stay." He'd be picking her up at nine forty-five so they'd be on time for the ten thirty check-in. The train left an hour later, and the experience would last three hours.

"Oh, you're going to have such a good time. I can't wait to go back." She shooed him. "Well, hurry up and finish, so you're not late."

Chuckling, he walked back over, stuck in his earbuds, and cranked up the power. As soon as he was done, he swept up, said his goodbyes, and drove home to shower and change.

Afterward, Gabriel walked over and rang Serenity's doorbell. The excitement he felt when she opened the door let him know he might be in trouble when it came time for him to return home for good. He'd realized that when he'd cut his trip short and had gone directly to her house on Wednesday. He'd never missed a woman—never missed *kissing* a woman—before, but he had with her. Even now, as she stood there in one of those cute sundresses and sandals that showed off her beautiful legs, he had to fight the urge to back her inside and go straight to her bedroom. Gabriel readily admitted to himself that he liked Serenity, but he had been asking himself all day why he was going through all this trouble for a casual relationship. It didn't help that he'd also spent a restless night trying to figure out how to proceed. He still hadn't come up with an answer and decided to go with the flow for now. They would go their separate ways when he left, and he'd move on, as would she. "Good morning."

"Good morning to you, too," Serenity said with a smile. "I'm ready."

She reached down for her overnighter, and he eased it from her. "I got it." He waited for her to lock the door, then led her to his car. After programming the address into the GPS, he got them underway. Fortunately, traffic was light and they would make it to their destination with time to spare. "How was your week?"

She rolled her head in his direction. "Busy. School will be starting next month, and parents are bringing in their kids for annual checkups, immunizations, and sports exams. It gets crazy like this every year."

"I can imagine. Yet you still took time to make dessert for a group's luncheon and those berries for Natasha." He'd never met a woman who did so much for others without expecting anything in return. No wonder everyone in town loved her.

"Oh, that was nothing. It didn't take long, or it *wouldn't* have taken long if Tasha hadn't kept eating the strawberries," she added with a soft laugh.

"I can't say I blame her because they're good, just like everything else you've made. I'm really enjoying the olive oil." Gabriel used the buttery and sweet one for cooking everything from vegetables and potatoes to meat and seafood. He'd used the lemon-flavored oil to grill chicken and shrimp, as well as in a vinaigrette. Both had given his food new life.

"How much do you have left?"

He slanted her a quick glance. "Not much. Which is why I've already placed another order."

Serenity burst out laughing. "I knew you'd be hooked. I'm so glad I'm not the only one. I just ordered more, too."

"Yeah, hooked." They shared a smile, and he refocused on the road. If he wasn't careful, the oil might not be the only thing he became hooked on. For the remainder of the drive, they discussed other potential ways to use the oil. When they arrived at the train station, Gabriel parked, then came around to help Serenity.

"How long is the tour?"

"Three hours. I chose one that serves lunch on the way up and makes a stop at a winery for a seated tasting. Dessert is served on the return train ride. I hope that's okay." It had been quite a while since he'd made plans for a date, and he had never done anything as elaborate as this. Everything from their dinner reservations later and the hotel room to another lunch and wine tasting tomorrow had already been booked.

"Sounds good. I kind of like being able to take my time at the winery."

Gabriel placed his hand on the small of her back and guided her over to check in. Once that task was completed, they still had half an hour to kill. He spotted a bench in a shaded area for them to sit. The weather had hovered near eighty degrees all week, but today's forecast predicted it to be somewhere around ninety. If the warm early temperatures were any indication, it would hit that mark easily.

"Have you ever done something like this before?" Serenity asked.

"No, but I've done a couple of food tours." She chuckled, and he said, "Hey, I told you I was sort of a foodie."

She bumped his shoulder playfully. "Yeah, you did. I guess I could be considered the same, since I love cooking and trying out new recipes." They lapsed into a brief silence. "You booked the hotel room already?"

Gabriel studied her, seeing a hint of uncertainty. "Yes. I didn't want to assume anything, so I got two rooms." She visibly relaxed, and he was glad he'd spent the extra money. He would be lying if he said he didn't want to make love to her. He did. Badly. But he'd let her set the pace, and if it didn't happen, he was sure he would enjoy being with her all the same. "This weekend is for you, Serenity. Whatever happens—or not—will be totally up to you. I just want you to have a good time."

"Thanks, Gabriel."

He slung an arm around her shoulder and pressed a soft kiss to her lips. Serenity laid her head against his shoulder, as if it were the most natural thing. Once again, he felt the stirrings of something in his chest. Choosing not to dwell on it, he pushed it aside and concentrated on his surroundings. Several people were in line, and others milled around, talking in small groups as they waited to board. "We still have a few minutes. Do you want to check out the Wine Shop?"

"Sure."

Gabriel led Serenity over, and they browsed the various wines, listened to the founding story on one of the TV monitors for a moment, then got cups of coffee.

They returned in time to hear the introductory lecture given by one of the wine specialists on Napa Valley and the wine train. Afterward, it was time to board. He'd upgraded their tickets to ensure they would have a table alone. He wanted her all to himself and didn't want to spend the trip having to make conversation with complete strangers. They ended up seated near the middle of the car, and the dining service began shortly after, starting with a Bibb salad.

Serenity studied the short menu. "I'm really torn between the seared beef tenderloin and the lemon and thyme roasted chicken."

"If you like, we can order one of each and share."

Her face lit up. "Great. Let's do it."

Every time she turned that beautiful smile his way and her eyes sparkled, it hit him square in the gut and made him want to do everything in his power to keep it on her face. When their meals arrived, he cut a portion of the beef and placed it on her plate, and she added some chicken to his. Gabriel forked up a portion of the chicken first and chewed slowly, letting the citrus and herb flavor explode on his tongue. "The chicken is really good."

Serenity took a bite. "Mmm, it is. Let me taste the steak." She ate a piece and angled her head. "This is good, too, but," she said, leaning forward and whispering, "yours is way better."

Her confession made his chest swell. "Thanks for the compliment. That's high praise, considering this meal was made by a gourmet chef. I'll make you steak anytime you want it."

Serenity wiggled her eyebrows. "I just might take you up on that, especially since you'll be leaving soon. So don't be surprised if I ring your doorbell this week asking for another one of your delicious meals."

He chuckled. "Let me know." Gabriel was smiling, but inside his stomach rolled at the mention of him leaving soon, and he didn't want to examine the reason. Instead, he focused on the fingerling potatoes and spring vegetables on his plate.

"I can't get over this view." Serenity braced her elbows on the table as she stared at the passing scenery. "Everything is in full bloom and gorgeous."

His gaze roamed over her face. "I agree." Sure, the greenery and colorful flowers were beautiful, but they didn't hold a candle to his dining partner. Once they finished and the server cleared the table, they spent the remainder of the short ride talking about everything and nothing.

After disembarking, the passengers were given a tour of the winery before settling on the patio for the tasting. Serenity said, "I'm really enjoying myself."

Gabriel gave her hand a gentle squeeze. "I'm glad."

"The first wine is a chardonnay," a wine specialist said. "It opens with fresh citrus aromas of lime and Meyer lemon, followed by ripe, juicy peach. And, finally, underlying notes of herbs, honeysuckle, and vanilla, making for an exceptionally fresh and vibrant wine."

Gabriel sipped the taste of wine in his glass and agreed. "What do you think?"

She nodded. "I like it. The citrus hits first, but the combination of floral and vanilla lingers."

They went through several more varieties—merlot, rosé, zinfandel. He ended up purchasing another chardonnay, which had notes of lime, mango, verbena, and rich vanilla. Serenity bought a rosé.

"I'm going to serve this at the next supper club dinner. And you're welcome to join us if you're not busy."

"I'll check my schedule and let you know." While he enjoyed the dinners, more and more Gabriel realized he'd rather share dinner with Serenity. Alone.

On the way back, dessert consisted of a strawberry tart and tea or coffee. "I love strawberries, and this tart is so good," Serenity said, slowly drawing the fork from her mouth and letting out a moan.

Fire shot to Gabriel's groin. "You're killing me, baby."

"I don't know what you mean." She gave him an innocent smile, then repeated the gesture, this time darting her tongue out to lick the bit of whipped cream from her fork. "I'm just enjoying my dessert, that's all."

"Keep it up and I'm going to be enjoying *you* for dessert." The more he got to know her, the more sides he saw. Never would he have thought she'd be a tease. He leaned closer. "How do you think you'd taste with whipped cream?"

Her eyes widened, and she cleared her throat. "Um…so, you don't think it's good?"

He smiled inwardly. "It's good, but I have to say those brownies you make are far better."

She eyed him. "Are you campaigning for more brownies?"

He reached across the table, grasped her hand, and placed a kiss in the center of her palm. "Maybe." She gasped softly, and his gaze went to the rapidly beating pulse in her neck. He wanted to place his lips there. To trail kisses there. Their eyes connected, and he saw the same desire he felt reflected in her eyes. Gabriel said she could set the pace, but the only pace he wanted right now was hot and fast.

* * *

Serenity had no idea what possessed her to tease Gabriel. She usually didn't flirt this way with men, and certainly never had with her ex. Maybe she could blame it on the wine she'd drunk, but that wouldn't be the truth. If she were being honest, she'd admit that there was something about the man sitting across from her that made her relax and lower her inhibitions. The gentle caresses, sweet kisses, and the fact that he'd gone out of his way to ensure she had a good time would challenge the sanest woman to remain unmoved. Plus, he looked so good in the black shorts and short-sleeved pale-gray button-down shirt. Her palm still tingled from the soft kiss he'd placed there, and every time he looked her way, heat thrummed through her body.

By the time the train arrived back at the station, he had her fantasizing about that whipped cream.

"Do you want to go back to the gift shop?" Gabriel asked as they stepped off the train.

"If you don't mind. There were a couple of bottles of wine I wanted to get." She hadn't wanted to leave them in the hot car and figured it would be easier to get them afterward, so she wouldn't have to carry them around all day.

"Not at all."

Several other people had the same idea, and it took a good fifteen minutes to make the purchase. "Are we heading over to the hotel now?" she asked as he pulled out onto the road.

"Check-in isn't until four, but we'll only be about half an hour early, so I'm hoping they'll just let us go ahead and do it. It's a bed-and-breakfast."

"I've always wanted to stay in a bed-and-breakfast just to see if they really do serve those big meals. I'm betting that's one of the reasons you chose it."

"You know me well," he said with a chuckle.

It took them less than ten minutes to get there, and Serenity was immediately entranced by the garden feel and even more by her room, which happened to be a secluded cottage not attached to any of the other rooms. She slowly toured the space with its gas fireplace, king-size bed, sitting area with leather chairs surrounding a small round table, and a Jacuzzi for two.

Crossing the floor, Serenity opened the door to

a charming balcony overlooking the creek and surrounded by lush gardens. Gabriel stood behind her and wrapped his arms around her waist. "This is beautiful, Gabriel. Thank you."

"You're welcome."

She turned in his arms and came up on tiptoe to kiss him. His tongue charged into her mouth, kissing her with a potency that weakened her knees. She slid her arms around his neck and held him in place as his hands moved slowly up and down her back, caressing and teasing. His lips left her mouth and skated along her jaw before claiming her mouth again. "Gabriel?"

"Hmm," he said, still trailing kisses along her shoulder while his hands caressed her breasts.

"We don't need two rooms."

Gabriel's head came up sharply. "Are you sure? I don't want you to feel—"

Smiling, Serenity placed a finger on his lips. "I'm very sure. After you cancel the other room, I want you to make love to me." He'd left it up to her to make the next move, and she was ready. She wanted this night with him, to have the memory once he went back to Atlanta. And she'd gladly pay the cancellation costs.

Without a word, he walked over to the desk, picked up the phone, and made the call. Gabriel faced her and slowly crossed the room to where Serenity stood. "Are you sure?"

Serenity nodded and was, once again, swept away. His hands roamed down her back and settled on her hips briefly before moving around to cup her buttocks.

She moaned, slid her arms around his neck, and drew him closer. He gripped her tighter and pulled her flush against his erection, turning her legs to jelly. She felt the slide of the zipper on her dress, then the warmth of his strong hands on her bare skin. He pushed the dress off her shoulders, let it drop to the floor, and then charted a path of butterfly kisses along the column of her neck and over her shoulder. She could do nothing but stand there and feel. He gently turned her around and trailed his tongue down the center of her spine while his hands caressed her breasts. Her breaths came in short gasps, and her knees buckled. "Gabriel," she pleaded.

"I love kissing you, touching you. Your skin is so soft." He spun her around and captured her mouth again in a hungry kiss while he unhooked her bra and dragged the straps down, freeing her breasts. He circled his tongue around a taut nipple and drew it into his mouth, then lavished the same on its twin.

Serenity grasped the back of his head and arched her body closer for more. Her legs trembled, and she could barely stand. After a few long moments, he lifted his head. She reached up, unbuttoned his shirt, and tossed it aside. Gabriel stepped back and, in the blink of an eye, shed his shorts and underwear. Her gaze traveled down his sexy body. She'd fantasized about having her hands on him, being able to touch him the way he did her. From the strong, defined planes of his chest and washboard abs to his lean hips and muscular thighs, the man's body was a pure work of art.

Gabriel picked her up and placed her on the bed, then stretched his body over hers. They both moaned. "I've dreamed about having you in my arms this way."

"So have I." Serenity ran her hands over the sculpted planes of his biceps, shoulders, and chest, wanting to feel his warm, smooth skin beneath her fingers. For the next few minutes, he treated her to sultry kisses, taking his time and driving her out of her mind with desire. Her eyes drifted closed, and she felt as if she were coming out of her skin. He gently kneaded and stroked her aching breasts and captured her mouth in a long, drugging kiss that set her aflame once more. She felt the heat of his mouth as he trailed a series of tantalizing kisses along her left ankle, her calf, and behind her knee, on her outer thigh and inner thigh, then on her right side, rendering her mindless. Never had she experienced such overwhelming sensations. "Gabriel." She moaned and writhed as he kissed his way up one inner thigh and then the other.

"I'm going to taste every inch of your beautiful body," he murmured, still kissing and licking his way back up her body. He hooked his thumb in the waistband of her bikini panties and dragged them down and off.

His confession pushed her closer to the edge. He charted a path down the front of her body with his hand and pushed two fingers into her pulsating core. She bucked wildly and raised her hips as his fingers probed deeper. Without warning, an orgasm hit, and she cried out.

Gabriel withdrew his fingers and kissed her once more. Standing, he dug a condom out of his wallet, donned it, and came back to the bed.

She skated her fingers over his broad shoulders and down his back, feeling the muscles contract beneath her touch. "Mmm, and I love the way your bare skin feels against mine."

"Me too, baby." He nudged her legs apart and, holding her gaze, guided himself inside her. He shuddered and held still for a moment before he started to move in slow insistent circles. He delved deeper with each rhythmic push, and Serenity wrapped her legs around him and lifted her hips to meet the next powerful thrust.

The sounds of their breathing increased, and he set a pace that had the bed rocking. She locked her ankles behind his back as he kept up the sensual tempo. What he was doing to her felt so good, she didn't ever want him to stop. His strokes came faster and harder, and she cried out with pleasure. She met and matched his thrusts, their breathing growing heavier and echoing in the quiet space. Serenity held him tighter as the pleasure built, this time even stronger. He gripped her hips tighter and went deeper. Her breath came in short gasps, and she convulsed with a loud wail. Gabriel locked his mouth on hers as the sensations continued to surge through her.

A moment later, Gabriel tore his mouth from hers, threw his head back, and let out a low, animalistic growl. His body shuddered, and he called her name on a ragged sigh. He collapsed on her, then shifted to his side, taking her with him.

After a few minutes, he said, "I'll be right back." He left the bed and went into the bathroom. When he came out, he started running water in the Jacuzzi. "How about we try this out?"

She smiled. "I say we should take advantage of everything this place has to offer."

Gabriel returned her smile. "I couldn't agree more." Once the tub was filled, he donned another condom, swept Serenity into his arms, and placed her in the Jacuzzi.

Serenity scooted over to make room for Gabriel. "Mmm, this feels so good."

He pulled her to sit between his legs. "The temperature's okay?"

"Perfect," she said, leaning back against him. It didn't take long for their passion to rise again. She turned and straddled him, then leaned down to kiss him.

He cradled the back of her head and deepened the kiss, his tongue slipping into her mouth. "Ride me, baby," he whispered against her lips. He grabbed her hips and guided her down.

Serenity's eyes slid closed from the exquisite feeling of him filling her. When she opened her eyes, she found him staring at her with an expression so caring it brought tears to her eyes. He kissed her tenderly, softly, and with an emotion that frightened her. She was in trouble.

CHAPTER 15

Gabriel sat in front of his computer Saturday morning working on his app. It was only eleven, but he'd been up since six. A week had passed since the trip to Napa, and to distance himself from his growing feelings for Serenity, he'd gone back to his twelve- and fourteen-hour workdays. Outside of a phone call and a couple of texts, he and Serenity hadn't talked. Yet each night, he went to bed with a hard-on and woke up the same way every morning. No matter how hard he tried, he couldn't stop thinking about her or the passion they had shared. Typically, his relationships, if they could be termed as such, never lasted past one or two dates, and he preferred it that way because no one got hurt. He tried to apply the same approach to his relationship with Serenity, but this time he had difficulty maintaining the distance he usually craved. He shook himself and turned his attention back to the screen.

A few minutes later, his concentration slipped again. Leaning back in the chair, he dragged a hand down his face. Visions of her riding him in the Jacuzzi flashed in his mind, and his hand stilled on the keyboard. His eyes slid closed as he recalled every sensual moment of that encounter. She had treated him to the most passionate night of his life and given herself completely. But Gabriel couldn't say the same for himself. As much as he'd enjoyed the sex, he could not bring himself to surrender his emotions totally and open the places inside him he'd purposely locked away to protect his heart. He couldn't risk it. However, he wouldn't mind having a repeat of the night. Gabriel pushed the thought away and went back to his work.

He managed to maintain his focus for another two hours before deciding to take a break for lunch. He rummaged through the refrigerator, but nothing jumped out at him. After a short debate with himself, he got in his car and drove over to Ms. Ida's for some barbecue ribs. The restaurant was crowded, as usual, but it took less than fifteen minutes for him to be seated and place his order. While waiting for his food, he sent an email to Darius to give an update on his progress.

"How's it going, Gabe?"

Gabriel glanced up from his phone to see Jon standing next to him. "Hey, Jon. It's going. You picking up something for you and Terri?"

"No. I just stopped in for a quick bite before I head

back to the office. I have to prepare for a couple of cases going to court."

Gabriel gestured to the chair across from him. "You're welcome to join me, if you're eating in."

Jon pulled out the chair and sat. "Thanks." The server came to take his order almost immediately. "So, have you and Serenity done any more food battles?"

Gabriel chuckled and wished their battles were as simple as food. "No. I think I'm going to just concede that Serenity is the better cook."

"I don't blame you. She could quit nursing, open up her own restaurant, and be as successful as this place." The server returned and placed a glass of lemonade in front of Jon. "Thanks."

"Probably, but I think she loves nursing more." He recalled how she'd comforted the fussy baby in the doctor's office. The woman had a way about her unlike anything he'd ever seen, and it was one of the reasons he found it hard to stay away. "Have you been to a supper club dinner since then?"

Jon took a long drink of his lemonade. "No, but not because Terri hasn't asked. My hours of late have been crazy, but then hers have, too."

Gabriel thought he heard something in Jon's voice, but he didn't know the man well enough to pry. "Hopefully, they'll slow down so you two can make it to one soon."

He toasted Gabriel with his glass. "We'll see."

Once their food arrived, the two men conversed about sports, politics, and just about every other subject. Gabriel found out that Jon and Terri had moved to town two years ago from Los Angeles. "How do you like living here?"

"It took some getting used to, that's for sure," Jon said with a little laugh. "It's not so bad, and I'm close enough to the Bay to get my fix when I need it. I still miss LA, but the promotion alone was worth the move."

Gabriel nodded. Yes, San Francisco, Oakland, and Napa weren't too far away, and he could experience everything he enjoyed back home. Yet it still hadn't swayed him completely. He wouldn't mind visiting, especially if it meant he'd see Serenity, but living here forever? Yeah. No. *Staying here would mean seeing Serenity every day, not just occasionally, and it's not like you're missing anything in Atlanta,* an inner voice chimed. He ignored it and continued eating.

After finishing their lunch and settling the bill, Gabriel and Jon went their separate ways. Gabriel stopped to get ice cream, then drove home. He scanned the front yard and noticed the grass needed to be cut. Almost immediately, his gaze strayed to Serenity's yard. From the look of it, the landscaping company had continued to drop the ball. He shook his head and went inside to change.

It took him almost two hours to cut his front and back yard and Serenity's front. He'd just finished trimming the edges when her car pulled into the driveway. Every reason he needed to keep his distance faded the moment she stepped out. His gaze made a slow tour down her body and back up. The sight of her beautiful, toned legs in her shorts conjured up more memories of their weekend, and it was all he could do not to haul her into his arms and reacquaint himself with the sweetness of her kiss. For a moment, they stood there awkwardly. "Hey."

"Hey, yourself. Thanks for doing the yard." Serenity glanced around. "It looks really good."

"You're welcome. How was your week?"

"Good. Yours?"

"Busy. I've been working overtime to get this program done."

"Oh. I hope you can get it done." She popped the trunk and removed two grocery bags.

Gabriel rushed over. "Do you need help?"

"I've got it. Thanks," she said quickly.

He moved back. For two people who had been enjoying each other's company over the past several weeks, they were now behaving like strangers. It made him wonder if she had any regrets. "Supper club tonight?" Gabriel asked, pointing to the bags.

"Yep. I should probably get started. Everyone will be here in an hour."

Gabriel waited for her to issue an invitation, but she didn't. He didn't know whether to be disappointed or not. "I won't keep you. Enjoy your evening."

"You, too. And thanks, again, for doing my yard. I really appreciate it."

"No problem." He stood there and watched the sway of her hips as she started up the driveway to her garage. It wasn't until she lowered the door that he resumed his task. As much as he should stay away from her, he couldn't. The casual relationship they'd agreed to seemed to be turning into something completely unexpected. Gabriel was falling fast, and he had no idea what to do about it.

* * *

Serenity placed the bags on the kitchen counter, then braced her hands over it and lowered her head. She figured not seeing Gabriel over the past week would give her time and space to put their relationship firmly in the casual friends-with-benefits category. But two minutes in his presence was all it took for everything she had begun to feel for him to come rushing to the forefront. It didn't help that he kept doing nice things for her, like mowing her yard. Serenity thought about inviting him to dinner but nixed the idea. However, she didn't know how long she could keep him at a distance because she truly enjoyed his company. Shaking herself, she emptied the groceries and got started on the meal she'd planned to prepare.

An hour later, Terri and Natasha arrived. Before the greetings were complete, Dana rang the bell. Serenity greeted her with a sisterly hug. "Hey, girl. Come on in. You look tired."

The women followed her to the kitchen, and Dana said, "I am. It seemed like every person in town brought their cars in. Then I had two piano lessons this afternoon. I'm thinking about making the lessons strictly for children and teens."

Serenity laughed as she poured a little oil in a pan for the sautéed spinach. "It couldn't be that bad."

"Trust me, it was. The first woman was fifteen minutes late and got mad because her lesson was cut short by the same amount of time. Not only that, but she kept trying to tell me what to do." She folded her arms and rolled her eyes. "Couldn't read a *C* from an *A* but acted like I was the one taking lessons. The guy who came in next paid more attention to my hands than what he was supposed to be playing on the piano. 'Your hands are so soft. I love how your fingers move on the keys. I see your left ring finger is empty. Does that mean you're single?'" she mimicked. "Ugh! I told him it would be better for him to find someone else to provide his lessons."

Natasha shook her head. "Girl, I don't know what's wrong with men these days. You'd think they would've come up with a better way to flirt by now."

Serenity laughed so hard, she almost burned the spinach. "Oh my goodness. What was he thinking?"

"I don't know what he was thinking," Terri chimed in, "but I do know what he was thinking *with*."

The women howled with laughter.

Dana waved a hand. "Whatever. Where's the wine?" She moved in the direction Serenity pointed and poured glasses for all of them.

After helping Serenity bring the spinach, mashed potatoes, and mesquite-marinated salmon to the table, they continued the conversation. As they sat around the table, she realized how much she'd come to value their friendship.

"You're not the only one who has men trying to come on to you on the job," Natasha said. "Mmm, this salmon is so good."

"It is," Terri echoed.

Dana lifted her glass in mock salute. "Just like everything she cooks. But getting back to the conversation, that wasn't the only time. A couple of weeks ago, I went out with a guy who'd brought his niece in for her lesson. When he found out I worked as a mechanic for my day job, his jaw dropped. And he had the nerve to tell me he didn't think that was some thing a *lady* should do and suggested I do something more in line with music since I was so good at it."

"Honey, I can top that," Natasha said with a wave of her fork. "I went to the movies with Waylon."

"From junior high school?" Dana asked with surprise.

She nodded. "You know, he called me half an hour before he was supposed to pick me up and told me not to worry about buying snacks because he was bringing popcorn and drinks from home to save some money."

Serenity almost choked on her wine. "Please tell me you went to the drive-in." Many cities had closed down their drive-in theaters years ago, but the one in town was not only still open but thriving.

"I'd be lying if I did. I should've canceled right

then, but I was trying to be nice since we'd gone to school together. Never again."

"We need to find us a good man or a husband like Terri, so we don't have to worry about these crazy-ass dates."

Terri held her hands up and shrugged. "Sorry to tell you, but with Jon and my work schedules, we haven't been on a date in months, aside from the Fourth of July festival and that dinner here a few weeks ago."

Natasha forked up some of the potatoes. "Well, Serenity doesn't seem to be having any of these dating woes with Gabriel."

No, her woes were of a different kind. Like falling for a man who had no plans to stay.

Dana leaned forward. "Spill it, my sister. And don't leave out any of the juicy parts."

Serenity chuckled. "We went to Napa last weekend and did one of the wine train tours."

"And they stayed overnight," Natasha said with a huge grin on her face.

Dana's and Terri's mouths fell open, and Terri said, "Girl, you've been holding out on us. One room or two?"

Serenity pushed her food around her nearly empty plate and mumbled, "One." They all screamed with excitement, and she shook her head. She decided to keep the part about it being her suggestion to get rid of that second room to herself. Though she had no regrets, that one night would be all they'd ever share. More nights like that one could get her into deeper trouble than she was already in and would complicate her life in ways she didn't need or want.

Natasha hopped up. "This calls for more wine." She plucked the bottle out of the refrigerator and topped off everyone's glasses before reclaiming her chair. "Okay, go ahead, Serenity. How was it?"

"It was great, and Gabriel was the perfect gentleman. I really enjoyed the ride, and the tour he chose came with a seated wine tasting at the winery. He also booked another tasting for the next day, which was nice, too." She held up her glass. "This is one of the wines I purchased there."

"I love it. It's light and crisp and goes nicely with this salmon," Terri said. "But we want to hear about what happened *between* those tours. You spent the night in one room, and as fine as Gabriel is, I know more went on than just sleeping."

Serenity had never been one to kiss and tell, but she scanned the eager faces of her friends and knew they probably wouldn't leave until she gave a few details. "We stayed at a bed-and-breakfast. The cottage had a private deck that overlooked a creek and was surrounded by beautiful gardens. It was so peaceful, I wish we could've stayed a few more days." She paused when she saw the knowing smiles on their faces. "It had a fireplace and a Jacuzzi...for two and—"

"Girl, please tell me you used the thing *for two* and not alone," Natasha interrupted.

"Yes, we used it." And she would never forget the erotic encounter. They'd used every inch of that Jacuzzi, and just the thought of all the ways Gabriel had cherished her body sent heat spiraling through her.

Dana chuckled. "By the look on your face, I'd say you more than used it. I'm jealous."

Serenity laughed and toyed with her glass. "Yeah, you could say that." She took a sip of her wine.

"Seems like you two are getting serious."

Serenity's smile faded. "We're not serious, Natasha." Sure, she liked him—a *lot*—but they'd set the guidelines of the relationship, and rules were rules. "And he'll still be leaving."

"Which will be when?" Natasha asked.

She shrugged. "He said end of the summer, so probably another month or so."

"In that case, I say you enjoy every sensual moment until he leaves." Dana toasted Serenity with her glass.

"Amen!" Terri and Natasha chorused.

"I don't know about y'all," Serenity said, trying to hide her smile. "But I think once is more than enough."

Dana scooted her chair away from Serenity. "In case lightning strikes from that lie you just told." Laughter broke out around the table. "With a man like that, every night wouldn't be enough."

Still chuckling, Serenity said, "Okay, you have a point, but sleeping with him again is probably not a good idea."

Terri stood, stacked their empty plates. and took them to the sink. "I don't know, Serenity. I've seen the way Gabriel looks at you. The man is totally into you, and I don't see anything wrong with the two of you exploring a long-distance relationship."

She whipped her head around. "Oh, *nooo*. Girl, if I couldn't make a relationship work when I saw my ex practically every day, there's no way I can do it with someone who I'd see every now and again." She wouldn't put herself through waiting around not knowing when she'd see Gabriel or for the day he decided to take his affections elsewhere.

"Gabriel isn't your ex," Natasha said. "And honestly, I don't see him doing any of those things. Who knows, he might even decide to stay."

Serenity couldn't dispute the fact that Gabriel was nothing like Lloyd, but she still didn't plan to get her hopes up. "I doubt he'll stay. Remember, Andrea said he's a city boy through and through." She rose from the table and joined Terri, who was rinsing out the plates at the sink. She placed the plates into the dishwasher. "Anyway, that's enough of that conversation. Tasha, how did the strawberries go over with your clients?" she asked, changing the subject.

"They were fabulous. I got calls telling me how much they enjoyed them. Next time I think I want to create a little gift basket to go along with it."

Dana divided a glance between Serenity and Natasha. "Strawberries? What strawberries?"

"I made Tasha a few of the boozy berries to give to her clients that closed on a property," Serenity answered.

"Are you talking about those chocolate-dipped ones infused with the whiskey and champagne?" When Natasha nodded, Dana said, "That's a nice touch. I bet old pinch-faced Kathleen was trying to figure out how to one-up you after hearing about it."

Serenity set out all the fixings for strawberry shortcake. "Remind me, who's Kathleen again?"

Natasha came over to the bar and picked up a plate. "She's one of the Realtors in the office—late forties or early fifties—and thinks because she's been there the longest out of the four of us, we should defer to her. She can't stand that I'm younger and lately more people have asked for me to handle selling or buying their properties."

"All the more reason for you to think about striking out on your own," Dana said, adding toppings to her shortcake. "Serenity, is this homemade whipped cream?"

"It is, indeed."

She tasted it and groaned. "This is divine. You're going to have me placing special orders for everything you cook if you keep this up."

Serenity gave Dana a quick hug. "Aw, that's so sweet, but it's easy and you can make it yourself."

Dana slanted her a sidelong glance. "Bite your tongue. I work on cars and play piano. The kitchen is not my domain. I've got the basics down and that's it."

Serenity laughed. "If you can fix a car, you can make whipped cream."

Terri came back to the table. "I meant to ask you about your yard, Serenity. It looks good. Did everything get straightened out with the mowing company?"

How did this conversation end up back on Gabriel? She was trying to keep him off her mind. "No. Gabriel did it earlier today." She kept her eyes focused on her plate because she knew they'd see it as one more thing added to the list of why Gabriel would be a great catch. Finally, she glanced up and found them all smiling at her. "Don't say one word."

"I wasn't going to say anything," Natasha said with feigned innocence.

"Mm-hmm."

"Not too many guys would mow your grass just because. Gabriel might be a keeper." Natasha dropped her head and shoved a spoonful of strawberry short-cake into her mouth.

Serenity eyed her friend.

"That's more than one word, so you can't get mad."

"Smart aleck." If only she'd met Gabriel before her ex. At this point the jury was still out on whether Serenity could risk opening herself up completely to another man, no matter how much she liked him.

CHAPTER 16

Gabriel woke up bleary-eyed Sunday morning and peered at the nightstand clock. He'd stumbled to bed at 5:00 a.m., which meant he'd gotten a whole four hours of sleep. He rolled over onto his back and blew out a long breath. He couldn't keep his mind from wandering to the woman who'd invaded his dreams for the past few nights. Dreams so erotic, he'd had a difficult time convincing himself they weren't real. Gabriel thought by working himself to exhaustion he'd be too tired to dream, but that wasn't the case. No amount of cold showers, running, or any other form of exercising had helped. As he lay there, he decided distance be damned, he was going to see Serenity today.

He drifted off to sleep for another hour, then got up to shower, dress, and find some food. Gabriel surveyed the meager contents of his refrigerator and realized he should probably go grocery shopping. Whenever he got focused on programming, everything else took a back seat, including food. There had been times when he'd gone an entire day without eating. Since being here, he'd done a better job of eating on a somewhat regular schedule. Until now. Closing the door, he went to put his shoes on. He'd pick up breakfast from Ms. Ida's place, stop at the ice cream parlor, and grocery shop afterward.

Once outside, his gaze automatically traveled to Serenity's house. Without stopping to think about what he was doing, Gabriel crossed the yard and rang her doorbell.

"Gabriel. Hey," Serenity said, clearly surprised to see him.

"Good morning."

"Is everything okay?"

He nodded. "I was on my way to Ms. Ida's for a late breakfast and wanted to know if you'd like to come with me."

A smile played around her mouth. "Any other time I'd be game, but I just made batter for waffles. You're welcome to join me, if you like."

Gabriel laughed. "I've never turned down a great meal, and I *know* yours will be exactly that. Do you need me to run home for anything?"

"Nope." She held the door open for him to enter, then led him to the kitchen. "I have everything for a lazy Sunday brunch—scrambled eggs, bacon, fresh fruit, and my homemade waffles."

On cue, his stomach growled. "What made you decide to make waffles? Not that I'm complaining."

"Somebody's hungry," she said with a chuckle. "I've been craving them for the past few weeks."

"Let me wash my hands and you can put me to work." He had no problem working for his breakfast. And he enjoyed cooking with her.

Serenity handed him a paper towel to dry his hands. "You can handle the bacon and the fruit. Just use this plate for the fruit." She had halves of a cantaloupe and watermelon, grapes, strawberries, and a pineapple.

"Got it."

"Do you mind if I put on some music?"

"Of course not." Serenity walked over to her phone, punched a few buttons, and Jill Scott's powerhouse voice poured through the portable speaker on the counter. Gabriel bobbed his head in time with the music as he sliced and diced the fruit. Once he finished, he joined Serenity at the stove, where she was adding brown and white sugar, a little salt, and water to a pot. "What are you making?"

"Vanilla maple syrup."

"Wait. You make your own *syrup*?" This woman never failed to amaze him.

"It's good, too," Serenity said with a little dance move in time with the beat. "And the best part is that it doesn't take long to make."

Smiling, Gabriel swung her out and moved his body in sync with hers. They danced for a minute, and then she went back to the stove. He watched in fascination as she brought the mixture to a boil, then turned it off and added maple extract. She grabbed another bottle from the cabinet. "What's in there?"

"Vanilla extract." She measured and added the liquid to the pot, then gave it a little stir. "That's it."

"Wow. That entire process took less than ten minutes. Where did you buy your vanilla extract from? I've never seen it in that kind of container." He held the bottle up in the light and noticed the long brown stems inside. He opened the lid and smelled. "Vanilla beans?"

"Yep. And I didn't buy it. I made it," she said, dancing her way back over to the waffle maker. "It's far cheaper these days with the price of extract going up in the stores."

He whipped his head in her direction. "I don't even know what to say. You are truly an amazing woman. I'd love the recipe to the syrup and extract, if you don't mind sharing."

"Sure." Serenity sidled up next to him. "But if you tell my secrets, I'm never feeding you again."

Gabriel threw his head back and laughed. He wrapped his arm around her and kissed her temple. "Baby, that's a serious threat, and as much as I love eating your food, I'm taking these recipes to the grave."

She joined his laughter, and it took them a few minutes to calm down. He'd missed being with her this way. He stroked a finger down her cheek. His gaze drifted to her mouth, and memories of kissing her flooded his mind—the plush softness of her lips, the sweet taste on his tongue. He had to kiss her again. He lowered his head and brushed his lips against hers. He'd meant it to be only a quick one, but the moment their lips connected, he was lost. Passion erupted, and he gathered her closer. Gabriel left her lips to trail kisses over her jaw, along her throat and the portion of her chest visible above her sleeveless top. Reaching up, he cupped her face and reclaimed her mouth. She gripped his shirt, meeting him stroke for stroke. He groaned. Feeling himself on the brink of losing control, he eased back.

"Um...we're supposed to be cooking."

They were cooking in his mind. With her eyes still closed and her lips moist from his kisses, she made an alluring picture, tempting him to have one more taste. His stomach growled again, ending the interlude. "I guess I should start on the bacon."

"And these waffles and eggs aren't going to cook themselves."

She gave him a smile that stirred something deep in his belly. He momentarily froze. *What the hell is going on?* He had never experienced these kinds of crazy emotions with a woman, particularly one he'd known only a short time. He dropped his hands, and Serenity backed out of his embrace.

Gabriel turned to the counter and busied himself with his tasks. They worked in companionable silence as Jill, along with Anthony Hamilton, sang about being so in love. "I take it you're a fan of Jill Scott."

She placed a done waffle onto a cookie sheet and

placed it in the warmer drawer on the oven. "I love her music."

"I was checking out things to do in the Bay Area and saw that she'll be at Yoshi's in Oakland next weekend."

"Are you *serious*? I've been trying to catch her in concert."

She'd just given him the opening he needed to ask her out again. "If tickets are still available, would you like to go?"

"Yes," she said, her eyes sparkling with happiness.

"I'll check and see while we're eating." He turned his attention back to the bacon and transferred the crisp strips to a paper towel to drain. Minutes later, they filled their plates, got glasses of orange juice, and took everything out to her deck. Serenity went back inside to bring out the warm syrup. Gabriel seated her, then went around the table and took his own chair. He was eager to try the waffles and the syrup. First he ate a piece of the fluffy waffle plain. It was crispy on the outside, soft on the inside, and slightly sweet. And delicious. Next he added the syrup. Unable to resist, he dipped his finger in for a taste before sampling them together. It was so good, he couldn't stop a groan. He glanced up to find Serenity watching him with a quiet smile. "This is the best syrup I've ever had, and I'm never eating the store-bought ones again."

Serenity smiled. "It really is hard to go back once you've tried it. I can't remember the last time I bought some. Jellies and jams, either, for that matter."

Gabriel paused with a forkful of eggs halfway to his mouth. "You make your own jams, too?"

She nodded and wiggled her eyebrows. "I see that gleam in your eyes. I take it you'd like to try some."

The corner of his mouth kicked up in a grin. "Hey, I can't help it. You know how I feel about food."

Chuckling, she rose to her feet. "I'll be right back."

While she was gone, he took out his phone and checked to see about the concert tickets. He smiled when he saw they hadn't sold out and quickly purchased two tickets. Briefly, he considered booking them a room for the night but changed his mind. He was already in too deep, and since he hadn't made any concrete decisions about the future of their relationship, he didn't think it would be a good idea.

"I have some strawberry jam you can try," Serenity said, setting a saucer with a slice of buttered toast, a knife, and a jar in front of him, then reclaiming her chair.

Gabriel spread some of the jam on the bread and took a hefty bite. He shook his head. "You're killing me here, Serenity. How am I supposed to go back to the other stuff after this?"

With a pleased look on her face, she bit off a piece of bacon. "Since you were nice enough to do my yard, you can take a jar home."

"Thanks. Oh, I got us tickets to the concert. I chose Saturday as opposed to Friday night, so you won't have to worry about rushing after work."

"I appreciate that."

"Maybe we can make a day of it and have dinner beforehand. The concert starts at seven thirty."

"If we can go to Everett and Jones in Jack London Square, you have a deal. I have a taste for some barbecue."

"You'll get no argument from me." They finished eating, and Gabriel helped Serenity clean up. Bringing her into the circle of his arms, he asked, "What are your plans for the rest of your day?"

"Relaxing for the most part, but I am going over to Splendid Scoops for some ice cream."

"Great minds think alike. I'd planned to do the same. Want to go now?" Serenity hesitated, and he wondered if she was still uncomfortable with them being seen together in town.

"That's fine. Let me change my shoes and we can leave." Serenity came up on tiptoe and pressed a kiss to his lips.

Gabriel quickly took over the kiss, slipping his tongue between her parted lips. His tongue moved deep in her mouth, staking its claim, causing her to moan. Too ravenous to be gentle, he devoured her mouth with an intensity that stunned him. But he couldn't stop. Her hands burned a path across his chest and wound around his neck. She gripped the back of his head and held him in place. Each stroke of her tongue against his brought him closer and closer to the brink of losing control. And Gabriel never lost control. A moment later, she released him.

"I'll only be a second," she murmured and strolled out of the kitchen.

He nodded and resisted the urge to pull her back into his arms for another kiss. When she was out of sight, he scrubbed a hand down his face. *Yeah, we need to get out of this house.*

* * *

In her bedroom, Serenity dropped down on the side of the bed and drew in a deep, steadying breath. Gabriel's kisses always seemed to make her lose all reason.

One week. It had been one whole week since she'd seen Gabriel after they'd shared a night of pleasure she hadn't been able to erase from her mind. She hadn't been prepared for the sensations that engulfed her then and had done her best to avoid seeing him because she needed to think about what it meant. Common sense told her now would be a good time to cut her losses, but how much she enjoyed being with him almost guaranteed she'd ignore that little piece of wisdom. Hence she'd invited him to breakfast and was now going into town with him for ice cream.

Serenity had been tempted to lead him to the bedroom to do just what Dana suggested—enjoy every sensual moment until he left. Shaking herself mentally, she stood and exchanged her flip-flops for a pair of low-heeled black sandals. She grabbed her purse and keys, then went back to the kitchen. Gabriel was standing at the sliding glass door with his hands stuck in his pockets, staring outside. She took a minute to study his tall, slim build. The navy tee he wore molded to his well-defined chest, abs, and arms, and his gray basketball shorts accentuated a firm, muscular butt that she could probably bounce a quarter off. As if sensing her presence, he turned and smiled. Her pulse skipped.

"Ready?"

"Yep." He followed her out the front door, waiting until she locked it, then led her over to his car. Once they were on the road, she asked, "Are you going to be working today? You've been putting in a lot of hours."

"I have been working a lot this past week. I should probably take the day off and pick it up tomorrow."

"You absolutely should. You can't keep working twenty-four-seven and not expect to get burned out at some point."

"You're right. I'm going to try to decrease my hours this week."

Serenity patted him on the thigh. "Good choice. You can't be productive if you're so tired you can't see straight, and I suspect with what you do, making mistakes means a redo."

Gabriel laughed softly. "Okay, you've made your point."

She smiled and resumed staring out the window. Less than ten minutes later, he parked a block away from the shop. As they walked up the street, she was struck by how different they were acting with each other now. Last weekend, everywhere they went, Gabriel held her hand, guided her with his hand on her back, or touched her in some gentle but possessive way. Today he walked at her side with a good foot between them and kept his hands to himself. Serenity knew it was because she'd told him she didn't want the townspeople in her business or to speculate on their relationship. But she missed the connection. *You can't have it both ways,* that irritating inner voice reminded her. She called out and returned greetings to the people she knew and did her best to ignore the speculative glances.

Gabriel opened the door to the shop and gestured her inside. "I guess everybody else had the same idea." A good fifteen people waited in line.

"It's been like this on the weekends since I moved here. It's only one. If we came around dinnertime, there would be twice the number of people here."

He leaned down to whisper in her ear. "What flavor are you getting?"

She shivered at his closeness. "Um…just vanilla this time to go with the apple pie I made last night."

His eyes lit up, and a smile spread across his face.

"Yes, I'll share." He took a step as if he was going to kiss her but seemingly remembered where they were and quickly turned away. Serenity's heart rate kicked up, and she took a furtive glance around to see if anyone had noticed. She relaxed when she saw everyone engaged in their own conversations and not paying attention to her.

"Ms. Wheeler!"

Serenity spun around just as Brianna launched

herself at her and wrapped her small arms around her waist. She hugged the little girl and pressed a kiss to her forehead. "How are you, Brianna?"

"I'm good. Mommy is getting me ice cream because I finished reading my book."

"That's wonderful. You'll have to tell me all about it next time I see you." She shifted slightly and spoke to Brianna's mother. "Hey, Pam."

"Hi, Serenity. Good to see you."

"Good to see you, too." Pam divided a curious glance between Serenity and Gabriel, and Serenity made the introductions. "Pam, this is Gabriel Cunningham. Gabriel, this is Pam."

"Nice to meet you, Pam," Gabriel said.

"Same here, Gabriel. Are you new in town?"

"I've been here for a couple of months. And who is this little one?"

"This is my daughter, Brianna. Brianna, say hello to Mr. Cunningham."

"Hi, Mr. Cunni…cummi…You have a big name."

Gabriel chuckled and squatted down to Brianna's level. "How about you call me Mr. C. That's easier. It's very nice to meet you, Brianna."

She shook his outstretched hand and shyly said, "Okay. Hi, Mr. C."

"Brianna, Mr. Cunningham is Mrs. Williams's grandson. Do you remember the lady who gave you the candy when you were at the doctor's office?"

She bounced up and down. "Yes. She was nice." Brianna looked up at Gabriel. "I like your grandma.

When you see her, can you tell her I finished my book?"

Smiling, he said, "I sure will. I've heard you have the best tea parties."

Her eyes widened, and she giggled, nodding vigorously. "I do. Ask Ms. Wheeler. She came to my house and she had a hat on. You can come next time."

Serenity's heart warmed as she viewed the exchange.

"Thanks for the invitation, but I didn't know guys could go to a tea party."

Brianna put her hand on her hip. "My daddy is a guy, and he always comes to my tea parties."

Pam rolled her eyes, and Serenity outright laughed, then said, "Well, there you have it."

Gabriel shook his head. "Since you put it that way, I'd be honored. Just let me know when and I'll be there." He rose to his full height.

She clapped. "Goody! Mommy, Mr. C is going to come to my house. Ooh, and Ms. Wheeler can come, too. It's gonna be fun."

"I heard, baby. Gabriel, I hope she didn't—"

"Like I said, I'd be honored," he said.

As they moved up in the line, Gabriel and Brianna kept up a steady stream of conversation. Serenity marveled at his patience and the way he gave the little girl his undivided attention.

"Does he have children?" Pam whispered to Serenity.

"No."

"You could've fooled me. I've rarely seen a man be

that thoughtful when it comes to someone else's child. He's going to be a great father."

Still watching them, Serenity agreed. And she felt herself fall for him a little more. After they purchased their ice cream and said goodbye to Pam and Brianna, Gabriel drove them home.

"Brianna is a beautiful little girl," Gabriel said, following Serenity inside. "And she can *talk*."

Serenity laughed and placed her dessert in the freezer. "Oh, you just got a little taste. She talks my ear off every time she comes into the doctor's office or when I visit. You were really good with her."

He shrugged. "I haven't spent a lot of time around kids, but I like them, especially kids like Brianna."

She had no idea why his confession made her happy. It wasn't like she planned to campaign for the role of mother of his children. "Let me cut you a piece of pie."

"Okay. Then I can get out of your hair. I don't want to mess up your relaxation day."

"I'm going to read and, later, take a long candle-lit bubble bath. I'll schedule a massage for sometime soon." She cut him a large slice and placed it into a plastic container.

Gabriel came up behind her and slid his arms around her. "I wish I'd remembered that last weekend. You could've gotten one at the bed-and-breakfast," he murmured, trailing kisses along the column of her neck. He spun her around to face him at the same time his head descended.

The kiss was electric and intoxicating. His mouth moved over hers, tasting, teasing, tempting. Serenity felt her control slipping and pulled back. Gabriel rested his forehead against hers, his breathing as ragged as hers.

"I'd better go. Thank you for brunch, the pie, and for spending part of your day with me."

Not trusting her voice, she merely nodded.

"I'll talk to you later, baby." He spun on his heel and strode out.

Serenity dropped her head on the bar. She closed her eyes, her breathing still ragged. She hadn't planned on meeting a man like Gabriel, one who had her guard dropping by the moment.

CHAPTER 17

So, how are things going with you and Serenity?" Nana asked casually as they ate dinner on Wednesday evening.

Gabriel should've known there was something up with her inviting him over in the middle of the week and cooking a spread he usually saw only during the holidays. "I'm not sure what you mean."

"Of course you are. You've been spending a lot of time with her and doing her yard every week."

He sighed inwardly and placed his fork on the plate. "Nana, I'm helping her out just like I'm doing with you. I think she has the same company." As far as spending time with her, any number of words came to mind—enjoyment, complicated, amazing, scary, confusing. His feelings were so muddled, some days he didn't know if he was coming or going. Serenity could make him lose control in the blink of an eye, something he'd never had an issue with before. In fact, he prided himself on his ironclad will and the ability to keep his emotions on lockdown.

"Driving off with her and suitcases in your car and walking through town to the ice cream shop don't have anything to do with helping her out. I may be old, but I'm not blind."

Obviously, Adele was back at her job. "I like her. Is that what you wanted to hear?"

Nana chuckled. "Was that so hard to say? Goodness, you act like there's something wrong with you dating Serenity. She's a wonderful girl."

"It's nothing serious." Gabriel cut a piece of ham and ate it. And he didn't plan to be around long enough for it to progress to that level. He thought about asking his grandmother about moving again but nixed the idea. After their last conversation, he assumed it would be a waste of time. He had yet to figure out what to do. Traveling back and forth could be an option, but it would also be expensive. And depleting his bank account wasn't on his list of things to do.

"Why not? You aren't getting any younger. Forty is just around the corner."

"Thirty-six is not that close to forty," he said, shaking his head and picking up his glass of lemonade.

"It is if you plan on getting married and having a few babies."

He choked on the drink, sputtering and coughing. *Marriage? Babies?* He struggled to draw in a breath. "You're getting way ahead of yourself, Nana," Gabriel croaked, trying to clear his throat. "I'm planning to go back to Atlanta soon, and Serenity will be here, so…" He let the sentence hang. She scrutinized him for a lengthy minute, making him squirm in his seat, but he didn't comment. They continued eating, and as soon as the plates were clean, she opened her mouth to say something else. When his phone buzzed, Gabriel sent up a silent thank-you and rushed to answer it. Until he saw his sister's name on the display.

"Are you going to answer it or not?" Nana asked, glaring at him.

"Hey, Drea. How's it going?"

"Hey, big brother. It's going well. Did I catch you at a bad time? I know you aren't still working, Gabe. It's after seven."

Gabriel chuckled. "I'm not working. Actually, Nana and I are just finishing dinner right now."

"Ugh. I'm so jealous. I know she cooked a feast," Andrea grumbled.

"That she did. Baked ham, roasted turkey, fresh green beans, mashed potatoes, homemade rolls—"

"Just stop. I can't stand you right now."

He laughed.

"How is she?"

"You can ask her yourself. I'll put her on speaker." He welcomed the distraction and getting the heat off him. "Okay."

"Hi, Nana."

"Andrea. How are you, baby?"

"I'm good. A little salty right now because I'm

missing all that good food. And I know you made dessert, too."

Nana's tinkling laughter floated through the room. "Just my pound cake."

Andrea groaned. "*See*. I knew it. Gabriel, don't eat it all."

"It's not like you're here to get it," Gabriel said.

"True. But Nana can send me some of it."

"I sure will, honey. I'll make you another one on Sunday and mail it on Monday, so it doesn't sit at the post office over the weekend."

"Thanks, Nana. I love you!"

"You're welcome."

Gabriel shook his head, but he couldn't blame her. He planned to have a large slice of that cake and, hopefully, take a couple of pieces home. He finished the last bit of food on his plate.

"Between yours and Serenity's food, I feel like I'm missing out on everything. Have you two been going to the supper club dinners?"

He froze and met Nana's widening smile. *So much for shifting the conversation.*

"I've only gone to a couple lately, but Gabriel's gone to quite a few," Nana answered. "As a matter of fact, they're dating."

"*What?* Oh my goodness! That's great, Gabe. I'm so happy for you. She's such a sweet person."

"Yes, she is." On that they agreed.

Nana sat back in her chair with a pleased expression on her face.

"But before you get all excited, it's not that serious. We're just hanging out."

"Whatever you say, big brother. I'll—"

"How's the job going?" Gabriel asked, cutting her off.

Andrea laughed knowingly. "It's going well. A lot of work some days, but nothing I can't handle. I have some great managers, so it makes things a lot easier."

"Good to hear."

Nana leaned closer to the phone lying on the table. "When are you coming to visit?"

"Hopefully, within the next month or so. I'm thinking I'll come for a weekend, now that everything has calmed down from the move. I kind of miss that small-town living."

Gabriel could honestly admit the town had some merits—the homemade ice cream, the ability to see the stars without lots of buildings, and of course, meeting Serenity topped the list—but he hoped to be back in Atlanta by then. However, the thought of not seeing Serenity, not being able to kiss or touch her, not sitting with her to watch the sunset while enjoying their favorite foods, somehow brought on an entire set of emotions, and he refused to analyze the reasons. "Sounds like a plan," he told his sister.

"Well, I'll let you get back to dinner. I know Gabriel is anxiously awaiting that pound cake."

"Yes, I am," he said with a little laugh. "I'm going to take a piece home to go with my ice cream from Splendid Scoops, too."

"It's really time for me to hang up now. A double scoop of strawberry would be *sooo* good right now."

"Guess you'll have to wait until you get here."

"Yeah."

Her dejected voice made Gabriel laugh even harder. "We'll talk to you later. Love you, Sis."

"Love you, baby," Nana said.

"Love you both."

Gabriel hit the end call button and stood to clear the dishes off the table. "If you want to get comfortable and watch your TV shows, I'll put the food away and clean up the kitchen. That'll give my dinner time to settle before I have some cake."

Nana slowly got to her feet. "I appreciate it. Take some of that food home and the cake. Oh, and make sure you cut a piece to take to Serenity," she called over her shoulder as she shuffled down the hallway.

His grandmother was persistent, if nothing else. It took less than thirty minutes for Gabriel to restore the kitchen to its former pristine state. As he reached for a knife for the cake, his phone buzzed. He went back over to the table where he'd left it and saw a text message from his sister.

Andrea: *I can't believe you've been holding out on me. How long have you and Serenity been dating?*

Gabriel: *Again, we're just hanging out. It's nothing serious.*

Andrea: *I wonder what Serenity would say if I asked her.*

Gabriel: *Don't even think about it.*

Andrea: *Oh, it's like that? Lol, okay. I won't say anything. For now. Tell Serenity I said hello when you see her, which I assume will be very soon.* 😊

He sighed and tossed the phone back on the table. The last thing he needed was his sister—or anyone else—interfering with his and Serenity's relationship, if that's what it could be termed. Hell, even he didn't know what to call it. Still, he couldn't wait for their trip to the Bay Area on Saturday.

* * *

"Gabriel will be here in about thirty minutes," Serenity said to her sister on speakerphone as she dressed on Saturday. "We're heading to Yoshi's to see Jill Scott."

"Ooh, I love Jilly from Philly. So, things are heating up between you and Gabriel, huh?"

More like exploded into something she hadn't planned.

"That silence says I'm right. Please tell me you're not still holding back because of that mess with your ex."

"Not really. It's more because he doesn't plan to stay here permanently. And before you say it, I'm not into long-distance relationships, not that he's said anything about continuing to see each other once he leaves." She applied mascara and lip color.

"So give him a reason to consider staying," Chandra said with a laugh. "I'm sure you can be very persuasive. If nothing else, cook him one of those fabulous meals. That definitely would do the trick. I know I'd stay."

Serenity chuckled. "You are truly a nut."

"Maybe, but what do you have to lose…other than a chance to find out if he's the one for you?"

"For your information, Miss Nosy, he's eaten plenty of my food, and he's even cooked for me." She clapped a hand over her mouth. *Just great.* That would be all her sister needed to hear. Groaning softly, she wiped the lipstick off her hand and reapplied it to her lips.

"Is that right? Hmm…what are you doing next weekend?"

"Why?"

"I'm coming to visit, so don't plan anything except maybe one of those dinners with your friends, and invite Gabriel."

"Chandra, I'm not going to—"

"Gotta go. Have a great time, and I'll text you with my travel information."

"Chandra, wait." Serenity glanced down at the phone display. Chandra had hung up. "That girl takes being the big sister way too far sometimes," she muttered as she went to the closet for her shoes and a jacket. Along with her heeled sandals, she grabbed a pair of flats, in case they decided to walk around Jack London Square.

Gabriel arrived exactly at two. "Hey, sweetheart." He bent and kissed her.

"Hi. I'm ready."

"You look beautiful," he said as they walked to his car.

"Thanks." She'd chosen a pair of black slacks and paired it with an off-the-shoulder fitted black and white top. "You don't look so bad yourself." He was dressed similarly in black slacks but wore a pale-blue button-down silk shirt and expensive loafers.

"Just trying to keep up with you." Gabriel winked and helped her into the car. After he started the engine and drove off, he asked, "Did you enjoy your cake?"

"You'd better believe it. I called your grandmother to thank her." She decided not to tell him about Ms. Della's trying to play matchmaker. She seemed to be more than excited about their dating, and Serenity had quickly ended the call without answering any of the woman's questions related to the seriousness of the relationship.

"By the way, I talked to Andrea the other night and she said to tell you hello."

"How is she doing? We spoke a few weeks ago and she was still getting acclimated."

"She said things have calmed down, and she mentioned maybe visiting for a weekend sometime next month."

"It'll be good to see her. I have to make sure everybody's available for dinner." She wanted to ask if he still planned to be here by then but changed her mind. Today she only wanted to enjoy some good music and food and the company of a really nice guy.

Gabriel merged onto the freeway. "I checked the traffic and it said we should make it to Oakland in about two hours."

"That's not bad, considering it's a Saturday. But I've known it to change in a heartbeat, so I'm going to make myself comfortable and enjoy the ride." They shared a smile, and he refocused on the road. Soft music flowed through the speakers, and Serenity leaned her head back and closed her eyes.

They'd been on the road for twenty minutes before he said, "I've been meaning to ask you this for weeks, but I keep forgetting. What made you decide on a career in nursing?"

She rolled her head in his direction. "I've always loved helping people, and nursing is one of the most respected professions around. And because it's always changing and evolving, I don't have to be stuck in one area. There's something rewarding about knowing my voice, my touch, and my care and time can help my patients make it through the tough moments in their lives. It's those little things, you know?"

"Yeah, I do. I noticed how caring you were at the Fourth of July festivities whenever someone stopped to ask about some ache or pain. You were amazing."

Her heart did a little flip. "Thanks. Like you, I've found my passion." From the time she entered high school, Serenity knew she wanted to become a nurse. She'd studied hard, earned her bachelor's degree, then went back for her master's. Initially, she had thought about working in the field for a few years, then moving into academia. However, more than a decade later, she still loved working with her patients, even more so after moving from the ER to family practice, and had no immediate plans to change her career path.

Gabriel reached for her hand and gave it a gentle squeeze. "And everyone is the better for it."

Serenity didn't know what to say. His sincerity touched her, and she felt the cracks in the wall surrounding her heart widening. They rode in silence for a while, then Gabriel's phone rang and she saw his friend's name pop up on the display.

He connected the Bluetooth. "What's up, D?"

"Nothing much. You busy?"

"I'm on my way to Oakland. Jill Scott is in concert tonight."

"Sounds interesting. I'm betting you're not taking this little trip alone."

"That would be a safe bet."

"And by these cryptic responses, I guess Serenity is sitting next to you."

Serenity bit her lip to keep from laughing at Gabriel's expression, which was a mixture of annoyance and exasperation. *At least I'm not the only one with nosy friends.*

"That would be a good guess." Gabriel slanted her a sidelong glance.

"Hey, Serenity. How's it going?"

"I'm doing fine, Darius."

"I have no doubts about that," Darius said with a chuckle. "You kids have fun, and I'll talk to you later, Gabe."

"Later." Gabriel disconnected, and the music started up again. "Sorry about that."

"No need to be sorry. He reminds me of my friends. They're the same way."

"Nosy and always in your business."

"Exactly." They both laughed. For the remainder of the drive, they swapped stories about their friends' antics.

When they made it to Oakland and Jack London Square, Gabriel said, "Since this is my first time here, I'll defer to you for parking."

Serenity had been there only a few times herself. "We can park in the garage next to Yoshi's. That way we don't have to worry about moving the car or adding more money to the meter."

"Works for me." He followed her directions to the garage. As they walked back out to the street, he stopped to glance in the window. "They have a restaurant?"

"Yes. If you eat there, you can get a reserved seat for the concert. Otherwise, it's first come, first serve."

"We can eat here if you want to do the reserved seating."

"Oh, no. I'm fine with standing in line. I've got my taste buds set for some barbecue. The doors open half an hour before the show, so we should probably plan on being back at least thirty minutes before then. Natasha came to a concert here, and she mentioned that the line gets long pretty quick."

He nodded. "Barbecue it is. Do you want to eat now, or a little later?"

Serenity checked her watch. "It's a little past four

now. Maybe we can walk for a little while or sit near the water, then head over to the restaurant in an hour or so."

"Sounds good." Gabriel took her hand, and they started toward the water. "How far is the restaurant?"

She pointed. "On the next block. Everything is in walking distance. There's a movie theater right across from the garage, a few more restaurants, and even a hotel or two."

"Now, that's convenient. I like this place," he said as they strolled leisurely down the street.

So did she. And she liked *him* even more. They ended up sitting on one of the wooden benches near the waterfront. With the weather in the high seventies, several people milled around, taking advantage of the late-summer weather. Gabriel scooted close and slung an arm around her shoulder. She leaned her head against him, and they sat enjoying the sounds of the water. A slight breeze blew across her face like a whisper, and she snuggled closer to Gabriel, feeling a closeness she'd never felt with another man. She closed her eyes briefly, inhaling deeply and letting the breath out slowly.

She had no idea how much time passed before she heard Gabriel whisper, "I could sit here all night with you."

Serenity lifted her head, and their gazes fused. "Then we should come back after the show."

He gave her a soft smile. "Whatever you want, sweetheart."

She resumed her position, and they stayed that way until he suggested they walk a little farther. The two of them went from one end to the other, then retraced their steps and headed for the restaurant. It was crowded, and they had to wait twenty minutes to be seated. After poring over the menu for several minutes, they decided to share one of the combination meals with chicken, ribs, and brisket, with sides of candied yams, macaroni and cheese, greens, and cornbread.

"Wow," Gabriel said when the food arrived. "This is a lot of food." He rubbed his hands together. "Okay, let's try this. Ladies first."

Serenity had to laugh. "You remind me of a kid in a candy store." She added portions of everything and shook her head when he filled his. "It's a good thing I got my food first."

He grinned sheepishly and shrugged. "You already know."

She waited for him to try everything. "Well? What's the verdict?"

"It's really good." He leaned forward and whispered, "But your yams taste much better."

"And *that's* why I brought you a little dessert." She tossed him a bold wink and went back to her food.

"Wait. I know that's not all you're going to say. What is it?"

"You're not even done with dinner yet. I shouldn't have said anything."

Gabriel lifted her hand and brought it to his lips.

"Come on, pretty baby, tell me." He kissed the back of her hand, turned it over and repeated the gesture on her palm.

Her breath stacked up in her throat. His lips were soft, and his hazel eyes teased and seduced her. If he kept staring at her like that, she was liable to hand him the dessert and anything else he asked for. "Brownies," she said breathlessly.

"My favorite." His smile turned wicked. "Next to you."

Serenity almost slid off her chair. *Trouble. I'm in so much trouble.* She slowly extracted her hand, but she had a hard time concentrating on her food for the next few minutes. She managed to get through and enjoy her meal without any more distractions. However, her palm was still tingling from his kiss later when they walked back over to the venue. Fortunately, there were only a few couples ahead of them in line, and she and Gabriel ended up with good seats on the floor less than twenty feet from the stage.

He scanned the space. "This is the perfect grown folks' venue."

"I couldn't agree more." The intimate club's floor level featured three rows of tables for four, while the upper levels had a choice of tables or booths. There wasn't a bad seat in the house. Animated chatter filled the air, while efficient staff moved through throngs of people, serving food and drinks, as music poured through hidden speakers. At exactly seven thirty, the announcer came on, gave some house rules, and introduced Jill Scott. Serenity couldn't remember the last time she'd had so much fun. She danced in her seat and sang along like she was one of Ms. Scott's personal backup singers.

Gabriel nodded in time with the beat and smiled at Serenity. "This was a good choice. I'm really enjoying myself."

"Me too. Can't you tell?" she asked, laughing and still moving to the beat.

By the time the concert ended, Serenity had to fan herself to cool down. She excused herself to the restroom.

"I'll wait near the exit." He pointed, almost shouting to be heard over the many people streaming out the doors.

She nodded and joined the always long line for the women's bathroom. After she finished, she met Gabriel.

"Do you still want to go back and sit by the water?"

"Yes, but can we go to the car so I can change into my flat shoes? And get your brownies."

"Absolutely." A smile lit his face and he all but dragged her to the car.

Serenity handed him the small Ziploc bag, then changed her shoes. He'd finished the first of the three by the time she stood. "I guess you wanted those."

Minutes later, after they were seated, Gabriel turned her way. "I enjoyed the concert."

"She was fabulous. Thank you for getting the tickets."

"It was my pleasure."

The kiss that followed was so achingly sweet and tender it brought tears to her eyes. She'd been falling for him since the first kiss, and she was in danger of losing the one thing she'd vowed never to give away again—her heart.

CHAPTER 18

"How was the Jill Scott concert last weekend?" Darius asked. "I figure since you skirted the topic every time we talked during the week, claiming we should be in *work mode*, you can't avoid it today. It's Saturday and we're off."

For the hundredth time, Gabriel wished he hadn't answered that call. He'd done so only because it might be work related and something he could solve quickly. "The concert was off the hook. She put on one of the best shows I've seen. We had a good time."

"Better than good, more than likely."

"Something like that," he murmured. As he'd said, the concert was great, but the time he and Serenity spent sitting near the water had been far better. The fulfillment he'd felt scared him to death because he could envision them sitting that way for years to come. And that wasn't supposed to be on his radar. At all.

"I have to say I'm really surprised you're still seeing

Serenity. Since your breakup, I can't recall the last time you went out with a woman more than a couple of times, if that. Yet it's been what, more than two months?"

"Thereabouts." Darius wasn't the only one surprised, and he'd described Gabriel to a tee. The difference? Those women weren't Serenity. Not one possessed the same sweet, caring spirit or could make him lose control simply from a kiss.

"I mean, I can't blame you. Serenity is a beautiful woman. All those curves packaged in one compact, stacked body, and—"

"You can stop right there, D." Something akin to jealousy if he were owning up to it rose fast and hard. Gabriel jumped up from the lounger he'd been sitting in on his deck and paced. *What is wrong with me?* It shouldn't bother him that Darius noticed Serenity's beauty, especially since he knew his friend wouldn't even think about trying to make a play for her, now or sometime in the future. That had always been one of their friendship rules. They did *not* go after a woman one of them had dated, no matter the circumstance.

"Interesting."

He dropped back down on the lounger. "What?"

"You. You know what I think?"

"No, and I don't particularly care. Not that it'll stop you," he added wryly.

Darius laughed. "I think you should extend your stay. It's not like we can't continue to handle things the way we've been doing. Brent and I can pop out there for a few days, or you can come home like you did a couple of weeks ago."

What Darius said made sense, but Gabriel had his schedule all mapped out, and now it had been blown to bits. "I don't know. Maybe. But for how long?"

"As long as it takes for you to decide what you want to do. You sound a lot like your grandmother," Darius said. "I mean, I can't really blame her for not wanting to move, though. I'm not sure I'd want to uproot my entire life at that age. Hell, you don't even want to do it now."

Gabriel frowned. "Whose side are you on?"

"No one's. I'm just sayin'. Look, man, just give it some thought. You said yourself that the town did have a few good points. Ms. Ida's, Splendid Scoops, and that lake we went to would make me reconsider. Then there's Serenity. Staying a little longer would give you a chance to see if she's your Mrs. Right."

He sighed. On one hand, he wanted more time with Serenity. On the other, more time could potentially be dangerous to his heart. "Hmm" was all he said. "I need to get going."

"Another hot date?"

"Not exactly. Serenity is having one of her supper club dinners."

"Man, maybe I need to visit more often. Maybe check out those three or four fine friends."

"Three. But remember Terri is married. I don't know if Natasha or Dana is seeing anyone. It hasn't come up. I could always put in a good word," Gabriel added with a chuckle. Then it would take the heat off him.

"Nah, I like to make my own introductions. Besides, I don't know if I want to trust what you might say."

He laughed. "On that note, I'm out. Talk to you guys on Tuesday." Gabriel ended the call and went inside. He changed out of his tank top and basketball shorts into a pair of navy linen shorts and a matching shirt. He got the bag holding two bottles of wine he'd purchased earlier out of the refrigerator, locked up, and went next door.

Serenity opened the door and gave him a bright smile. "Hey, Gabriel." She came up on tiptoe and brushed a kiss over his mouth. "We're out back."

The kiss wasn't nearly long enough for him, and he pulled her flush against him and crushed his mouth against hers. As soon as their lips connected, he was lost. His tongue stroked hers and delved deeper to claim every area of her mouth. Finally, he eased back, gifting her with butterfly kisses along her jaw, then lifted his head. "Hi."

"Um...we should...probably..."

Gabriel smiled faintly. "Yeah, probably." Except he needed a minute to get his body in order. "But we'll never make it to the backyard if you keep standing there looking at me like that." The woman was temptation personified.

She shook her head but was smiling. "I don't know what I'm going to do with you."

He lifted an eyebrow.

"Behave and come on."

Chuckling, he followed her out to the back, where her three friends and another couple he didn't know sat laughing and talking.

"Hey, Gabriel," Dana called out. "I hope that bag means more wine."

He held it up. "It does, indeed. And it's already chilled."

"Now, that's what I'm talking about." She hopped up from her chair and claimed the bag.

Smiling, he greeted everyone.

Serenity led him over to the couple. "Gabriel, I'd like you to meet my sister, Chandra, and my brother-in-law, Mark."

Gabriel stuck out his hand, and both rose to shake it. "Nice to meet you."

"Same here, my brother," Mark said.

Gabriel repeated the gesture with Chandra. The two sisters were similar in looks and color, but Chandra was a few inches taller.

Chandra studied him and smiled. "It's very nice to finally meet you, Gabriel. I've heard a lot of good things about you."

He shifted his gaze briefly to Serenity, who lowered her head, then back to Chandra. "Oh?" He really wanted to know what Serenity had told her sister about them. She merely smiled and nodded, then hooked her arm in his and steered him toward the table filled with various appetizers. *Uh-oh.* "How long are you going to be here?" he asked, hoping to head off any interrogation.

"Just the weekend." She gestured to the spread. "Go ahead and fix yourself a plate. Everything is delicious."

"If your sister cooked, I have no doubt." Gabriel scanned the offerings, which had been labeled— bacon-wrapped scallops, crab-stuffed shrimp wrapped in bacon, mini teriyaki beef skewers, lamb rib chops, barbecue chicken bites, vegetable and fruit trays, cheese and crackers, and spinach dip with sliced baguettes. He looked at the dessert-size plate in his hand. This wasn't going to work.

"Problems?"

"Nothing that a bigger plate won't solve."

Chandra stared at him, then burst out laughing. "My husband said the same thing." She handed him another plate. "Take two. That's what he did."

"Good idea." He accepted the plate and between the two got some of everything.

"So, Gabriel, how do you like living off the beaten path?"

"It's not as bad as I originally thought it would be, but I prefer being closer to the city."

"So do I. Serenity told me you cut her grass when I mentioned how good it looked. That was nice of you."

"Just trying to be a good neighbor."

"And do overnight trips, concerts, and kisses fall in the category of being a good neighbor?"

Gabriel should've known those other questions were just lead-ins for what she really wanted to know. Before he could answer, Mark joined them. *Saved!*

Mark slid an arm around Chandra's waist and kissed her temple. "Babe, are you over here scaring Gabriel?" He turned to Gabriel. "You'll have to forgive my wife. She takes her big sister role seriously, and she's a psychologist who'll lure you in without you even knowing."

Chandra swatted at Mark. "Hey."

"You know it's true. Leave the man alone. He just got here, and you couldn't even wait until he fixed his plate before you started in on him. Besides, whatever is going on with Gabriel and Serenity is their business."

"I just need to make sure he's not—"

Mark cut her off with a kiss. "Hush, baby. Not your business. Remember what you said when my sister tried to do the same thing with you?"

"Why are you always bringing up old stuff?" She rolled her eyes.

"Hey. What's going on?" Serenity asked as she approached, dividing a wary glance between Gabriel and her sister.

Mark let out a short bark of laughter. "Nothing other than your sister being her nosy self."

"No harm done," Gabriel said, sensing Serenity's unease. "Everything looks really good, and I know it's going to taste the same. You wouldn't happen to have a few of those brownies for dessert?"

A smile blossomed on her face, and she visibly relaxed. "You never know." She pointed to the two plates.

"I couldn't fit everything on one."

She placed a hand on her hip. "You can come back for more, you know."

"That's exactly what I plan to do." They slipped back into their usual playful banter, and he momentarily forgot about her sister and brother-in-law standing there.

Serenity shook her head. "Come sit down. What do you want to drink?"

"I can get it. You're the one who should be sitting. With all this food, I know you've been on your feet all day." As he followed her to the table, he looked over his shoulder and met Chandra's amused expression. She gave him an imperceptible nod, as if she'd given him a temporary pass. He couldn't decide whether that was a good thing or not.

* * *

Although she laughed and contributed to the various conversations flowing around the table, Serenity kept one eye on her sister. She hoped Chandra hadn't said anything crazy to Gabriel and was grateful to Mark for the rescue.

"Okay, Serenity, this is so good." Natasha held up one of the lamb rib chops. "I didn't think I liked lamb, but it must have been the way it was prepared the other times I had it. Because I love these, just like I did the last time you made them. We need to add these to the supper club rotation more often."

Terri waved a hand. "Amen, sister. Amen."

Everyone around the table laughed, and Serenity said, "See, that's why y'all are my BFFs."

"I hope there's enough for leftovers," Mark said around a mouthful of scallop.

She patted his arm. "I'll make more for you to take home."

He grinned. "Best sister-in-law *ever*."

Serenity leaned back in her chair and found Gabriel watching her. He smiled and winked.

"Well, now," Chandra said, sotto voce.

She skewered her sister with a look. They were definitely going to have to talk when everyone left.

"Oh, yeah. I love this song." Dana jumped up with her wineglass and started dancing to "Shame" by Jill Scott.

Terri joined her, and the two belted out the lyrics while the group clapped and encouraged them.

"These lyrics are pretty appropriate for the moment. I hope you and Gabriel don't miss out on a good thing," Chandra whispered to Serenity. "Now, that *would* be a shame."

Of all the songs to play, it had to be this one. "I don't know what you're talking about. Don't you remember what I told you? Casual. Temporary. The end."

"Girl, I've been watching the two of you, and there's a lot more going on than you care to admit."

She angled her head. "Or maybe it's more than either of you realize or planned."

Yeah. *Way* more than she'd planned. And she had no idea how to make it stop.

Gabriel came around the table and pulled her to her feet. "We didn't get a chance to dance last weekend."

Serenity heard her sister laugh but ignored it. Never missing a beat, Gabriel danced her over to an empty spot on the deck. She'd never seen him dance, but the fluid movement of his hips had her mesmerized, reminding her how those same hips moved as he made love to her.

As if interpreting her thoughts, he said, low and sexy, "I can't wait to have you to myself. I think I'd like a private dance...*horizontally*."

She gasped and missed a step. He moved closer and wrapped an arm around her to steady her but didn't let go, his body grinding against hers in a way that made her want to tell everybody to go home. By the time the song ended, her body was so on fire, she needed a minute. Make that five minutes. Serenity snatched her wineglass up, tossed back the remainder, and set it down with a thud. Putting what she hoped looked like a genuine smile on her face, she said, "I'm going to bring out dessert." She spun on her heel and headed for the sliding glass door leading to the kitchen.

"I'll help," Gabriel said.

She didn't want him to help. What she needed was a minute away from him to get herself together. But she said instead, "Great. Thanks."

"Are you okay, Serenity?" Gabriel asked as soon as they were in the kitchen alone.

Serenity opened her mouth to give the standard, "I'm fine" line, but changed her mind. "No, I'm not okay. You holding me and touching me has my body all in an uproar, and I want everybody to go home so you can finish what you started. Any other questions?" She almost laughed at his shocked expression. He stood speechless for several seconds. "I thought not." She washed her hands, then uncovered the pan of brownies, cut them, and placed them on a plate.

He came and stood close to her. "Would it help if I told you I wanted everyone gone the moment I walked in the door?"

They stared at each other for a lengthy moment, then both burst out laughing, releasing some of the tension. She grabbed two more plates and lined one with mini peach cobbler bites and the other with bite-size molded chocolate cups.

"What's going in these?"

Serenity retrieved a container from the refrigerator and handed it to him. "These chopped strawberries and raspberries. The little cups are all chocolate."

"You mean the entire thing is edible?"

"Yep."

Gabriel got a spoon out of the drawer, scooped some of the mixed fruit into one of the cups and popped it into his mouth. His eyes widened as he chewed.

"Good?"

He placed a hand over his heart and groaned

pleasurably. "Beyond. If I can have these and the brownies for the rest of my life, I'm never leaving."

As soon as the words left his mouth, she saw the excitement in his eyes dim, as if he hadn't meant to blurt it out. It was on the tip of her tongue to tell him if that's all it would take, she'd gladly make them. But rather than make things more awkward, she kept her mouth shut. Instead, Serenity removed a large container from the freezer. "Oh, that's cold!" She hurried over and nearly dropped it onto the counter. "I always forget to use a towel."

"I can't believe you made homemade ice cream, too," Gabriel said, finishing filling the last of the chocolate cups with the fruit. "The stuff from the shop in town is good."

"It is, but you know me when it comes to food. I don't do anything by half."

He smiled. "No, you don't. Okay, all done. Are we ready to take these out?" He picked up a plate. "I'll get the ice cream, too."

"I think so." The plates and utensils were already outside. She waited for him to move, but he just stood there. "What?"

Placing the plate back on the counter, he closed the distance between them. "I need one more kiss to hold me."

"Yeah, I could use one, too," she murmured.

"Good."

Before she could blink, his mouth was on hers. His lips were incredibly warm and soft, and his tongue stroked hers with the confidence of a man who had perfected the art of pleasing a woman. Her head fell back and her breaths came in short gasps, and she lost all sense of time and space. Nothing else mattered except this moment with him. She moaned his name, grabbed his head, and took over the kiss.

At length, he eased back. "We should probably stop before the ice cream melts."

"Mmm, probably." Serenity inhaled deeply and let the breath out slowly. "Okay, let's go." They managed to take everything outside in one trip.

"Here, let me take that." Chandra jumped up and relieved Gabriel of the plate holding the chocolate cups. "Oh my. These are new, Sis. Is this *chocolate*?"

"It is. You can eat the whole thing."

"Say no more." She bit into it, chewed, and moaned. "Well, I'm keeping this plate. You all can have the rest. This is divine." Laughter followed her statement.

"Girl, hand me that plate," Natasha said, leaning over the table to snag one. She ate it and pretended to swoon. "I don't know which I like best—these or the chocolate-dipped strawberries."

Dana opened the lid to the container Gabriel placed in the center of the table. "I know you didn't make homemade vanilla ice cream. I'm going to need to work out every day this week to offset these calories because I'm getting some of everything."

Around the table, everyone chorused their agreement.

Gabriel brought over the plates, napkins, and

utensils from a smaller table, and they were all but snatched out of his hands. He chuckled. "I guess everybody's a little eager."

Serenity couldn't hold back her laughter. *This* was her happy place—seeing her family and friends enjoying the food, music, and fun. Yes, it had taken her the better part of last night and today to prepare, but she didn't care. She loved it. After another hour, one by one, her friends departed with hugs and promises to talk during the week.

When she came back from walking them out, she went still when she saw Gabriel and Mark in the kitchen, rinsing out dishes and stacking them in the dishwasher. "Wow. Thanks, guys."

Mark smiled her way. "Hey, you did all the cooking, so it's the least we can do."

"You know I'm always down to help with the cleanup if I can eat this good food," Gabriel chimed in.

Chandra entered with the remainder of the food trays, and the two women began storing the leftovers. With the four of them working, it didn't take long to clean up everything.

"Do you need me to do anything else, Serenity?" Gabriel asked.

"No."

"Okay. I'm going to take off. Mark and Chandra, it was a pleasure meeting you."

"Same here, man," Mark said as they went through one of those ritual handshakes.

Chandra smiled. "I hope we get to see you again."

"I'm going to walk Gabriel to the door. Be right back," Serenity said. She and Gabriel made their way out front. "I appreciate you always staying to help with the cleanup."

"Anytime, baby." He dipped his head and covered her mouth in a gentle kiss. "I'll talk to you later."

She nodded, closed the door behind him, and laid her head against it.

"Serenity? You okay?"

Serenity startled and whirled around at the sound of her sister's voice. "Yeah. I'm fine."

Chandra leaned against the wall in the entryway and scrutinized her like an organism under a microscope. "Hmm. So that was Gabriel. The brother is one good-looking man. And with those hazel eyes and that beard hugging his face like a shadow giving him that sexy, dangerous kind of edge...*yummy*. I see why you're having trouble remembering that agreement."

"I'm not having—" The pointed look on Chandra's face stopped the lie in its tracks.

She came into the living room, sat on the sofa, and patted the space next to her. "Talk to me, Serenity."

Sighing, Serenity went over and sat. "He makes it hard not to fall for him."

"Him helping clean the kitchen wins points in my book any day. Though I'm sure he probably just did that to make a good impression with us."

"He does it every time we eat together." Along with doing whatever is needed to assist with the meal, cutting her grass, checking on her when he knew she had long days. All the things she'd wanted when she'd been looking for that kind of special relationship.

Chandra's eyebrows shot up. "Are you serious? Honey, he might just be a keeper. And don't forget, he did your yard today."

She leaned her head back and closed her eyes. "And last week and the week before that. Pretty much every week since he moved here."

"So help me out, Sis. What's the problem?"

"The problem is I don't want to be the only one risking my heart. And what part of he's not planning to stay here didn't you understand?" *If I can have these and the brownies for the rest of my life, I'm never leaving.* Gabriel's words came back to her. She knew he hadn't been serious, but her traitorous heart leaped at the prospect anyway.

"If it helps any, I think he's right there with you. And I think there's more going on between you than either of you realize. I saw the way he looked at you."

Serenity had seen it, too. Felt it as if he were touching her. Each moment they spent together chipped away at the layers over her heart and challenged her resolve, and she had no idea how to make it stop. Or even if she wanted to at this point.

CHAPTER 19

Wednesday, Serenity rushed down the hallway to the next examination room. They'd been back-to-back with patients since the doors opened that morning, most of them children and teens needing physical exams and vaccinations for the upcoming school year. She heard the crying before she turned the knob.

"Good morning, Mrs. Martin. Hello, Danielle." She smiled at the little girl cuddled into her mother's side. The girl's wary gaze met Serenity's, and she burrowed deeper. It was going to be a long day. Serenity spent more than ten minutes administering the vaccines Danielle would need to enter kindergarten. It might have taken less time if she hadn't had to calm the mother first.

When she finished, Serenity dated and marked the vaccination card and dropped the chart off. She made her way to the staff room and found Starr leaning back in a chair with her eyes closed. "Is everything okay, Starr?"

Starr rotated the chair in Serenity's direction. "I'm

worn out and it's only noon. Did I miss the sign that said today was kinder vaccination day or something? Because I can't believe how many of these kids have come in today. Shoot, I didn't even know we had that many kids living in this little town."

Serenity laughed and retrieved her purse from her locker. "I have to admit, I wondered the same thing a time or two this morning. I'm glad to be getting out of this office for a little while."

"Lunch date?"

"I'm meeting Natasha and Dana at Ms. Ida's."

"I haven't seen them in a few weeks. Tell them I said hello." Like Natasha and Dana, Starr had grown up in Firefly Lake.

"I will. Do you want me to bring you something back?"

"No, thanks. My husband is coming to have lunch with me."

"That's so sweet. He's still working at the hospital?" Serenity recalled Starr mentioning her husband being a respiratory therapist.

Starr smiled and nodded. "I have to admit he's a great guy, and I couldn't be happier."

"I'm sure you'll enjoy your lunch. See you in a while." Starr threw up a wave, and Serenity left. During her short walk, she thought about her co-worker's words. Hearing the love in Starr's voice, Serenity felt a pang of envy. She'd told herself she'd be okay going at it alone, that she didn't want a committed relationship or love, but now she wasn't so sure.

"Hi, Serenity." The hostess greeted her with a wide smile. "Table for one?"

"Not today, Norene. I'm meeting Dana and Natasha." She searched the restaurant and spotted them in the middle of the room. "I see them." She navigated through the tables, and responded to *hello*s as she passed. Serenity slid into the empty chair at her friends' table. "Hey. Have you been here long?"

"No," Natasha said. "But I went ahead and ordered you a shrimp Caesar salad because I know you're on a time limit."

"Thanks. It's been a madhouse."

Dana nodded. "School is about to start, and the garage has been crazy busy, too."

"I'd think that would be at the start of summer, not the end, since that's when people take vacations." Serenity took a few sips of water.

"Oh, it's hectic then, too."

Serenity turned to Natasha. "What about the real estate business?"

"Every season is busy, but for different reasons. Winter and fall tend to be a little cheaper because not many people sell during those months. It's the holidays, school has started, and parents don't particularly want to uproot the children, so it's probably a better time to buy for someone who's strapped for cash. In the spring and summer, it may be more expensive, but with the better weather, houses tend to show better. And those folks who couldn't sell in the winter are eager to get it done."

Serenity had no idea of all that went into the real estate market.

"I do have some good news," Natasha said excitedly.

"What?" Dana and Serenity said at the same time.

"A friend of mine asked me to be her interior designer. She said she'd be more than happy to provide referrals when I'm done."

Serenity's mouth fell open. "That's great, girl."

"It is," Dana agreed. "You've been wanting to do this for a long time. I'm glad you're finally getting a chance to put that degree to work."

Natasha nodded. "You and me both. If it works out, I'll think about doing it part-time."

The server returned with their food. They all thanked the young man and started in on the meal.

"This is good," Dana said, "but I really want more of those crab-stuffed shrimp wrapped in bacon. That's the first time you've done an all appetizer spread for our supper club meets. What made you decide on that?"

Serenity shrugged. "I just wanted to do something different. I'm thinking for the next one, a brunch menu for dinner—homemade waffles, bacon, smoked sausage, scrambled eggs, fruit, sautéed potatoes with peppers and onions, cinnamon rolls."

Natasha groaned. She glanced down at her salad, then at Serenity. "There is just something wrong about you sitting here talking about all that good food while we're having salads. I want *all* of that menu *now*." She shot Serenity a glare as she shoved a forkful of chef salad in her mouth.

Serenity almost choked on her water. "I'm sorry. I was just thinking out loud." Too late it dawned on her that she'd basically recited most of the same brunch menu she and Gabriel had shared. Images of their time together filled her mind—from cooking together and dancing in her kitchen to relaxing with full plates on the deck. It startled her to realize that he'd become an integral part of her beloved cooking. Only this time, there was no criticism. Just appreciation. Deciding not to dwell on it for now, she went back to her conversation. "I don't have anything planned for the next couple of weeks, so let me know when you want to do the next meetup."

"Tonight!" both Natasha and Dana said, bringing on another fit of laughter.

"Seriously though," Natasha said, "let's check with Terri first to see when she's off. She'd be too mad if she missed out." The three continued to eat for a few minutes, and then she asked, "Did Chandra and Mark get home safely?"

"They're not headed home until the weekend. Mark surprised her with a trip to Napa and San Francisco. They spent Monday and yesterday in Napa and are heading toward the Bay today." Serenity smiled remembering the shock on her sister's face. Rarely was someone able to pull one over on Chandra, and Serenity couldn't have been more excited for them. What moved Serenity most was Mark's words. *Baby, you work so hard helping everyone else find balance. This week I'm helping you find yours.* The kiss they'd shared after had been so filled with passion, Serenity had felt it clear across the room.

Dana sighed wistfully. "That is so wonderful. Does Mark have any brothers?"

"Two sisters," Serenity said with a chuckle. She'd wondered the same thing the first time she'd met Mark.

"Speaking of men, that was some serious heat you and Gabriel were generating on Saturday."

She pretended to focus on her salad and forked up a big bite. Silence rose, and she finally lifted her head, meeting Natasha's and Dana's expectant gazes. "Yeah, heat."

Natasha fanned herself. "Girl, with how close you two were dancing and the way he was staring at you, I fully expected him to kiss you right then and there."

"I know that's right," Dana said. "I don't know if I would've had the restraint you had, Serenity. I might've taken the decision out of his hands and kissed *him*."

Serenity's body tingled with the memory, and she laughed. "Believe me, I was tempted." The man put the *T* in temptation. She pushed away her nearly done salad and rubbed her temples. "This has gotten so out of control."

"It's hard *not* to be out of control with a man like Gabriel," Natasha said. "But that doesn't mean it's a bad thing. And based on everything I've seen, I think he feels the same. I know he's not planning to stay, but I really hope things work out between you two. You seem so happy, and it would be a shame to just give it up without giving the relationship a chance."

"I was happy before he came to town." *But you're happier now,* her inner voice countered. She wanted to refute it but couldn't. Serenity took a peek at her watch. "I need to head back and get ready for the afternoon crowd." She fished some bills out of her purse, put them on the table, and stood. She gave both women a brief hug. "I'll see you later."

"Okay," Natasha said. "And think about what I said."

"I will." She hurried out of the restaurant and started up the street at a brisk pace, putting all her musings aside. Her mind needed to be focused on her patients.

The afternoon proved to be as much of a whirlwind as the morning, and Serenity was more than ready to kick her feet up when she got home. Thankfully, she'd made some chicken salad last night and didn't have to worry about cooking dinner. As she pulled into her driveway, Gabriel was coming out of his house. By his attire, she figured he might be going for his daily run. He waited until she got out of the car and sauntered over.

"Hey, sweetheart. You look exhausted. Long day?"

She smiled tiredly. "Beyond."

Gabriel rubbed her arm. "Do you want me to bring you something for dinner? I was going over to the lake for a run, but I can throw something together real quick before I go."

Her heart melted. "Thank you for offering, but I've already got it covered."

"You sure?" When she nodded, he said, "Okay, but if you need anything, just call."

"I will." She leaned up and kissed him. Belatedly, she remembered she was standing in the middle of her driveway, giving a prime time viewing to Adele, who would no doubt be on speed dial with Gabriel's grandmother and anyone else who'd stand still long enough to listen.

"I'll check on you later." Gabriel blessed her with one of his knee-weakening smiles and strolled off toward his car.

Serenity felt the scales in her heart tilt a little further in his favor. The past two months with Gabriel had been amazing, and if she were being honest with herself, she didn't want it to end. And that was the crux of her problem because she knew it would end. And soon. Every time she considered asking for space, he did some thoughtful thing, like just now, that made her say, "One more day won't hurt." Except, in the end, it would hurt.

* * *

Thursday morning, the slip-slap of Gabriel's running shoes hit the pavement as he kept up a steady rhythm. As he jogged, he mentally went over his schedule for the rest of the day. He'd gotten up at seven and worked for three hours to finish his part of the note-taking app and decided to go for his run now to clear his head for the meeting with Darius and Brent at noon. They had originally planned to meet on Tuesday but had to postpone it until today due to Brent needing to take care of some personal business. After his meeting, he'd work for another four or five hours, then go grocery shopping.

His thoughts shifted to Serenity, and he wondered how her day was going and whether it would be as tiring. He'd called to check on her last night, as promised, but they spoke only briefly because she was already in bed, despite it being before ten. Gabriel increased his speed until he reached a fast sprint and kept up the pace for the next few minutes. He slowed, reversed his course, and went back the way he came. When he got to his car, he took a moment to cool down and drink the bottle of water he'd brought before sliding behind the wheel and driving home.

Gabriel showered, ate a bowl of fruit, and downed a protein shake, then booted up his computer and clicked on the videoconference link. While waiting for his friends to log on, he made a few more notes on the new video game he and Darius would be starting on next.

"What's up, G?" Brent said.

He moved back to the screen. "Hey. Everything okay with your dad?"

"Yeah. It turned out to be heartburn, not a heart attack, thank goodness. Mom was freaking out, and I had a hell of a time trying to keep her calm. She kept saying he couldn't leave her here alone. Man, these have been the longest two days of my life." He ran a hand over his head. "They're both okay, so I'm relieved."

"I'm glad to hear it. Tell them I said hello." Brent's parents had been married for over forty years and were still passionately in love. He could imagine how hard the loss of one would be for the other. Had his own parents lived, Gabriel knew they'd be the same. They'd never hid their love from him and Andrea, and it wasn't uncommon to see their parents sharing a kiss, a tender touch, or a dance, even though no music would be playing. Gabriel had yet to experience that kind of deep love. An image of Serenity flashed in his mind, along with them dancing in her kitchen. He had done his best to remain detached, but somehow she'd worked her way into his psyche and was inching toward his heart. "Where's Darius?" he asked, shifting back into work mode.

"He's finishing a call."

As soon as the words left Brent's mouth, Darius appeared on the screen. "Sorry. Hey, Gabe. Did you guys start yet?"

Brent shook his head. "I was just giving Gabe an update on my parents. I'll start with the business and then leave you two to talk." He went over the company's financials and projected income. Because of the last two projects, the firm was solid so far, which made them all breathe easier. "Darius mentioned that you two are pretty much finished with the note-taking app."

"We're going to do a practice run once you're done," Gabriel said. "You staying on to see it?"

"You'd better believe it. With all the elements you two included, we should have no problems launching it. Actually, I'm done, so go ahead."

Darius chuckled. "Eager?"

"I'm eager for anything that's going to make us some money."

"True that," Gabriel said. He clicked a few keys, activated the share screen option, and launched the program. His excitement grew with each passing moment. He typed a test sentence on the page. "The beauty of this app is that the notes can be accessed by multiple people if necessary."

"This is fabulous," Brent said. "Will they have to access it from their computer or laptop only?"

Darius shook his head. "It should work across all platforms. I'm going to log on from my phone."

A minute later, Darius's words flew across the screen. Gabriel hit the "share" button and sent it as an email. "Brent, I just sent the note to your email. Let me know if you get it."

"It came before you finished your sentence. Is this the final version, or do you think you'll need to tweak some things?"

"I think it's as close to finished as we want," Darius answered. "We'll play around with it for a couple of days to see if there are still any bugs to be worked out."

"Sounds good. I'm going to start working on a marketing angle. Can you send me all the specs?"

"I'll bring it to your office when Gabe and I are done."

"Thanks. Anything else you need from me before I log off?"

Gabriel and Darius had nothing else for him.

"Okay. See you in a bit, D. Oh, before I go, how is the relationship with Serenity going, G?"

Gabriel should've known he wouldn't be able to conduct the call without one question. "It's fine."

"Fine, as in it's no big deal, just a friends with benefits kind of thing, or fine, as in you finally realize you really like her and she has potential for something more?"

As much as he wanted to say it was the former, he was marching toward the latter and couldn't do a thing about it. "I don't know."

A slow grin spread across Brent's face, as if he didn't believe that lie any more than Gabriel did. "Whatever you say."

Darius shook his head. "I told him he should think about staying a little longer to decide, especially since Nana said she wasn't moving. Period."

Gabriel sighed. "In case you forgot, we have a company to run. In Atlanta."

"True," Brent said. "And we've been running it just fine these past two months. It'll continue to be that way, regardless of location. The last time I checked, technology is pretty advanced that way. By the way, you said you didn't know whether the relationship had the potential for more, but everything you've done with her points to exactly that. See you later." And he was gone.

Gabriel shot Darius a dark glare.

"Don't look at me like that. You know I'm right, bro. Glenn did the same thing when he was fighting falling in love with Toya. You see how that turned out."

Not wanting to dive into his muddled emotions or the fact that Brent had been correct in his assessment, he changed the subject. "I made some notes on the new video game."

Darius laughed. "Okay, I can take a hint. Whatcha got?"

For the next two hours, they discussed the game that would take place on an island where a player tried to reach a safe zone. The beauty of the game would be that each time a person logged on, they'd have a different and new experience. No two games would be the same.

"I like this. We can vary the experiences from fun to survival. Since it's on an island, we can include pirates and jungle animals." Darius angled his head thoughtfully. "I'll see what else I can come up with. When do you want to start?"

"A couple of weeks maybe. That'll give us time to figure out all the specs. And I wanted to get started on the kids game." Gabriel noted the time. It was already after three, and he'd planned to start writing the codes for the children's educational game. He thought about Brianna and wondered if it would be something the little girl would like.

"What are you smiling about?"

He hadn't realized he was smiling. "I was just thinking about a little girl I met, Brianna. She's one of Serenity's patients she's known since birth. She invited me to a tea party."

Darius threw back his head and roared with laughter. "Are you going?"

"Who knows. I haven't received an official invitation yet. And I'm not sure I can see myself sitting at a little table sipping tea out of one of those kiddie plastic teacups."

"Me, either. I'm glad it's you and not me."

"Anyway, I'm going to get started. I need to run to the grocery store later. If you think of anything, let me know."

"Will do."

They ended the meeting, and Gabriel stood to stretch. He also wanted to see Serenity but knew if he'd divulged that information, he would've had to endure more teasing. He picked up his phone to send her a text: *Dinner is on me tonight. Just come on over whenever you're ready.* Potential for more? Yeah. Maybe. He felt like a car careening down a hill with no brakes. He'd never met a woman like her and he suspected he never would.

CHAPTER 20

After the long week, Serenity was glad to see the weekend. She, Natasha, and Terri had piled into Dana's car, and the four of them drove to Napa for a mini spa day. After full-body massages, they sat in chairs clothed in robes while enjoying manicures and pedicures.

She sighed in pleasure. "I so needed this."

"So did I," Terri said. "The ER has been crazy these past three weeks. A couple of nurses called out, and I had to put in far more hours than I wanted."

"That's exactly why I'm glad to be out of the hospital."

"If it keeps going this way, I may look into something similar. Between my erratic shifts and Jon working on this big case at the law firm, I doubt we've seen each other more than three hours this *week*."

"That's not good," Dana said. "How long have you guys been married?"

"Four years."

Natasha leaned forward. "You two are still newly-weds."

"Close. I just hope our schedules level out. I miss spending time with my husband."

"Terri, I'll keep an eye out in the office and let you know if something opens up."

"Thanks, Serenity."

The conversation turned to the changing season and them taking a trip up to Apple Hill. The area had several orchards—some where you could pick your own apples—and wineries. Serenity said, "I can't wait. Those apples are so good, and I'm looking forward to making pies and apple bread and stocking up on my cider."

"Oh, that apple bread is so good," Dana said. "Last year, I ate that entire loaf in less than a week, and I think I gained five pounds."

Natasha waved a hand. "Same, girl. Oh, I almost forgot—Terri, the next supper club is going to be brunch for dinner. Serenity's making waffles."

Terri whipped her head in Serenity's direction. "From scratch?"

"Of course."

"If I'm on the schedule for next weekend, I might have to be the one calling out." They all laughed, and she said, "Y'all think I'm playing. I love waffles, and I'm not missing out on those."

"You do know we'll plan it around your schedule," Serenity said.

"Mm-hmm, and my schedule says I need those waffles sooner rather than later."

Serenity shook her head. "Well, since it won't be today, are we going to get a late lunch somewhere around here or wait until we get home?"

"Since it's already close to two, I vote for eating here," Dana said.

"Ditto," Terri said.

Serenity looked at Natasha.

"You already know my vote. I'm not in a hurry to go back."

"Napa it is." They finished their treatments, dressed, and sat in the locker room to Google nearby restaurants.

"I've been eating good all week, and I really want a juicy hamburger," Natasha said.

Serenity scrolled to one of the listed spots. "This place serves burgers. They also have salads and sandwiches."

"Sold."

They drove the short distance to the restaurant and were seated almost immediately. While Natasha and Terri got their burgers, Serenity and Dana opted for the crispy teriyaki chicken sandwich.

"Are you and Gabriel hanging out tonight?" Dana asked Serenity.

"We're probably just going to have a movie night at home." She enjoyed those times with just the two of them snuggled close and stuffing their faces with popcorn. She'd never been able to do that with her ex because he saw it as a waste of time. He'd preferred being surrounded by people. Even when they did dine out, somehow he always saw someone he knew and had occasionally invited the person to join them, not caring about the fact that it was supposed to be a date. Gabriel was so different, and in a good way. She had finally been able to experience all the things she'd seen her parents and Chandra and Mark do.

"Movie night sounds like fun."

"It's nice to just chill every now and again. He's choosing the movie this time, so I have no idea what we're watching."

Natasha lifted a hand. "Hold up, missy. *This time?* As in you already had a movie night and didn't tell us?"

She felt her cheeks warm, remembering those amazing kisses they'd shared. Serenity waved her friend off. "It was a few weeks ago. We just watched *The Shawshank Redemption.*" The server returned at that moment with their food, saving her from further explanation.

"Oh my goodness. This hits the spot." Natasha closed her eyes and groaned as she chewed the first bite of her food.

"This chicken teriyaki sandwich isn't too bad, either," Dana said.

Serenity agreed. She hadn't taken more than three bites when her cell rang. She wiped her hands on a napkin and fished the phone out of her jean shorts pocket, smiling when she saw Pam's number. "Hey, Pam."

"Hi, Serenity. It's Bri."

She could tell that Bri had been crying. The hairs on the back of Serenity's neck stood up. "What's going on, Bri? Is Pam okay?"

"It's not Pam. It's…Brianna," Bri said haltingly. "She fell off the slide, hit her head, and is still unconscious."

"No," Serenity whispered. She didn't realize she was on her feet until Natasha touched her hand. "What are the doctors saying?"

"Not much yet. We're still in the emergency room, and they're running tests. Pam and Reggie are devastated. We all are." Her voice cracked. "But Pam wanted me to let you know."

She felt her own emotions rise and tried to keep her voice steady. "Thanks for calling. I'm in Napa, but I'll be there as soon as I can."

"Thanks, Serenity."

Serenity ended the call and slowly dropped back into the chair. "Brianna fell off a slide and hit her head. It's serious."

"Then we need to get on the road," Terri said. "We all know how much that little girl means to you. And her family adores you."

Dana had already asked for to-go boxes and settled the bill while Serenity was on the phone. The ride back was done in almost complete silence, and Serenity prayed the entire way.

"Serenity, I'm going to go straight to the hospital," Dana said when they reached the town limits.

"Thanks, Dana." By the time they pulled into the hospital lot, Serenity was a bundle of nerves. She was out of the car before Dana came to a complete stop. "I'm sorry our day got cut short." She could barely hold it together.

"Don't worry about any of that," Natasha said, stepping out and hugging Serenity. "Just call when you're ready for us to pick you up."

She nodded.

Terri got out. "I'm going in with Serenity to see if I can find anything out. I'll call Jon and ask him to come get me."

Serenity and Terri rushed inside and straight to the emergency department. She frantically searched and spotted Bri on the far side of the already crowded room. Bri saw her at the same time and met Serenity halfway. They shared a tight hug. "How are you holding up?" Bri's eyes were red and puffy.

"Barely. We still don't know anything. Hey, Terri."

Terri hugged Bri. "I'm so sorry about Brianna. I'm going to go back and see what I can find out. It may not be anything yet, but I'll let you know as soon as I can."

"Thanks."

Serenity led Bri back over to where she'd been sitting. "Where are Pam and Reggie?"

"They came out about fifteen minutes ago and said they were going down to the coffee shop."

The two women sat, not talking, both lost in their own thoughts. Several minutes later, she spotted Pam the moment she entered the waiting room and crossed the room in a flash.

"Serenity." Pam engulfed Serenity in a hug as she sobbed. "My baby, my baby."

It was all Serenity could do not to break down. Hearing her friend crying broke her heart. She held on and murmured that Brianna would be okay, but she didn't know who she was trying to convince more. At length, she eased back and noticed Reggie off to the side. She embraced him, too.

"Thanks for being here, Serenity."

"You know I wouldn't be anywhere else."

Terri came back after about fifteen minutes, but she didn't have any news. She sat next to Serenity. "I can stay with you, if you want."

"No. You need to go home to your husband and try to get a few of those minutes in," she added with a small smile.

"All right, but call me if you need me to come back."

"I will. I promise." She watched Terri disappear around the corner with her phone to her ear, then resumed the wait. She hoped it was nothing more serious than a slight concussion and a few bruises. Serenity wanted to ask what happened, but the family was so distraught at the moment, she didn't dare. It took another hour before the doctor came out. Along with a broken arm and bruises, Brianna had a concussion. She had awakened briefly, and he considered that a good sign. They were keeping her in the hospital, and the family could visit once Brianna was moved to a room.

By the time they were allowed to visit, another two hours had passed and the sun had begun to set. Serenity had planned to get the update from Pam once she'd seen her daughter, but Pam insisted Serenity accompany them to the room. At the first sight of Brianna lying so still in the big bed, the tears she'd held back all day finally broke free. Serenity swiped at them and fought to keep her composure. When Pam gestured her forward, Serenity ran a careful hand over the little girl's face and placed a soft kiss on her forehead. "You're going to be okay, sweetie. You have to get well for our tea party." The last words were choked out by her tears. She faced Pam and Reggie. "I'm going to go so you can spend time with her. Please let me know if anything changes or if you need me to come back."

Pam nodded.

Serenity hugged them both and gave their hands a squeeze of encouragement, then slipped out quietly. She successfully made it to the bathroom before breaking down completely. When she emerged several minutes later, Gabriel was leaning on the opposite wall. He didn't say anything, just opened his arms. Without thinking, she flew into them and buried her face in his chest. The tears started again, and he held her. She needed this. No other man, outside of her father, had made her feel safe and comforted.

"How is she?" Gabriel asked.

"Still not awake, and it's pretty serious. She has

a broken arm, bruises, and a concussion." The tears welled in her eyes again.

"She's going to come through this." He kissed her temple. "Come on, baby. Let me take you home."

She wiped her face with the tissue she'd gotten from the bathroom. "How did you know I was here?"

"Jon and I met up for a run, and I was there when Terri called. I told her to tell Dana and Natasha that I'd pick you up so they wouldn't worry."

Serenity stared up at his concerned features in wonder and lost her heart completely. How could she not love this caring man?

* * *

Gabriel parked in his driveway and led Serenity into his house. He could have just as easily walked her over to hers, but for some reason, he wanted her close. Brianna meant a lot to her, and this couldn't be easy. He'd only met the bubbly little girl once and had been taken in by her sweet smile, so he could imagine what Serenity was going through right now.

He sat in the oversize recliner and pulled her onto his lap. She laid her head on his shoulder and released a deep sigh. Her stomach growled softly. "When was the last time you ate?"

"This morning. We had just started lunch when I got the call."

It was nearly eight, and she had to be starving. "I'll fix you something. Is there anything in particular you want?"

Serenity sat up. "Not really. I don't have an appetite at the moment."

"I know, but you can't take care of anyone else unless you take care of yourself." Gabriel caressed her face and kissed her softly. "I made shrimp and pasta in a white wine and butter sauce for dinner. How about a little of that?"

"Okay."

He eased her off his lap and onto the chair, then stood and headed for the kitchen. Taking down a plate, he dished up a small portion of the pasta and heated it in the microwave. When it was done, Gabriel put it, along with a glass of wine for each of them, on a tray and carried it to her.

His heart constricted at the sight of her curled up in the chair. Suddenly, Brent's words came rushing back: *You said you didn't know whether the relationship had the potential for more, but everything you've done with her points to exactly that.* The knowledge that his friend was right slammed into him and weakened his knees. Gabriel hadn't hesitated to volunteer to pick Serenity up from the hospital—more like he'd insisted on it. Those weren't the actions of a man involved in a fling. Neither was cooking for her or going out of his way to find tickets to a concert because she mentioned liking an artist. In fact, every single thing he'd done indicated that this was more. *She* was more. And the voice that had been whispering in his head for the past couple of weeks that extending his time would be a good thing kept getting louder.

As if sensing his presence, Serenity sat up and smiled at him. "That smells good."

He placed the tray over her lap and picked up his glass. "Can I get you anything else?"

"No, thank you." She took a sip of the wine. "I know we're supposed to have our movie night, but..."

"We'll do it another time." He'd been looking forward to snuggling up with her while they watched the movie and enjoyed some snacks, but he understood.

Her face transformed as she ate, softening as a smile curved her lips. "This is wonderful, Gabriel."

"Thanks." He sat back, sipped his wine, and silently contemplated what made her different from all the other women he'd dated. It all came back to one word: everything. From her giving spirit, confidence, and intelligence to her engaging smile, sense of humor, and authenticity—she had never wavered from who he thought her to be—she'd captured him totally. Gabriel didn't even need to think about how much they had in common, especially food and music. Those things added icing on top of a decadent cake. "All done?" he asked when he noticed her empty plate. Placing his glass on the end table, he stood and reached for the tray. "Would you like anything else?"

"Yes. I'd like for you to hold me again."

Her simple request shouldn't have pleased him so much, but it did. "I can do that. Let me put this away, and I'll be right back." Gabriel left and returned quickly. After turning on some soft music, he lowered himself onto the recliner and shifted her until she sat on his lap, adjusting her until she was comfortable. He pushed the side button to lift the leg rest and didn't try to initiate any conversation. Gabriel simply wrapped her in the shelter of his arms. He didn't know how long they'd been sitting when he heard a phone buzz.

"I think that's my phone." Serenity sat up and grabbed her purse off the end table. She dug it out and answered. "Hey, Pam. How's our girl?" She didn't say anything for a few seconds, then whispered, "Thank goodness. I know you and Reggie are relieved. I'll stop by tomorrow for a few minutes, and I appreciate you calling." She disconnected. "Brianna woke up for a longer time and spoke briefly."

"That's good news." Gabriel smiled and dropped a kiss on her lips.

"It is." Serenity ran her hand up his chest and around his neck, then kissed him. "Thank you for being here. It means a lot."

"I didn't want to be anywhere else." The words were out before he could stop them, but they were the truth.

"Gabriel," she whispered, pulling his head down for another kiss.

What started as gentle changed in intensity to *hot* in the blink of an eye. Hearing his name whispered from her lips spiked his arousal. Her mouth parted slightly, and his tongue found hers. He removed the band from her hair, and her braids cascaded around her face. He fisted his hands in her hair and crushed his mouth against hers, plunging deep, swirling and feasting on the sweetness like a starved man. His hands roamed down her back, over her hips, and found their way to the silken flesh of her thighs and curvy bottom. He slid a hand beneath her top and skimmed a thumb over her breasts. She trembled beneath his touch, fueling his passion, and the kiss intensified. Her hands came up to stroke the nape of his neck, and he groaned deep in his throat. Gabriel had only planned to be here for her tonight, but the way she was making him feel negated any chance of the quiet, relaxing night he'd envisioned. "Serenity."

"I don't want you to talk, Gabriel."

He lifted his head, and their gazes locked. "What do you want?"

"You. Tonight, I just want you."

Gabriel hit the side button, lowered the chair, and with her in his arms, strode purposefully down the hallway to his bedroom. He placed her in the center of his bed and followed her down. The rapturous expression on her face combined with the sensual picture she made lying on his bed almost pushed him over the edge right then and there, and he had to close his eyes to steady himself. At that moment, he'd never wanted another woman more. Slowly, methodically, he stripped away each piece of her clothing, kissing and licking his way down her body, and was rewarded with her passionate cries.

Serenity pushed his shirt up and over his head, tossing it aside. She trailed her hot tongue as she went, sending sharp jolts of electricity straight to his groin.

Too impatient to wait, Gabriel stood, kicked off his shoes, and removed his slacks and briefs in one smooth motion. He searched for and found the condoms in his drawer, tore one off and tossed the others on the nightstand. After rolling it on, he crawled onto the bed and lowered himself onto her. He shuddered from the pleasure of feeling their bodies skin to skin. He kissed her with a hunger that both excited and frightened him, and she returned his kiss, giving as good as she got. He kissed his way down to her beautifully formed breasts and captured a chocolate-tipped nipple between his lips. He laved and suckled first one, then the other, charted a path down the front of her body with his hand and slid two fingers into her slick, wet heat until she was writhing and moaning beneath him.

Serenity let out a loud moan, then leaned up and skated her tongue over his jaw, neck, and shoulder.

Unable to wait any longer, he eased inside, inch by inch until he was fully embedded. He withdrew to the tip and thrust again, repeating the action several times. A tremor raced through his body.

"More, Gabriel," she begged.

Gripping her buttocks in his hands, he stroked deeper and harder, giving her everything she asked for. Her body trembled around him, and her inner muscles clenched him, almost snapping his restraint. You feel so good, baby," he whispered against her lips.

"Mmm. So do you."

He closed his eyes and let the sensations take over as he kept up the pace.

She wrapped her legs around his waist and pulled his mouth down on hers, their tongues tangling and dancing.

Their breathing grew ragged and sweat broke out on his body as she arched up to meet him stroke for stroke. It felt so good being inside her. He could feel his orgasm building and knew he wouldn't last much longer. Gabriel drove into her until she cried out wildly, her inner walls contracting around him. Pleasure ripped through him with an intensity that almost blew his head off, and he yelled her name. His eyes slid closed, he groaned her name again, shuddering above her as the spasms racked his body. She reached up and stroked the sides of his face. He opened his eyes, and when their eyes connected, he felt it again—that tug on his heart. Gabriel could no longer deny what it had been telling him. He loved her.

* * *

The following Tuesday, during her lunch, Serenity drove over to the hospital to see Brianna and was pleased to learn the little girl would be able to go home the next day. Serenity stayed longer than she'd planned and made it back to the office with five minutes to spare. With back-to-back patients, she kept busy, but Gabriel was never far from her mind. He'd stayed there for the rest of that day, all through the evening, and when she went to bed later that night.

Now, tonight as she lay in bed, she reflected on how different he was from her ex.

With Lloyd, everything had been fine so long as she fit neatly into the space he'd carved out for her in his life. And as a doctor, he had never been very sympathetic or held her when she lost a patient. She could still hear his caustic words. *This is a hospital, and sometimes people die. You can't afford to be upset and crying every time one does. So toughen up, accept it, and move on.* And in hindsight, she recognized that she'd settled for being Lloyd's entertainment hostess, instead of holding out for the love she deserved. But Gabriel had done just the opposite, providing the solace she'd needed. The contentment she'd felt in his arms was unlike anything she'd ever experienced.

She glanced over at the clock and sighed. *I need to go to sleep.* Shifting to a more comfortable position, she closed her eyes. As soon as she did, Gabriel's handsome face appeared in her mind, and memories of their lovemaking awakened her desires once more. She wanted to call him, ask him to come over and put out the flame he'd started. Despite her best efforts, Serenity had fallen in love with him. How could she not? A part of her wanted to hope he felt something for her, as well, and that, maybe, what they had didn't have to end.

CHAPTER 21

After finally admitting to himself that he'd fallen in love with Serenity, Gabriel had gone back to working fourteen- and sixteen-hour days. The emotions she evoked in him were stronger and deeper than he'd felt with any other woman he'd dated, including his ex, and it scared him. He feared that if he put his heart on the line again, he would come away with it broken into little pieces. So he did what he did best—work. Aside from the two short visits with Brianna and his daily run, he'd stayed in. Running into Serenity at the hospital during one of his visits yesterday had made things worse because all he'd wanted to do was wrap her in his arms forever. The word *forever* and a woman had never been used by him in a sentence at the same time. Yet, with her, he'd begun to want it.

He hadn't been able to cut off communication completely and had sent her texts to make sure she was okay. His friends' suggestion to extend his time played over in his head like a refrain from a song. But what would happen after that extra month or two? Sure, he'd warmed to the town, but could he live in Firefly Lake permanently? Or would he grow tired of it after a while? And if he did, what would happen to his relationship with Serenity? The questions bombarded his mind, and he squeezed his eyes shut to try to block them out. However, they kept coming, demanding answers he didn't have. The only things he knew for sure were that he didn't want to spend weeks or months away from Serenity and that his heart had been steadily opening to the possibility of staying.

For the rest of the week, Gabriel kept up the grueling pace, but no matter how hard he worked, he couldn't outrun his feelings. And outside of a couple of brief text messages, he'd stopped answering Darius's and Brent's calls, not wanting to answer their questions, either. By Friday, he couldn't take it anymore. His friends would probably laugh themselves silly if they knew he was running around acting like a lovesick fool. At the moment, he'd accept the name because he *had* to see her, kiss her.

Thirty minutes later, he stood on her doorstep, ringing the bell.

"Gabriel, hi," Serenity said when she opened the door.

For a moment, Gabriel could only stare. He didn't understand why this one woman got to him. Today she wore a low-cut tank top and shorts that showcased her beautiful body. She'd left her hair down, and her braids swirled around her face and down her back. The memory of his hands fisted in the mass as he feasted on her mouth appeared in his mind, and he fought back the urge for a repeat.

She folded her arms, an amused expression on her face. "Are you going to say something, or stand there staring all day? This isn't the first time you've seen me wearing shorts."

He dropped his head and chuckled. "Sorry. Hi. Can I come in for a minute?"

She unlocked the screen and held it open. "What's up?"

When Gabriel passed, his body brushed against hers, and the contact sent heat thrumming through him. "I just wanted to see you. I missed hanging out with you."

Serenity stared up at him, seemingly contemplating his words, then said softly, "I missed you, too."

He'd planned to broach the subject of them maybe continuing to see each other once he returned home, but the words got stuck in his throat. Instead he asked, "Are you busy right now?"

"Well, I was about to change clothes and go to Ms. Ida's for a late dinner."

"Would you like some company?" He observed the play of emotions on her face and knew she was probably thinking about them being seen together. Outside the trip to the ice cream parlor, they still hadn't done anything in town. Since he'd been in town for almost three months and Adele had pretty much put out a news bulletin every time she saw the two of them, he figured they should be old news by now.

"Sure. Give me a few while I change."

"I'll wait here."

She nodded. "I won't be long."

Gabriel crossed the living room and sat on the love seat. His phone buzzed, and he sighed when he saw a message from Darius: *You okay, bro? We're worried about you.* He sent back a short reply and hoped it would be enough to appease him: *Fine. Just focused on the program.* He breathed a sigh of relief when no other message came through. Serenity returned a minute later, and he swiftly came to his feet. She'd changed into a sleeveless V-neck top, a pair of crop pants, and wedge-heeled sandals.

"I'm ready."

"Have you seen Brianna?" he asked once they were on the road.

"I went by yesterday, and she is steadily improving and getting back to her old self. Her mom is having a time keeping her from jumping around so much."

Gabriel laughed. "Yeah, I don't know any six year-olds who understand the definition of 'slow down,' 'stop running,' or 'be still.'"

Serenity joined his laughter. "Exactly."

He grasped her hand. "I'm really glad she's doing well. I know how hard it was on you to see her hurt. I remember you saying you've known her from birth."

"Yes. I'd only been here three weeks and was working in the ER at the hospital. I helped deliver her right in the back seat of her parents' car. We didn't even have time to get her in the door before Brianna came into the world."

"No wonder you're so close to her family." It also explained why she always got invited to family gatherings and had been on the call list when Brianna was injured. Gabriel turned onto the street and found parking a few doors down from the restaurant.

"This is rare for a Friday night," Serenity said. "But it's past the dinner rush, so hopefully, it won't be crowded. I'm starving."

He got out of the car and came around to help her. "You haven't eaten today? It's almost eight o'clock."

"Not since about noon, and I only had a boiled egg and half a banana."

He shook his head.

"What? I had another long day, and then I got caught up reading this mystery thriller when I came home and forgot to eat." She rolled her eyes playfully. "Don't act like you don't ever skip meals when you're on that computer working on some video game or program."

Gabriel didn't say a word, especially since he'd skipped more meals this past week than he had the entire time he'd been in town. The balance he worked hard to achieve had been thrown out the window, and he'd reverted to his old ways.

"Mm-hmm, that's what I thought," she said with a chuckle.

He opened the door and gestured her forward first.

"Table for two?" the hostess asked.

"Yes." The phrase "table for two" summed up everything good about his relationship with Serenity. In his mind, the times they spent with just the two of them around their love of food had been perfect.

She led them to a booth near the back and handed them menus. "Your server will be with you shortly. Enjoy."

"Thanks." Gabriel had dined there enough that he had a few favorites and already knew what he wanted to order. "Do you know what you're getting?"

"I thought I did," Serenity murmured. "But now that I'm looking at the menu, I want some of everything. What do you have a taste for?" she asked, not looking up.

"Besides you? I'm having the fried catfish, macaroni and cheese, and green beans, with cornbread."

Her head came up sharply and her eyes widened. She quickly glanced around, as if trying to determine whether anyone had heard him.

"You asked," he said with a lazy grin.

"You know I meant the food. What am I going to do with you?"

Chuckling, he said, "Another loaded question." He'd been asking himself the same thing about her and was afraid to hope for what he wanted.

"I think I'll have the gumbo and sweet tea."

He leaned forward and said softly, "And have you decided what you're going to do with me?"

"I'm not answering that question."

She didn't have to say a word. Her eyes told him everything he needed to know—passion, desire—it was all there, tempting him beyond reason. He hadn't expected to fall for his sexy neighbor, but he couldn't help it. The server came and took their drink and food order. Once the young man departed, he asked Serenity, "What does your weekend look like?"

"Nothing exciting. I'll probably catch up on my cleaning and laundry. What about you?"

"Probably spend it working, unless you save me. We never got around to our movie night."

Eyes sparkling, Serenity said, "Well, since I'm such a good neighbor, I'll help you out. As long as the movie you pick isn't one of those gory horror movies," she added with a shudder.

Gabriel laughed and waited until the server placed the drinks on the table and walked away before continuing the conversation. "No horror. Since you mentioned being a Marvel fan, I figured we'd watch *Endgame* and I can still have the action movie I want."

"Count me in. If you had said *Infinity Wars*, we would've had to start early so I could watch both. There's no way I'd be able to sleep unless I got the resolution."

He'd seen the movie and remembered the outcries in the theater at the end. "I'm glad I could help." Although, the prospect of them watching a double feature that would last almost six hours sounded good to him. As he'd told her earlier, they needed to maximize the time they had left.

When the food arrived, Serenity let out a soft moan after the first bite. "Mmm, so, so good."

He smiled and started in on his food, loving that her appreciation of good food mirrored his. They'd been eating and laughing for a few minutes when a woman he'd never seen came over to the table.

"Well, hello, Serenity." She divided a speculative glance between Serenity and Gabriel.

"Hi, Mrs. Satterfield."

"Who's this handsome young man?"

"This is Ms. Della's grandson, Gabriel."

"How are you, Mrs. Satterfield?"

"Doing well for an old woman," she answered with a huge grin.

Gabriel chanced a glance at Serenity and saw her roll her eyes. He sensed her rising irritation.

"You two make—"

"Um…Mrs. Satterfield, we don't want our food to get cold," Serenity cut in.

"Oh, yes, yes. You're right. Enjoy your dinner, and it was nice to finally meet you, Gabriel."

"Nice to meet you, too, ma'am." The woman stood there a moment longer, as if she wanted to say something else, then strutted off. "You okay, sweetheart?"

"Yeah. That woman is always in somebody's business."

Wanting to reclaim their relaxed camaraderie, he said, "Look on the bright side: she's not as bad as Adele, and we won't have to worry about her sitting in the window."

A small smile peeked out. "I guess." The tension lining her features lessened, and she went back to eating.

A few minutes later, a second person wandered over to ask about them dating and commented on what a nice couple they made. Shortly after, a third person stopped by. Each time, Gabriel felt her withdraw more, and the nice dinner he'd hoped to have had been shot to hell. Serenity left half her food on the plate, and his appetite had waned considerably, so he had the remainder boxed up to go. By the time they made it back to her place, she had all but shut down.

At the door, Serenity said, "Thanks for dinner."

"Anytime. I'm sorry about all the interruptions."

"It wasn't your fault. I guess that's the price we pay for living in a small town. You want to come in for a few minutes?"

"Sure." Gabriel followed her to the kitchen, where she placed her leftovers in the refrigerator, then to the family room. He placed his container on the end table and sat next to Serenity on the sofa.

After turning on some music, Serenity scooted close to Gabriel and rested her head on his shoulder. They sat in companionable silence for a while, and then she asked, "Do you plan to come back and visit once you return to Atlanta?"

The question threw him a little because he didn't know where the conversation was going. "Yes. Nana was adamant about not moving, so I'll be in and out to check on her. Why?"

"I know you're planning to leave soon, and we said what we have would end. But I was wondering about us...I mean...I like hanging out with you and thought maybe we could still see each other."

Gabriel sat up, his heart pounding. *Is she saying what I think she's saying?* He studied her for a lengthy moment. "You mean like a long-distance relationship?"

"I guess. But you don't have to answer right now." She shrugged. "It's just something to think about."

Not that he could. She'd rendered him speechless. He'd been afraid to hope for this very thing, and his emotions swelled with the prospect that they might be on the same page. He also understood how hard it was for her to even make the suggestion, particularly after seeing how uncomfortable she'd been with all the townspeople stopping by their table, knowing what happened with her ex and wondering if the outcome would be the same with them. "Serenity—"

Serenity shook her head and stood. "Just think about it."

Not wanting to make her uneasy and hoping she hadn't changed her mind, he just nodded, grabbed his food, and started for the front door. Once there, Gabriel covered her mouth in a gentle kiss. "Get some rest, and I'll call you tomorrow about a time for the movie. We can talk more then."

"Okay. Good night." She closed the door softly.

Sighing, he shoved his hand in a pocket and headed home. He had a lot to think about and sat up most of the night agonizing over what he should do. It had taken his mind a while to get on board with what his heart had been telling him, and the sun had already made its ascent into the sky when he finally admitted what he wanted. Serenity. Only her. With an exhausted smile, he fell across the bed and was asleep before his head hit the pillow.

Saturday morning, Gabriel jerked upright in bed at the sound of pounding on his front door, followed by the incessant ringing of his doorbell. Bleary-eyed, he checked the time and saw that it was nine. He'd gone to bed only two hours earlier. Groaning and flipping the covers back, he got up, pulled on a pair of basketball shorts, and stumbled toward the front door, preparing to give whoever was banging on it a piece of his mind if it wasn't an emergency. He snatched the door open.

"What the—"

"You look like hell."

He muttered a curse and glared at Darius. *I do not need this today.* "What are you two doing here?"

Brent pushed past Gabriel and entered the house, with Darius following. "You stopped answering our calls and texts," Brent said, as if that explained everything.

"I responded to Darius's text yesterday."

Darius grunted. "You mean that sorry-ass response you sent?" He sprawled out on the sofa. "And you can dial down the glare, bro. Might as well make yourself comfortable and tell us what's going on."

"Because we're not leaving without answers. *Real* answers," Brent emphasized as he sat on a chair. "Glenn couldn't make it because his parents are flying in today, but he said he might call later."

The three men engaged in a stare down until Gabriel relented and flopped onto the sofa at the opposite end from Darius. He leaned his head back and closed his eyes.

"The last time you did this was after the mess with Christine, so I assume things aren't going well with Serenity."

His jaw clenched at the mention of his ex. Darius had always been the most outspoken of the four friends, so it didn't surprise Gabriel that he'd be the first to speak. He cracked an eye open. "Things are fine between us." Or they would be once he talked to her.

Brent leaned forward, braced his forearms on his thighs, and clasped his hands together. "Then help us out, G. What's going on? You haven't been talking to us, and you look like you haven't slept in a week."

Darius held up a hand. "If this is going to take long, we need to do it over food. That bagel and coffee I had earlier is gone." He studied Gabriel. "Yeah, I can see this will be a while."

Gabriel opened his mouth to suggest they go back to Ms. Ida's, since both his friends had enjoyed the food, but changed his mind. The last thing he wanted or needed was a repeat of last night. "Where do you want to go?"

"San Francisco. I figure we can hang for the next

couple of days. We don't leave until Tuesday morning." He must have seen the look on Gabriel's face because he added, "Unless you have other plans."

"Serenity and I are supposed to get together to watch a movie, but I'll call her and see if we can do it another time." He was disappointed, but these were his best friends, and they'd flown across the country to check on him, the same way he would have if he thought one of them was struggling with something. It was the least he could do.

CHAPTER 22

After the night she'd had, Serenity got up Saturday morning needing to put some distance between her and Firefly Lake and headed to Vacaville Outlets for some retail therapy. She stopped first at a café for breakfast and enjoyed an omelet filled with spinach, mushrooms, bell peppers, bacon, and cheese, along with some fruit, while reading the book she'd brought along.

Fortified for her shopping spree, she drove over to the mall and found a reasonably close parking spot. As she turned off the engine, her cell rang. Gabriel. Her hand hovered over the accept call button for a few seconds before deciding to let it go to voicemail. She'd thought about the way he'd pretty much frozen when she'd proposed them continuing to see each other and wondered for the millionth time if it would have been better for her to refuse that first date and keep her friends-only stance.

Dropping the phone in her purse, Serenity decided to put all thoughts of Gabriel aside and focus on her me time. Two hours later and smiling, she headed to her car loaded down with all her purchases.

Serenity felt much better by the time she returned, but hoped Gabriel wasn't home. Her heart rate kicked up when she saw his car, and she didn't relax until she was safely inside. Then she remembered their movie night date. She fished her phone out of her purse and listened to his message telling her that his friends had flown in unexpectedly and were taking him to San Francisco for the weekend and that he'd probably be flying to Atlanta afterward. She waited for him to continue. To say something, *anything* about them, but he didn't. He just ended it with a lame "I'll call you." The part of her that loved him and wanted to spend time with him was disappointed that he seemed to be running. The part that had warned her not to get close said, *I told you so.*

She did her laundry and tried to go back to her book but gave up after reading the same page three times. Needing to find her Zen zone, she decided to invite her friends over for an impromptu dinner. Serenity sent a text to all three women: *Hey, sisters. How about dinner tonight around six thirty?* The time frame would give her two hours to plan an easy menu, shop for what she needed, and cook. Before she could put the phone down, it buzzed twice.

Dana: *Girl, you know I'm there. I'll bring margaritas!*

Natasha: *Count me in. Since Dana beat me to the drinks, let me know what you need me to bring.*

Serenity smiled and typed back: *Margaritas are perfect, and don't worry about bringing anything, Tasha.*

She knew what she was going to do for dinner—a fajita bar with homemade guacamole, salsa, and tortilla chips. Going into the kitchen, she checked her ingredients and made a list on her phone's note app. Another text popped up as she typed.

Terri: *Ugh! Just started a shift, so can't make it.* 😣 *All I know is it better not be those waffles!*

Serenity chuckled and responded as she walked back to her bedroom: *No waffles. Promise.* 😊

Terri: *Whew! Gotta run. Have fun.*

After putting on her shoes and grabbing her purse and keys, she retraced her steps to the kitchen and out to the garage. When she got to the grocery store, she went directly to the meat department. She usually sliced her own meat but opted to have the butcher do the chicken and steak to save time. While waiting, she picked up all the other things she needed, then circled back to get the meat. On her way to the checkout, she saw a couple of people she knew and threw up a wave. One of the women rushed down the aisle toward Serenity.

"I saw you and Ms. Della's grandson at Ms. Ida's last night," she gushed. "How long have you two been dating?"

"We're just neighbors and friends. I have to run. Have a good evening," Serenity called over her shoulder as she hustled toward the cashier. *Great. Just freaking great!* This was exactly what she'd wanted to avoid. Thankfully, she made it out of the store before anyone else said anything.

As soon as she arrived home and started cooking, her tension started to melt away. Before long, the sweet and smoky smells of the chicken, steak, and shrimp filled the kitchen. Once they were done, she made the condiments and fried the chips. Serenity sampled the guacamole to see if it needed more salt or lime juice. "Mmm, perfect." She had to push the bowl away to keep from eating it all. For dessert, she decided to chop strawberries to fill the chocolate cups she had left over from the last supper club. Automatically, an image of Gabriel's expression when he ate one of the desserts floated through her mind, which opened the floodgates to everything else that had happened, from the dance to the fiery kisses.

Stop thinking about him! Cook for your girls. That. Is. All. The doorbell rang, interrupting her trip down fantasy lane. *Thank goodness.*

"We're here!" Dana said, holding up a large tote bag.

Natasha hugged Serenity. "Hey, girl."

"Come on in." Serenity hugged Dana, and the trio walked back to the kitchen.

"Oh, my goodness, fajitas." Natasha inhaled deeply. "Those margaritas are going to be perfect."

A smile played around Serenity's mouth. "That's what made me think of it. Everything's ready, so we can eat as soon as Dana makes the drinks."

Dana unloaded the bag. "You have a choice of mango, pineapple, or strawberry."

"Mango," Serenity and Natasha said at the same time, then laughed.

While Dana blended the drinks, Serenity and Natasha plated everything and took it all outside. Serenity went back for plates, while Natasha set the table and lit candles.

For the first few minutes after everyone fixed their plates, the only sounds heard around the table were moans and comments about how good everything tasted.

"This margarita is delicious," Serenity told Dana.

"I agree." Natasha lifted her glass in a toast. "To Dana, the official bartender."

They all touched glasses and finished eating.

"Not that I'm complaining because I was seriously trying to figure out what to eat for dinner, but what's going on?" Dana asked, polishing off the remainder of her margarita. "Brianna didn't have a setback, did she?"

"No. She's doing well."

"Then it must be Gabriel."

Serenity forgot how perceptive Dana could be, especially since they'd grown so close over the past several years. "Yep, it's Gabriel."

Natasha frowned. "Did he end the relationship?"

"No. Last night I suggested us having a long-distance relationship, and today he called and said his friends surprised him and are taking him to San Francisco for the weekend."

"Okay, but that's not—"

"Then he said he's probably flying back to Atlanta. The end. I feel like he's ghosting me."

Dana touched her arm. "You've fallen in love with him."

She nodded. "It was supposed to be no strings, no emotions, but…"

"But you couldn't help falling for him because he's a great guy," Natasha finished. "Have you told him?"

Serenity stared at her friend as if she'd lost her mind. "Absolutely not, and I won't. Especially since he didn't even mention whether he wants us to continue seeing each other."

Natasha sighed. "I still think you should talk to Gabriel. Maybe he just didn't want to say anything in front of his friends. I know he cares about you."

"Whatever. I'm done. I've set myself up for my last heartbreak." Truth be told, her room at Heartbreak Hotel had been booked since the first time he kissed her. "He called again, but I just let it go to voicemail. There's nothing else to say."

"When he comes back, he's going to want to know why you haven't returned his calls," Dana pointed out.

"I know." But she had a few days to come up with an answer.

Natasha and Dana stayed around for another hour and, after helping to clean up, left with Serenity promising to listen to Gabriel if he called. Now, if she could only get through that conversation without him knowing her feelings…

* * *

Gabriel enjoyed hanging out with his friends, but he missed Serenity. She hadn't returned any of his calls or responded to his text messages, and his anxiety had climbed steadily throughout the day. As he sat eating dinner with Brent and Darius, he tried to put on a good front and contributed to the conversation when necessary, but his mind was back in the small town, where, in the past, he never could leave fast enough.

"Still nothing from Serenity?" Brent asked.

"No." He pushed his half-full plate away.

Darius placed his napkin on the table. "If you're done, we can head over to the hotel." When Gabriel nodded, he signaled for the server.

They'd booked connecting suites that had a living room area in between. Gabriel lowered himself onto the sofa, leaned back, and closed his eyes.

A few minutes later, Brent said, "Okay, G, we've given you time. You need to tell us what's going on. And don't try to tell us it's nothing. We've known each other way too long. Did you and Serenity break up?"

He let out a short bark of laughter. "If only it were that easy." Gabriel sat up, braced his elbows on his thighs, and buried his head in his hands. "I'm in love with her," he mumbled.

"We figured as much," Darius said. "And you're running scared."

"Yes…no…hell, I don't know."

"Have you told her how you feel?"

"No. And last night she mentioned us trying long-distance, since I was supposed to be going back to Atlanta in a couple of weeks. It caught me off guard, and I didn't answer right away. Before I could open my mouth, she seemed to backpedal and ushered me out. I've been thinking about what you guys said about extending my time by a month or two to see where this thing could go. Or even think about staying." And he wondered whether she would still have pulled away if he'd said something sooner.

Brent shrugged. "Maybe she's just as scared as you are."

"She had a bad breakup, which is why she said she wanted to keep it light with us in the beginning." Gabriel scrubbed an agitated hand down his face. "We went to Ms. Ida's for dinner last night, and more than one person came over to the table to ask about our relationship. I could tell she was getting uncomfortable, and by the time we got back home, she had pretty much shut down." Until the proposal.

"I think you should do more than think about staying. You should just do it."

"Man, so it really is true what they say about small towns, that everybody knows everybody's business." Darius shook his head and muttered, "Unbelievable. But I agree with Brent. If you love her, you have to stay and work it out." He opened his mouth to say something else, but Brent's phone rang.

"It's Glenn," Brent said as he connected. "Hey, Glenn. I've got you on speaker."

"Hey. Everything okay with Gabe?"

"I wouldn't say that," Darius called out. "G slipped and fell in love."

Glenn's laughter came through the line. "That's not a bad thing, Gabriel."

"I can't be sure," Gabriel said. For the first time in a long while, he wished his father were still alive. He'd always given Gabriel good advice, and Gabriel could use some right about now.

"I thought things were going well with you and Serenity."

He filled Glenn in on everything he'd told Darius and Brent, including Serenity's breakup. "And then there was the whole issue of me maybe going back to Atlanta."

"We told him he should've told her how he feels," Brent said.

"I don't always agree with these two, but this time they're right. If she's still nursing that broken heart, she's not going to readily put herself out there. Chances are she's waiting for you to make the first move."

Men didn't want their hearts broken any more than women did, and he was no exception. In hindsight, he realized that maybe he should've made that first move and spoken up the moment she made the proposition because he wanted the same thing. "How did you handle it with Toya?"

"I didn't handle it at first because I refused to believe I'd fallen for her so fast," Glenn said with a chuckle. "But when I couldn't go more than a few minutes without thinking about her, I knew something was up. I'd like to tell you that this thing called love isn't scary, but I'd be lying. It's scary as hell, but it's also the best risk you'll ever take with the right person. Only you know if Serenity is that person for you. Oh, and as far as the issue surrounding where you'll live, you can do your job just as well in Firefly Lake as you did in Atlanta."

Darius threw up his hands. "Thank you! That's exactly what I said. And we'll have a permanent vacation spot."

"Ha ha. If you must know, I'd already been considering staying and was heading to Atlanta to let you all know."

Brent and Glenn chuckled, and Brent said, "It's about time."

Gabriel sat digesting his friend's words. Everything Glenn said expressed how Gabriel felt. Now he needed to determine only one thing—was she worth risking his heart? Every moment of his time with Serenity played in his head like a movie reel, and the answer came back a resounding *yes*. He leaped up from the sofa. "I need to call her. I need to tell her I'm staying."

"So, Doc, when I have a momentary lapse while pursuing my Mrs. Right, can I count on you for some of this good advice?" Darius asked.

They all laughed, breaking the tension.

"Yeah, bro. I got you. Gabe, go call Serenity and let me know if I need to dust off my tux."

Gabriel snorted. "Thanks, Glenn, but I think you're getting way ahead of yourself."

"We'll see. Later, y'all."

Gabriel pulled out his phone and prayed she would answer this time.

"We'll be in the other room," Brent said, walking toward the connecting door.

Darius clapped Gabriel on the shoulder as he passed. "Good luck."

Gabriel waited until they'd left the room to call. The phone rang several times, and his heart sank. He prepared to leave a message, then heard her voice.

"Hello."

"Serenity, baby. Are you okay?" He breathed a sigh of relief.

"Hi, Gabriel. I'm fine. I thought you were with your friends."

"I am, but we need to talk." She seemed distant. "Are you sure everything is all right?"

"Yes, and you're right. We do need to talk. I know what I said last night about us continuing to see each other when you leave, but I don't think it's a good idea now. We both knew that it would end, and I think now is a good time."

"Serenity, I know what we agreed to in the beginning, but you have to know I care about you." He held back on saying he loved her because he felt the first time he said it should be in person.

"I know," Serenity said. "But—"

"I don't want it to end. I want more with you."

"Gabriel, I don't think it's going to work. It'll be too hard."

He heard her voice crack, and his heart clenched. "Baby, is this about what happened at the restaurant last night?"

"Yes…no. I mean partly. I just can't put myself through this again, wondering when the other shoe is going to drop and you get cold feet and ghost me again."

Ghost her? Then it dawned on him. In his first message, he said he might be going to Atlanta, but he didn't explain why. He bowed his head and closed his eyes, realizing she'd been hurt by her ex far more than she'd shared and thought Gabriel was doing the same. "Serenity, I know you're afraid. But I—"

"I have to go. Goodbye, Gabriel." She said it so softly, he had to strain his ears to hear her.

"Serenity, wait. *Serenity*." Gabriel glanced down at the display. She'd hung up. He slammed his hand down on the table. *"Dammit!"*

Darius and Brent rushed into the room and asked what happened.

"She ended it. I know she's afraid, but she hung up before I could convince her I'm not like her weak-ass ex."

"Then there's only one thing to do." Darius withdrew the car keys and held them up. "You need to tell her in person."

"But you already booked these rooms for two nights."

He shrugged. "Brent and I can always come back tomorrow, but this is more important. So let's go."

Gabriel stood there, momentarily stunned. But he shouldn't have been surprised because they'd had each other's backs for almost two decades and would do whatever was necessary to help one another. "Thanks, man. I owe you."

"Make me the best man at your wedding and we'll call it even."

Brent laughed. "Hold up. Why do you get to be the best man? I rented the car."

Gabriel shook his head. "Can we go now? Neither of you will be a best man if I can't convince Serenity to give us a chance."

Darius made a show of thinking. "Good point. You've got at least an hour to come up with a way to get it done, my brother."

That hour turned out to be one of the longest in his life. The fact that they'd left after ten in the evening and missed all the traffic was the only thing that kept him sane during the drive. When Darius turned into Gabriel's driveway, Gabriel barely waited for the car to stop before he hopped out. He tossed Brent the house key. "I don't know what time I'll be back."

"Hopefully, sometime tomorrow," Darius said with a grin.

"You guys can be a pain in the butt sometimes, but I'm glad you have my back." They did a fist bump and went in opposite directions, them to his house and Gabriel to see Serenity. He rang her doorbell and waited anxiously. He took a surreptitious glance over his shoulder to see if Adele was in her usual spot, but the house was dark. He spun around when he heard the door open.

"Gabriel." Serenity's eyes went wide.

"May I come in?"

She hesitated briefly, then stepped back for him to enter. "What are you doing here?"

Any doubts he had about his feelings disappeared. He loved this woman more than his own life, and it took all his control not to kiss her, especially seeing her in the skimpy tank and shorts set. They needed to talk first. "I came for you, baby." He stroked a finger down her cheek, grasped her hand, and led her to the sofa. For a moment, he sat and tried to gather his thoughts. Still holding her hand, he brought it to his lips and placed a kiss on the back. "I know you're afraid. So am I. But I love you, Serenity, and I can't give you up." Okay, so he had an entire speech he was supposed to say before blurting out those three little words, but apparently, his heart said otherwise.

She brought her hands to her mouth, and tears filled her eyes. "What did you say?"

"I said I love you and probably have since you tossed those brownies at my head."

A little laugh escaped her. "I was so mad at you." Serenity reached up to touch his face. "But you turned out to be that angel, and I couldn't help but fall in love with you. I was afraid to want more because I broke the rules."

He understood. He'd broken them, too. They'd agreed to keep it casual, but love had other ideas. And he couldn't be happier. "Some rules are meant to be broken. So what do you say about us keeping this going?"

Serenity got up and paced in front of him. "I have to think about a long-distance relationship. They never seem to work out. And then there was your message about going back to Atlanta without an explanation."

"I know. I'm sorry. But what I needed to say couldn't be said in a voicemail message."

She stopped and whipped her head in his direction. "What are you talking about?"

Smiling, Gabriel stood and gathered her in his embrace. "Ours won't be a long-distance relationship."

She stared up at him, frowning. "Are you saying…?"

He nodded. "I've been thinking about it for the past few weeks, and I don't want to be without you for months at a time. I *can't* go without seeing you for that long. I'm staying here."

"Yes!"

He swept her into his arms, kissed her with all the love in his heart, then strode down the hallway to her bedroom. Gabriel wanted her to be part of his life forever and knew the perfect way to seal their commitment. Nana would be happy to know that he hadn't let his blessing pass him by.

CHAPTER 23

Serenity opened the door to Natasha. "Come on in. I'm almost ready."

"Girl, your smile is so bright, I need my sunglasses," Natasha said, pulling them off her head and sliding them over her eyes.

Serenity laughed. "I know, and I can't help it. I didn't think I could be this happy." It had been exactly three weeks since Gabriel's declaration of love that Saturday, and they'd spent just about every evening together sharing dinner and talking about what they wanted for their future.

"I'm so happy for you and Gabriel. When are you guys going to Atlanta?"

"We're flying out on Thursday. I'm coming back on Sunday, and his friends are going to help him drive back." He'd put his condo on the market, and they were going to pack everything up.

"Then I'm glad we're having our supper club

tonight." Natasha and Serenity shared a smile. "Thanks for going with me to take pictures of Crystalwood Lake and Brookshaw Cove. I promise it won't take long because I know you've got to get things ready for dinner."

Serenity squatted and tied her tennis shoes. "It's no problem. I think what you're doing is a great idea." She slung her purse on her shoulder and picked up her keys.

"So do I. We need more tourism here, so I figured doing a little brochure about our best-kept secrets might help. The land development company is going to break ground on the new condos next spring, and I'm doing everything I can to be the exclusive Realtor, so the brochure will be good for that, as well."

"You'll get it. This isn't going to be one of those huge multi building complexes, is it?" Serenity asked as they got into Natasha's car.

"No. Only about twenty units. The town council is all for a little growth, but they're adamant about keeping the town *small*."

"Good. I like this place. You know, I'm sort of having second thoughts about you adding Brookshaw Cove to your brochure. I kind of think of it as my and Gabriel's special place."

"Aw, that's so cute. I never even knew it existed until you told me."

"That's because it's pretty much hidden."

"And exactly why I need your directions." As Natasha drove, she continued to share her vision for the travel pamphlet.

"You can park in this lot." Serenity pointed. "It's much closer to the inlet." They parked and got out. A light breeze blew across her face. The calendar had just turned to fall, and the temperatures hovered near eighty degrees.

"I'll do the cove first, then come back and take pictures of the lake area."

"Okay." She took her friend down the path leading to the cove and through the archway. Ten steps in, she froze. Gabriel stood next to an elaborately set table.

Serenity turned her surprised gaze to Natasha. "You tricked me."

Natasha shrugged. "Not really. I am planning to do the brochure, but I agree, this place belongs to the two of you. Hi, Gabriel. Bye, Gabriel."

"Thanks for your help, Natasha. We'll see you at dinner."

Natasha smiled, gave Serenity a quick hug, and disappeared the way she'd come.

"Your table for two awaits." Gabriel held out his hand.

Still in shock, Serenity slowly walked toward him and grasped his hand. "It's beautiful. *Amazing*. Thank you for this." He bent and kissed her with a sweetness that brought tears to her eyes.

He seated her, then rounded the table and sat. "Since you're going all out tonight for the supper club dinner, I thought we'd keep it light this time. I'll go all out next time."

She didn't care what was under those domes. That

he'd gone out of his way to prepare her a special lunch made her love him that much more. They dined on chicken Caesar salads and French bread, with sparkling lemonade. He'd even brought a portable speaker and made a playlist with her favorite Jill Scott songs.

When they finished eating, Gabriel stood. "Let's go for a walk." He entwined their fingers and took the same path as their first date, stopping on the golden sand to watch the waves.

Serenity walked closer to the water and inhaled deeply. She didn't think she'd ever tire of this place's beauty. "I still can't believe you found—" She turned to see Gabriel down on one knee, holding a black velvet box with a diamond solitaire that sparkled like stars in the sunlight. Her heart started beating double time.

"Serenity, you are a rare blend of beauty, brilliance, and grace, all wrapped up in the most compassionate heart I've ever known. These past few months with you have brought more joy and happiness to my life than words can ever say. And I want to spend my forever showing you how much I love and cherish you. Will you marry—"

"*Yes*," she shouted and launched herself at him, knocking him backward on the sand and kissing him.

Laughing, Gabriel sat up. "Does that mean you want the ring?"

She giggled and stuck out her left hand. "Oh yeah." He slid it on her ring finger, then kissed it. Serenity couldn't stop staring at its beauty. "I love it. And I love you."

"I love you, too, baby. Forever."

Serenity sat snuggled in Gabriel's arms, feeling more content than she ever had in her life. "Gabriel, I was thinking about what you said earlier about the table for two, and I realize the times we've spent cooking and sharing meals have been some of the best for me." That he loved cooking and food almost as much as she did still amazed her. She couldn't get enough of those quiet times of talking and listening to music, and she didn't want it to end.

"Same here."

"Can we always make a point of having our table for two?"

"Absolutely. However, since tonight will be a table for many more, we'd better head back and get to work."

She laughed softly. "I guess so." She left his lap, stood, and pulled him to his feet. "I still can't believe Natasha was in on this."

Gabriel grinned. "Hey, a brother has to do what a brother has to do. And she was more than willing to help me out."

"Yeah, I bet." They walked back to the table, packed everything up, and drove home.

In her kitchen, they cranked up the music and started in on the brunch for dinner menu. Gabriel had asked if she minded him adding fried chicken, and she readily agreed. "Before that chicken hits the table,

I'm going to need you to put about three of those wings aside for me to have later."

"Whatever my baby wants." He winked and continued moving to the music as he cooked.

They'd just finished with the preparations when the doorbell rang. Serenity hurried to answer the door. "Andrea!" Each woman let out an excited squeal as they hugged and rocked. "Oh my goodness. I thought you said you weren't going to be able to make it this weekend."

Andrea smiled. "I wanted to surprise you."

"I'm more than surprised." Serenity reached out to hug Andrea's grandmother. "Hi, Ms. Della. Come on in. Everything's ready." She led them to the kitchen.

"Hey, big brother," Andrea said, reaching for Gabriel.

Gabriel swung her up in his arms and kissed her cheek. "Hey, Sis. You look good." He hugged and kissed his grandmother. "Hi, Nana. Have a seat."

Both women sat at the kitchen table, and Serenity and Gabriel shared a look. She gave him an imperceptible nod.

He grasped Ms. Della's hand. "Nana, remember the night I came to dinner and you were telling me how you and Grandpa fell in love? You said that if I found a special lady not to let my blessing pass me by."

The older woman's eyebrows shot up, and she divided a curious glance between Serenity and Gabriel. "What are you saying?"

He held Serenity's left hand out and said, "Serenity and I are getting married."

Andrea screamed and grabbed them both up in a crushing hug.

Ms. Della rose to her feet as quickly as her seventy-eight-year-old body allowed and followed suit. "Oh, I'm so happy," she cried. "Wait." She searched Gabriel's face. "Does this mean you're staying here?"

He nodded. "Can't leave either of my favorite girls."

Ms. Della's tears made Serenity's come faster. Their celebration was interrupted by the doorbell. Serenity wiped her eyes and went to let her three friends in. She was beyond excited to see Jon with Terri. Soon, laughter competed with the fragrant food as they fixed plates.

"Be right back," Gabriel whispered to Serenity. "I left something at the house."

"Okay." He was gone and back in a flash, and another round of tears started when she saw her sister and brother-in-law, along with Gabriel's three best friends and a woman she assumed was Glenn's wife. Gabriel had introduced her to Glenn via a video-conference shortly after their reconciliation. She was further shocked when Pam's family walked in behind them. She grabbed her sister up in a big hug. "What are you doing here?"

Chandra touched the ring on Serenity's finger and winked. "Mom and Dad said to tell you congratulations and they'll call you tonight." Their parents had left for DC earlier in the week.

"You knew?" Chandra nodded, and Serenity turned her stunned gaze to Gabriel, who merely shrugged and smiled. The day couldn't get any better. She went around and greeted everyone else.

Gabriel's sharp whistle cut through the chatter. "Can we have your attention, please?" He waited until the conversation quieted. "Serenity and I have an announcement."

He nodded her way, and she whipped her hand out, wiggling her fingers.

The room erupted in cheers and calls of "congratulations" and "it's about time." Everyone crowded around to get a better look at the ring. Serenity smiled so hard her cheeks hurt. But she didn't care. Brianna tapped Serenity on her arm, and she hunkered down in front of the little girl.

"Can I be the flower girl when you get married?"

"You sure can."

"*Yay!* Mommy, I'm gonna be Ms. Wheeler's flower girl." Brianna bounced up and down, then threw her arms around Serenity and hugged her tight.

"Okay, everyone. This calls for a toast," Natasha said.

Official bartender, Dana produced bottles of champagne, and Darius helped her fill everyone's glasses. Brianna held a flute of sparkling apple cider.

Natasha held up her glass. "To Gabriel and Serenity and Serenity's Supper Club. Good food, great friends."

Gabriel whispered to Serenity, "And a taste of passion." He touched his glass to hers and, instead of sipping the bubbly, lowered his head for a kiss.

Serenity wrapped her arm around his neck and held him close, trying to infuse all the love she had for him in it. She'd risked it all this time, and won.

RECIPES

Vanilla Crisps

Makes 24 crisps

- 1⅓ cups all-purpose flour, plus more for the sheet
- 1 teaspoon baking powder
- ½ teaspoon salt
- ¼ cup margarine
- ¼ cup solid vegetable shortening, plus more for the sheet
- 1 cup granulated sugar
- 2 eggs, beaten
- 1½ teaspoons pure vanilla extract

Preheat the oven to 400°F. Lightly coat a cookie sheet with shortening and dust with flour. You may be tempted to use a nonstick flour spray, but old school is best as the cookies tend to burn.

Sift flour, baking powder, and salt into a small bowl. Set aside. In a medium bowl, using a hand or stand mixer, cream the margarine, shortening, and sugar until light and fluffy. Add the eggs and mix, then stir in vanilla. Mix in dry ingredients a little at a time. Drop the dough by tablespoonfuls onto the prepared cookie sheet, leaving about 2 inches between each. Bake approximately 8 minutes or until edges of the crisps are lightly browned. Transfer the cookies to racks to cool.

Homemade Vanilla Extract

Makes 8 ounces

- 1 ounce grade A Madagascar vanilla beans
- 1 cup vodka (80 proof alcohol), see note

Special Equipment

- 8½ ounce swing-top glass bottle
- Funnel

Split each bean lengthwise to expose the seeds (do not scrape) and place the beans into the bottle. Add enough vodka to cover the beans completely by at least half an inch, leaving a little headspace in bottle. Secure the top on the bottle and give it a shake, and then store in a cool, dark cabinet. Shake the bottle every week or so (or when you remember). It *can* be used in six months, but for optimum flavor, aging twelve months is best. Once it's ready, you can remove the beans, or if you'd like to get more flavor, you can leave them in, as the extract will continue to strengthen.

NOTE: While the odorless and tasteless vodka allows the full flavor of vanilla to shine, you may also use white rum (yields a sweeter vanilla flavor) or bourbon (yields a slightly sweet and smoky vanilla flavor). I say make one of each!

Make reservations for Sheryl's next delicious book!

COMING SUMMER
2023

ACKNOWLEDGMENTS

My Heavenly Father, thank You for my life and for loving me better than I can love myself.

To my husband, Lance, you will always be my #1 hero!

To my children, family, and friends, thank you for your continued support. I appreciate and love you!

They always say to find your tribe and I've found mine. They know who they are. I love y'all and can't imagine being on this journey without you. Thank you for keeping me sane!

Tracy Hale, thank you, thank you for your encouragement. Love you, girl!

A very special thank you to my agent, Sarah E. Younger, my editor, Junessa Viloria, and the entire Forever team. I can't tell you how much I appreciate having you in my corner.

A special thank you to Sciabica Family gourmet olive oils for their gracious donation (www.sunshineinabottle.com).

To all my readers, thank you for your support and encouragement. I couldn't do this without you!

ABOUT THE AUTHOR

SHERYL LISTER is a multi-award-winning author and has enjoyed reading and writing for as long as she can remember. She is a former pediatric occupational therapist with over twenty years of experience and often says she "played" for a living. A California native, Sheryl is a wife, mother of three daughters and a son-in-love, and grandmother to two special little boys. When she's not writing, Sheryl can be found on a date with her husband or in the kitchen whipping up delicious meals and desserts to satisfy her inner foodie.

Find out more at:

SherylLister.com
Facebook.com/SherylListerAuthor
Twitter @SherylLister
Instagram @SherylLister

Looking for more second chances and small towns? Check out Forever's heartwarming contemporary romances!

THE TRUE LOVE BOOKSHOP
by Annie Rains

For Tess Lane, owning Lakeside Books is a dream come true, but it's the weekly book club she hosts for the women in town that Tess enjoys the most. The gatherings have been her lifeline over the past three years, since she became a widow. But when secrets surrounding her husband's death are revealed, can Tess find it in her heart to forgive the mistakes of the past...and maybe even open herself up to love again?

THE MAGNOLIA SISTERS
by Alys Murray

Harper Anderson has one priority: caring for her family's farm. So when an arrogant tech mogul insists the farm host his sister's wedding, she turns him *and* his money down flat—an event like that would wreck their crops! But then Luke makes an offer she can't refuse: He'll work *for free* if Harper just considers his deal. Neither is prepared for chemistry to bloom between them as they labor side by side...but can Harper trust this city boy to put down country roots?

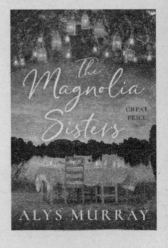

HER AMISH PATCHWORK FAMILY
by Winnie Griggs

Martha Eicher, formerly a schoolteacher in Hope's Haven, has always put her family first. But now everyone's happily married, and Martha isn't sure where she fits in...until she hears that Asher Lantz needs a nanny. As a single father to his niece and nephews, Asher struggles to be enough for his new family. Although a misunderstanding ended their childhood friendship, he's grateful for Martha's help. Slowly both begin to realize Martha is exactly what his family needs. Could together be where they belong?

FALLING IN LOVE ON SWEETWATER LANE
by Belle Calhoune

Nick Keegan knows all about unexpected, life-altering detours. He lost his wife in the blink of an eye, and he's spent the years since being the best single dad he can be. He's also learned to not take anything for granted, so when sparks start to fly with Harlow, the new veterinarian, Nick is all in. He senses Harlow feels it too, but she insists romance isn't on her agenda. He'll have to pull out all the stops to show her that love is worth changing the best-laid plans.

Discover bonus content and more on
read-forever.com

STARTING OVER ON SUNSHINE CORNER
by Phoebe Mills

Single mom Rebecca Hayes isn't getting her hopes up after she has one unforgettable night with Jackson, a very close—and very attractive—friend. She knows Jackson's unattached bachelor lifestyle too well. But in his heart, Jackson Lowe longs to build a family with Rebecca—his secret crush and the real reason he never settled down. So when Rebecca discovers she's pregnant with his baby, he knows he's got a lot of work to do before he can prove he's ready to be the man she needs.

A TABLE FOR TWO
(MM reissue) by Sheryl Lister

Serenity Wheeler's Supper Club is all about great friends, incredible food, and a whole lot of dishing—not hooking up. So when Serenity invites her friend's brother to one of her dinners, it's just good manners. But the ultra-fine, hazel-eyed Gabriel Cunningham has a gift for saying all the wrong things, causing heated exchanges and even hotter chemistry between them. But Serenity can't let herself fall for Gabriel. Cooking with love is one thing, but trusting it is quite another...